OUR ETERNAL SOULS

sands press
Brockville, Ontario

OUR ETERNAL SOULS

A NOVEL BY P. L. JONAS

sands press

sands press

A Division of 3244601 Canada Inc.
300 Central Avenue West
Brockville, Ontario
K6V 5V2

Toll Free 1-800-563-0911 or 613-345-2687
http://www.sandspress.com

ISBN 978-1-990066-22-1
Copyright © P.L. Jonas 2022
All Rights Reserved

For information on bulk purchases of this book or any book published by Sands Press, please call 1-800-563-0911.

To book an author for your live event, please call: 1-800-563-0911

Sands Press is a literary publisher interested in new and established authors wishing to develop and market their product. For more information please visit our website at www.sandspress.com.

DEDICATION

To my late friend Arleta, who opened my mind to a cosmic understanding of life.

PART ONE: ZORATHIA
Millions of Years Ago

PROLOGUE

A tremendous explosion on the planet's surface sent the ship spiraling out of orbit and into the cosmos. One-hundred passengers witnessed the destruction of their civilization, caused by the greed and self-serving practices of warring nations.

Many years had passed when they discovered a planet to colonize. Lush with vegetation, oceans, and mountains, their preliminary assessments determined the atmosphere was minimally habitable. Their bodies needed only minor adjustments their advanced technology could provide, and it was the perfect location. Unfortunately, while transporting equipment to the surface, the ship imploded from an unknown cause, taking with it most of the technology they needed and more lost souls.

In order to survive long term, they extracted DNA from the primitive, indigenous humans living on the islands along the coastline. By becoming part human, they adapted well, yet retained their alien longevity and telepathic ability.

Determined not to make the same mistakes as in the past, they created a utopian realm based on peace and happiness devoid of negative emotions.

They called themselves Zorathians and named the planet Earth. And they lived and prospered for thousands of years.

CHAPTER ONE

Xenia and Yonan's Eternal Love

The last touches of Xenia's brush had just swept across the silk canvas as she finished the painting, when the house shook and the ground moved. Dropping the brush, she grabbed the table, waiting for the motion to stop. The sounds from the swaying crystal pendulums and metal chimes on the veranda drifted through the open door. It was not uncommon for the earth to tremble, since active volcanoes existed on distant islands. But the occurrences were becoming more frequent. This time, paintings tilted and the brush container crashed to the floor.

Startled, Xenia picked up the container and glanced at the painting. She frowned at a large blotch left from her brush when she was jolted by the shaking. There was not much time before her husband, Yonan, arrived home and she was determined to finish. Rushing to make the correction the best she could, she hoped he would not notice, since it was a special anniversary present.

She hung the still wet painting on the wall and hurried to change into her best silk tunic for the occasion. At her dressing table, she gazed at her reflection in the polished metal mirror, unchanged in all the centuries. Gray eyes stared back at her, the flecks of white flashing from her excitement in stark contrast to her golden-brown complexion. After she had brushed her straight black hair, which hung to her waist, she fastened on a necklace of tiny white crystals strung on a fine wire Yonan had given her on their wedding day.

The sound of firm footsteps made her smile as powerful arms wrapped around her and strong hands pulled her hair aside to trail lips along her neck.

"Yonan, my love," Xenia said, turning to give her husband a deep and passionate kiss on his full, sensuous lips. "Happy Anniversary," she whispered in his ear while running her fingers through his long black tresses.

"And to you, my heart." He gazed into her eyes. "How many is it now? I've lost count," he teased.

"You have not!" She pushed a finger into his broad chest. "How could you possibly forget it is our four-hundredth anniversary?"

"Each year has been gloriously happy. Has it not?"

Xenia snuggled her nose into his neck again. "Yes, every one of them."

"And you are beautiful as ever." He twirled her around and pulled her into the living room. "How was your day, my heart?"

"The usual. I worked at the design studio this morning. The new altar is coming along nicely and its completion will be next month."

"Excellent." Yonan guided Xenia to the deep yellow cushions placed around the room.

"Anything new at work?"

"Only a shipment of silkworms to Tenant 102. They are starting their own silk production there, finally." He pointed to the wall. "What is this?"

"Your gift, of course."

"It is glorious and deftly painted. I am there and it is very real."

"I am pleased you like it." She sighed with relief that he had not noticed the flaw.

"It goes well with the others of the waterfall and those from our travels. Thank you. Your artistic talents continue to amaze me." He kissed her cheek while reaching down to a small basket on the floor. He pulled out a similar crystal necklace to the one she was already wearing and hung it around her neck. The two strands sparkled together in the light.

"It is beautiful." Her fingers ran across the pale-yellow stones. "These are more brilliant than the white ones."

"A new stone discovered recently. They are harder than any of the other crystals we've found. It was difficult to drill holes to string on the wire."

"I love it, and I love you . . . forever and ever."

"Forever and ever. As we promised on our wedding day, to live together in this beautiful world, always."

"Yes." She leaned in for another kiss when he pulled away.

"Wait . . . did you hear that?"

Xenia perked up, looked at Yonan, and nodded.

Motionless, they waited for the telepathic message to begin.

<To the community of Tenant 101, please present yourselves at the Temple of the Glowing Light this evening after sunset for an urgent message from the Supreme Creator. In light and love, your high priestess, Gayeena.>

"That's unusual," Yonan said. "When was the last time this happened?"

"Was it about the meteor decades ago? It ended up crashing on an unpopulated part of the continent."

"Now I remember. Come, let's have dinner first. We have time."

~ ~ ~

Xenia and Yonan's graceful golden-brown bodies took the steep mountain path with ease, their colorful silk tunics fluttered in the breeze. They followed, along with hundreds of other Zorathians, headed toward the Temple of the Glowing Light to hear the message. Under the full moon, they picked berries and fruit to eat along the lighted path, smiling and laughing, the sounds of the waterfalls flowing from the cliffs into the stream below. Zorathians lived in a beautiful world of joy, love, peace, and contentment. Negative emotions, such as fear, were unusual in their utopian existence.

The Temple rose from the top of the mountain, glowing like an incandescent pyramid. Its walls of crushed crystals shimmered from the light within, demanding obeisance, and the enormous wood beams supported the walls like fingers pointed in prayer to the Supreme Creator.

Yonan and Xenia chose seats next to their neighbors and best friends, Seema and Tahn, and the two couples held a quiet conversation as the rest of the community took their places.

Once everyone arrived, Gayeena entered, gliding along the floor with slow, determined steps. A natural healer, her aura was blue, which only she and the Elders could see because of their higher soul vibration. Although a thousand years old, her face remained ageless, with uncommon pale skin glittering with silvery sparkles to match her silver hair worn in a single thick braid down her back. Her hair was so long, her heels would kick up the tail end with each step.

She took her revered place in the center of the hall and raised her arms. The finely woven white silk caftan fluttered as she turned in circles, humming her personal mantra. The room grew quiet. Everyone waited for her words.

A pillar of golden light streamed through the open ceiling, engulfing her and transforming her bluish glow to a bright, pulsating golden glow.

Gayeena's voice reverberated throughout the hall as she channeled the message from the Supreme Creator.

"There is change coming. A great cataclysm will cause the Earth to shift on its axis. Earthquakes of increasing magnitude and volcanic eruptions will taint our air. All will be lost. We must prepare ourselves for the coming end of Zorathia. Our land will sink beneath the oceans, never to rise again."

Shocked gasps and muffled cries spread through the congregation. Zorathians could live as long as they wished. Yet now, they must prepare to die?

Xenia and Yonan turned to each other with confused expressions. Xenia reached for Yonan's hand, squeezing it until nearly numb. Fear rising within her.

She whispered, "How can this be?"

Yonan shook his head, and they returned their gaze to Gayeena for guidance.

Gayeena opened her eyes to the unfamiliar fear in the faces of her people and spread her hands in front of her. "You will experience unusual emotions like fear, anguish, loss. Support one another with love, as we face the end of our world."

"When will this happen?" shouted several people and murmuring spread through the congregation.

Gayeena clasped her hands together. "Please, please, calm yourselves. The exact time is not yet known. You experienced the signs today of Earth making its plans known to us as it has for some time. These things will occur more often with stronger shaking and upheavals." She paused and took a deep, clearing breath. "This part of the planet will sink. There may be other parts which will survive. More communications will go out to you as we learn more information. Try to stay calm."

She lowered her hands and hung her head, allowing the golden light to dissipate and her bluish glow to return. The room fell silent at her words. The energy had changed to a vibration of worry and fear. They turned to comfort one another and to calm the surge of unfamiliar emotions.

"Let us say a unified prayer," Gayeena said, "to calm our spirits and ease our minds in preparation.

Oh, Supreme Creator,

Give us the strength to endure this coming change.

Help us maintain our peace and steadfastness in your love.

Oooom, Neeee, Ooooom, Naaaaa, Ohm.

In your greatness, we commend our spirits."

The high priestess stepped down from the altar and walked among the congregation, showing her compassion and to say personal blessings.

One by one, the people left the temple. Their moods had changed from happiness and joy to foreboding and fear, whispering is hushed voices among each other, their faces tense with worry and many crying tears of sadness.

Xenia and Yonan promised their friends they would visit soon, hugging and kissing each other, trying desperately to ease each other's concerns without knowing how.

As soon as they entered their home, lamps lit up automatically powered by an energy source fed from the sun. Xenia stood in the middle of the room staring at her paintings of the beautiful mountains, beaches, and rivers, and crumpled into a ball on the cushions, sobbing.

Yonan rushed to her side. "My heart, I have never seen you this upset. What can I do?"

"I have not cried like this before." She sputtered between sobs. "Only from joy have I ever shed tears. This pain. What are we to do?"

"Maybe it will pass. You saw how affected the others were. We are all in shock. And the idea of us ever separating." He clutched his chest. Then he hugged Xenia tightly, burying his face in her hair, taking in her scent of jasmine flowers. "I could not bear it."

"We will lose everything, my art, your silk business, our friends, family. You must visit your father and your aunts."

"There is time. Gayeena is not sure when it will happen exactly. Let me think. There is something I was told long ago."

Xenia leaned back into his arms while he rocked her gently. His soothing energy calmed her.

"I remember the first day I saw you. Do you?" She spoke in a soft tone.

"Of course."

"You were like you are now. Young in spirit and mind. You had much to learn. Standing proud, you almost swaggered."

"I did not swagger," he laughed. "Well, maybe a little."

"I first noticed you under the waterfall."

"And you fell in love with me instantly," Yonan taunted.

"Not instantly. The love grew. You enamored me and it was like we were one. As if we had known each other from before. Is it possible?"

"I suppose. Wonder why we had not considered it."

"When we joined in marriage, we never wanted to be apart. Maybe it came from having lived a previous life together."

"Perhaps. I am so glad we agreed not to procreate, though they do allow us to have one child. Ours will not have to suffer this terror."

"True. Our people were so concerned with controlling population growth . . . and to what end . . . this?"

"What do we do now? Sit here and wait for the end?"

Yonan squeezed her hand. "We wait for more information from Gayeena and the Elders. That's all we can do."

CHAPTER TWO
Escape Plan

Against the advice of the Elders, hordes of panicked Zorathians piled into the existing small fishing vessels and ventured out to sea to find safer ground. But earthquakes and volcanic eruptions caused the seas to rage, and within days, telepathic contact had been lost. The realization that all had perished crushed the hopes of everyone in the community that there might be a way to escape their impending death.

The Elders called a special meeting with builders and planners at the Design Center. Xenia was among those called to join the specialists, including her assistants Darmu and Sharna, around the large worktable in the middle of the room. Xenia's unfinished altar towered next to them.

Ziros, the Chief Elder, spoke first, his face lined with worry. "We are gathered here today in hopes of constructing larger boats to carry our people to safer ground."

"Would it take much time? We have never built boats larger than the fishing vessels," said Xenia.

"Gayeena will be scrying the sacred crystals to scan the globe for safer lands and to see when the Great Shift will occur. In the meantime, we need to do what we can. We will use the existing plans for the smaller vessels and expand the capacity and accommodations."

"Will those on the other side of the continent travel with us?" Darmu asked.

"They have communicated to me they are working on a similar building project," Ziros said.

The others mumbled agreement, tasks were delegated, and some began sketching. Ziros was unrolling the plans of the smaller vessels, when a loud bang startled them, and the building shook as the earth jolted.

"Another earthquake," Darmu shouted.

The new altar rocked back and forth. The walls bent and the windows bowed as if they might burst. Xenia and Darmu had started to run to the altar to stop it from teetering over when the tall structure cracked.

"Xenia, stop!" Darmu cried as he ran. "Take cover everyone."

The group scattered in confusion. Some fled outdoors. Xenia rushed to the other side of the room, but could not find anything to serve as protection from the altar should it fall. She grabbed Sharna's hand and dragged her out the back door. Ziros and Darmu were behind them, stumbling along the shaking path, dodging the bending trees and falling branches. There was a loud crash, and they turned in time to see the roof cave in on top of the altar. Then the movement of the ground came to a rolling stop.

"No!" Xenia started for the workshop.

Darmu held her back. "It is dangerous to go in there unless you want to die today."

His words struck her in the heart. She knew he was right.

When the shaking stopped, Ziros waved everyone around him. "This is most unfortunate, but we must not give up hope. Let's clean this up and salvage what we can and continue our planning."

Sharna turned to the elder. "We should make contact to see if there is any other damage to our homes or shops?"

Ziros nodded and closed his eyes, sending out mental messages to those in the village. After a few minutes, he opened his eyes. "There is minor damage to structures, but everyone is safe. Let us proceed. Time is of the essence."

CHAPTER THREE

Future Lives

"Yonan!" Xenia hurried through the house until she found him on the veranda. "There you are. What a relief you and our home survived that quake."

"My heart, I am fine, and you?"

"The altar was destroyed."

"Sadly, it is the beginning of many losses we must bear. We can see the smoke from the volcano out here. It is a frightening sight and makes our impending death more real."

"It is so upsetting, but you are right. This is only the beginning. The committee is planning to build big ships to attempt traveling to safer land. It might work." Snuggling into his shoulder, she wrapped her arms about his waist as they gazed at the hanging clouds of smoke around the distant volcano.

"I figured it was the plan. We need to decide what we want. Attempt to save ourselves and join those on the ships . . . or wait until the end."

Her eyes watered. "I have been thinking the same. We are connected. What do you want to do?"

"There is no guarantee we will find safer ground on the big ships. We could put our names on the ship manifest, in case the venture fails. I've been thinking about our future.

"Future?"

"After we leave this life. I want to ensure we find each other in our future lives when we reincarnate."

"What do you mean by ensure?"

"I remembered something I was told long ago about when we die and our souls reincarnate into future lives."

"Because we are part human. But we wanted to live forever."

"And now it is not possible. Gayeena uses special crystals to see the future. That is how she will discover the timing of the Great Shift. Why not see into our own futures to find where and when our souls reincarnate?"

"How would we do it?" Her smooth, broad forehead furrowed.

"In our astral bodies. I learned this from an ancient sage when he had tired of living and chose to die. He said it is possible to travel in the astral plane to the future."

Her eyes grew large. "Why did you not tell me?"

"It is not common knowledge, and it never occurred to me we would need the information. He told me traveling forward in time is through a special gateway."

"Would we use the crystals? I am confused."

"Sorry if I am talking too fast. We will use the crystals to look into the future. I guess the chances of us incarnating in the same time and place are slim, and only one of the many challenges."

"What other challenges? My mind is spinning."

"One step at a time. If we find ourselves together in a future lifetime, it would be wonderful."

"And if not?"

"We keep searching until we find ourselves near each other. Then we travel to the future to get them, I mean us, together."

"It all sounds complicated and uncertain. Will we be able to do it before the end comes?"

"Hopefully. I think it is worth trying. Otherwise, we may never see each other again after we die." Strong emotions overcame Yonan. His eyes glistened with unshed tears. "I am unsure of my emotions right now. When I think of losing you, I hurt here." He placed his hand over his heart. "It has never done this before."

"A lot of new emotions are flooding through me, too." Xenia drew him into the house and they cuddled in each other's arms on the cushions, rocking back and forth to calm their energies. "Tell me more." Her voice was barely audible.

"We may not be male and female as we are now. Or of the right ages."

"I see. We will search until we find the right combination. But we have known other Zorathians who decided to leave this Earthly plane. I do not recall any of them being concerned about their future lives. Have you?"

"I remember a couple who said they believed their souls would reconnect in future lives and they were satisfied."

"I guess they had faith. You have no faith we will?"

He sighed. "I want to know that at least once we will live a long and happy life together in the future. It is peace of mind I seek. Does it make sense to you?"

"I suppose. How do you plan we do all of this, if it is possible? Can we see the future in the crystals we have?"

"I do not think so. We need one of the special crystals Gayeena uses."

"Are you going to ask her for one?"

"We must keep this a secret. We cannot let Gayeena find out what we are doing. She could disrupt our plan and it would go awry."

"Keep a secret from Gayeena?" Xenia pulled away from him. "I am very uncomfortable lying to anyone, especially the high priestess. How can you think of such a thing? And how do you plan to get one of her crystals without asking?"

"It is drastic, but these are drastic times. Everything is changing. I'll take only one."

"Steal a crystal? This is unlike you. We should talk to Gayeena."

Yonan sat there saying nothing, for he was thinking. He did that sometimes until he had his thoughts arranged just right.

"Well?" She gave him a pleading look.

Yonan knew she was right, but he resisted at first. "I will talk to her alone, since it is my idea. I am convinced she would be unhappy with my plan. There must be a reason she has not shared this information with everyone."

"It would be better with her approval. Besides, we need help to accomplish these things. Maybe she will help us."

The two lovers sat huddled together. "I will miss this beautiful world." Xenia said.

"If we succeed, we could be together in a place as beautiful."

"I hope you are right about everything, my love. Being separated from you pains me, too. I have never felt this kind of pain. Will it go away?"

Yonan kissed her with an intensity saved for special unions, and their passion ignited their auras into a blaze of golden glow vibrating pure love. "The pain should leave once we are sure of a future together."

~ ~ ~

The couple hurried along the road through the village, passing others chatting in hushed voices. They overheard some lamenting over the lost lives of friends and family on the fishing vessels. Their strained expressions showed the mood and energy in the community had shifted because of the impending losses. The usually happy and carefree world was already changing.

The two continued to their special place. As soon as they reached the waterfall, they were more relaxed. "Ah, much better." Yonan smiled.

"It is wonderful here and we are lucky no one else is around. I will miss this place, but I am glad we have a plan. It gives me hope."

"Yes, hope." Yonan pulled her toward the water, slipping her out of her tunic and he out of his. They dove into the cool pond, meeting underwater in a gentle embrace before rising to the surface.

"How much time do you think we have left, Yonan?"

"Not sure, but we must start soon with our plan. I mean, talk to Gayeena."

"I agree. After we enjoy this time together." She pushed Yonan's head under, laughing.

Seconds later, the surface of the water vibrated, and the trees surrounding the lagoon shimmied. When a roaring sound came from underground, it startled the two lovers. They jumped out of the water and pulled on their tunics, hurrying away from their special place. All the way home, there were intermittent rumblings in the ground beneath their feet.

"I'll go tonight to the Temple of the Glowing Light." Yonan said in a low voice as they entered their home.

"My love, you are trembling. Are you afraid? Should I go with you?"

"No, my heart. I am not afraid. I will see you soon." He kissed her and left.

CHAPTER FOUR
Taking the Crystal

The moonlight shone on the vacant path as Yonan made his way to the temple, wondering why the path lights were not on and where the others were. Considering the situation, he expected the temple to be full of people meditating or praying.

Yonan struggled whether to tell Gayeena his plan, despite his promise to Xenia. Guilt filled him. He had never lied to his wife. Yet his desire to try it on his own and not tell the high priestess consumed him.

When he reached the temple, a strong white light shot out of the opening at the top. He knew someone was inside and he wanted to remain unseen. He crept to a window made of crushed crystal and kneeled by a bush. Through a small, smooth and clear crystal, he could see inside.

Gayeena stood facing the altar. Behind her, several Elders dressed in white silk caftans, like Gayeena's, were sitting in the front pew, their palms up in the air, meditating. Her hands cupped over an enormous white crystal set on a metal stand. It glowed with an intense white light illuminating the entire hall and shot the beam of light up through the ceiling. She was speaking.

Yonan inched as close as he could, straining to hear her, convinced she was scrying for when the end of Zorathia would come. Her voice was loud and clear, but the words were unfamiliar. Yonan realized she was speaking in another language. The only other language Yonan had heard was that of the natives who lived on the nearby islands. He tried using his telepathic ability, hoping he could understand, but Gayeena blocked her thoughts. She must have been speaking in a special language used by the Supreme Creator.

On the altar were a multitude of white crystals of all shapes and sizes. He was confident he could take a small one Gayeena would not miss.

When the beam of light died down, Gayeena turned to the Elders. Speaking in Zorathian, she told them what she saw. "Within three full moons, our beloved Zorathia will be gone."

There were murmurs among the Elders with shaking and nodding of heads. They left through the main entrance. Yonan watched them pad their way down the mountain and out of sight before he moved.

Three moons? Yonan faltered, stumbling from the imbalance at his core. It was beyond his comprehension that the Great Shift would occur so soon. Would there be enough time to build the big ships and travel to a safer location? Would he and Xenia accomplish their goal before the end?

Turning to go straight home to tell her, he stopped himself. First, he must get one crystal—and since Gayeena had left, he could not talk to her, anyway. There was no time to waste.

They locked no doors in Zorathia, since their people did not steal. Yonan cringed at the realization of the first crime he was to commit, but he validated his action with the urgency of the situation and continued on with his plan. He entered the temple through the main entrance and strode up to the altar. Soft moonlight from the opening in the ceiling illuminated the hall. The crystals vibrated a soft white glow, and the energy helped to center Yonan. He regained his balance and confidence that he was doing the right thing.

He worked from the left to the right, unsure how to select a crystal, figuring he would sense which one to take by the level of vibration. Over each stone he hovered his right hand, waiting for a sign. If nothing, he moved down the altar table. All the stones had a distinct vibration and sound. One had a low dull tone and warmth, though he was not touching it. Another felt cool and vibrated in a high-pitched tone. Finally, he reached the end of the altar.

Which one? Or did it matter? Making another pass in the opposite direction with his eyes closed, he hoped one would signal him to stop. A crystal changed its tone. He opened his eyes. The color shifted from white to a slight blue and the sound was like Xenia's voice, a soprano. *Is this a sign? It has to be.* The stone was small enough to fit into the bag he had brought with him slung over his shoulder. He checked to make sure the glow was not visible from outside of the bag. There was nothing. He looked inside and the crystal was still, no longer vibrating or glowing. Heaving a sigh of relief, he was turning to leave when he heard the sound of the front doors opening. In came Gayeena. He froze.

"Yonan, why are you here? Is there a problem?" She approached him with her smooth steps.

"Uh, well I—" Unnerved and consumed with guilt, he dropped the bag on the floor and the crystal fell out.

Without a word, she picked up the crystal, turning in over in her hands. "What do you plan to do with one of my special crystals?" Her voice was calm, with no anger, malice, or any accusations.

As if she had put a spell on him, Yonan could not help himself, and the story tumbled from his lips. "Forgive me, High Priestess. We wanted to see into our future lives. You remember how much Xenia and I love each other and had planned to live together forever? We want to time-travel through a gateway to get our future selves together." He stopped. How was it he had told her everything?

"Come, sit down." She guided him to the front row pew. "I understand your dilemma. None of us wants to die, myself included. But stealing the crystal is unnecessary. You may have it, freely. We have no more rules. There will be no Zorathia. We must work together to help one another until the end."

"Forgive me." He slumped his shoulders like a child. "Stealing the crystal was not the way to go about this. I expected you would be angry and punish me."

"Angry?" she chuckled. "In a thousand years, when have I ever been angry? Besides, punishment is a thing of the past." She gave him a gentle and loving smile. "We are all having unfamiliar emotions because of the Earth's changes."

"I should have known you would only show me love. You are right. It is these emotions, and I was not thinking straight."

"Do you even know how to scry into the future?"

"Not exactly."

"How did you hear about time travel?"

"Many years ago, I met one sage before he chose to die. He told me the ancient ones traveled to the future through a Gateway. It did not interest me at the time, but I found it interesting the capability was not shared."

"Ah, you mean Elder Simon. It surprises me he told you."

"We were talking about where our people came from, our beginnings. I was young and had begun school to learn the teachings and asked him many questions."

"Did he tell you how the time travel worked?"

"No."

She patted his hand. "Well, my son. You did not have this planned out very well, did you? Bring Xenia to the temple tomorrow and I will tell you everything you need to know and show you how to accomplish your desire."

Flooded with relief, Yonan stood and bowed deeply before Gayeena. "Thank you, High Priestess. Your willingness to help us will be forever appreciated."

"Well, forever is coming soon, my son. Come at mid-day." She rose and glided away to her residence next to the temple.

~ ~ ~

Xenia was waiting at the door when Yonan arrived home.

"I tried not to worry and to stay calm, but I could not." She embraced him. Her arms held him tight, not wanting to let go. "Did you talk to her?"

They settled on the deep cushions. "Yes, but first, I want to share with you what I witnessed."

"What do you mean?"

He told her about Gayeena and the Elders and the strong white light emanating from the crystal during the scrying, and then he stopped.

"Why are you looking at me that way? Did something happen?"

"I have news you will find upsetting."

Xenia braced herself and held Yonan's hands in hers. "Ready."

Yonan looked into her gray eyes with intent to steady her. "The Great Shift is coming in three full moons." He squeezed her hands and could feel her energy wane, and she quivered. "It will be fine, Xenia. Do not be distressed. My plan will work. Do you believe me?"

"I believe you, but the end is coming sooner than I expected? I am afraid. We have done none of these tasks before. How will we accomplish everything in time?"

He took a deep breath. "We must go to the temple tomorrow at mid-day."

"The temple?"

"Gayeena has given us approval."

"How wonderful! You talked to her about our plan?"

"Well, after she caught me at the altar taking a crystal."

"You told me you would not take it."

"I am sorry. But it has all worked out. She was not upset. Instead, she is going to help us. She even let me keep the small crystal I tried to steal. I have it in my bag."

"Really? This seems too easy."

"Yes, a little, I guess. I am excited now and not stressed. I must admit, I was not sure if it would work and am glad she caught me. She knows exactly what to do." He gave an awkward laugh. "With her help, we will succeed."

"I hope you are right."

CHAPTER FIVE

Choices

Gayeena sent a telepathic announcement to the community that it would be three moons until the Great Cataclysm destroyed Zorathia. There was little time to build the ships and attempt the ocean travel. Emotional chaos spread among many Zorathians. Others took the news with a relative calm since they had lived long lives and were not as fearful of their impending deaths.

Gayeena explained it would affect different parts of the continent at different times. Tenant 101 would be affected earlier than others. She suggested bidding farewell to friends and family in other parts of Zorathia. Or, move to other parts not affected until later if they chose not to travel on the ships. The end was inevitable, regardless.

There was also the option of choosing to die of their own accord in an early End-of-Life Ceremony.

The Elders visited the community, expressing their concern for the people's welfare and helping them to make their decisions on what to do. They encouraged everyone to gather at the temple daily and meditate to raise their consciousness, which would stabilize emotions. Telepathic messages from the other parts of the continent flooded the people's minds as well, saying farewell or wanting to visit. Others signed up on the big ships in hopes of a success, though there was no guarantee.

~ ~ ~

On their way to meet with Gayeena, Xenia and Yonan paid a visit to their friends Seema and Tahn.

"I am wondering if we should let them in on our crystal scrying. They should have the same opportunity as us. Do you agree? They are our closest friends, after all." Xenia peered at him through her lashes.

He frowned. "If you want to ask them about their thoughts on future lives, yes, do that. We told Gayeena we wouldn't tell others about our plans."

She nodded in agreement as the door opened and Seema stood smiling ear to ear. "I heard your voices. Come in, please."

"You look happy today, Seema," Xenia said.

"Yes, I am, because we have decided."

"What decision? About whether to join the others on the ships?" Xenia asked.

Seema and Tahn clasped hands. "No, we do not want to attempt the ocean voyage. We fear it is a lost cause. We want both of you to attend our End-of-Life Ceremony," Seema said.

Xenia's face fell, "You are not going?"

"It might be as bad a death as waiting for the end. We want a peaceful end to our lives."

"We understand, right?" Yonan cast his eyes to Xenia, and she nodded.

"My dear friend." Seema took Xenia's hands. "You are sad."

"I do not want to say goodbye, yet. I want more time with you." Xenia's eyes glistened.

"We can spend time together, the two of us. Perhaps a whole day before the ceremony?"

"I would love to, Seema," Xenia said.

Tahn and Yonan were quietly chatting together and took hold

of each other's forearms, showing their friendship and understanding.

"We will be there to support you." Yonan acknowledged with a smile.

"Also," Xenia turned to Seema, "we were wondering if you ever considered what will happen after you die? I mean, about your souls reincarnating into the future?"

"What a surprising question. Of course, we will have future lives."

"Are you concerned you might not find each other again in future lives?" Yonan asked.

"We love each other very much. Though there is no guarantee our future selves will be together again, we accept it," Tahn said.

"Ah, I understand." Yonan regarded them. "That is a good way to view it.

Seema reached over and patted Xenia's knee in comfort. "It must be particularly devastating for the two of you, since you planned to spend eternity here together. Are you concerned whether you will ever see each other again?"

"In a way, yes. Only . . . what if you could travel to your future lives?" She glanced at Yonan, who looked stunned at her words.

Seema's eyes grew large. "It is not possible. Why want something that cannot be?"

"It can. Yonan and I are going to attempt it."

"You are?" Tahn said.

"Uh, soon," Yonan said, not wanting to share more.

"How?" asked Seema.

Xenia told them what she and Yonan were planning and then waited for their response.

Seema and Tahn communicated with each other mentally before responding. Tahn spoke first. "We are happy for you and understand how important this is. We sincerely hope you succeed." He paused, glancing at Seema, who smiled and nodded.

"Like you said, there is no guarantee. It has never been done before, and we are willing to take our chances," said Xenia.

Xenia gave Yonan a knowing glance. He accepted Seema's and Tahn's decision and looked at peace. "We will miss your friendship. You have been very special to us."

"And you as well, my dear friends," Seema replied.

"Maybe we will reconnect in a future life," Yonan said.

"And hopefully we will realize the connection," said Xenia.

"We hope so too," said Tahn.

They bid farewell until the ceremony. Once outside, Yonan stopped Xenia.

"At first, I thought you were making a mistake, and I was almost angry."

"Angry?"

"Almost, but then I realized you did the right thing by giving them a choice. I was honestly surprised they did not want to try. But they differ from us. I hope they tell no one else about our plans."

"Sometimes, you surprise me, like now. I love you with all my heart." She hugged him tight and kissed him.

CHAPTER SIX

Scrying the Crystal

Xenia and Yonan arrived at the Temple, where Gayeena was waiting at the altar. He handed her the crystal he had taken the night before.

"You can keep it. We will use one of my very special ones for this task." She turned to the altar and selected a flat clear crystal about ten inches in diameter. Its surface was smooth and pristine, with an intense white glow. "Ah, this one will do nicely."

Yonan peered at the crystal in her hands. "What makes these different from the others we use in our daily tasks?"

"First they have been cleared of all negative energy and then charged with our energy source to increase their vibration. We do not perform it on all crystals." Gayeena said.

"I never really understood, but it does not matter now, since we cannot use them for much longer. Will we?"

"Unfortunately, no." Gayeena motioned them toward her. "Come, follow me."

The couple gave each other a questioning glance, but followed Gayeena out the back way of the temple and down a path to a small round building. To their surprise, they found the entrance bolted. Gayeena pulled out a set of oddly shaped tools, unlocked the bolt, and pulled open the door.

Once inside, the lights came on. Along the circular wall were several large armchairs with headrests, made of a silver metal. In the center was a round table where Gayeena placed the crystal on a wire stand.

"What is this place?" asked Yonan.

"We call it our atheneum, a place which promotes learning about this world and a repository of all our knowledge and history. When the ancient ones first came to Earth from another planet, they brought knowledge with them, such as the technology they used to build the energy source we use today, as they taught you in school when you were youths."

"We did not know about this place. Why was it kept a secret?"

"At the time it was no longer needed. However, all subsequent high priestesses and elders were told, in case we should need the knowledge again, like now. Because of what happened to their planet, the future of Earth was important to the early Zorathians. They scried with the crystals, and with the use of these devices, they traveled forward in time."

"Did they discover what was going to happen to Zorathia? I mean, the Great Shift?"

Gayeena paused, as if forming the right words in her mind, before answering. "Yes, they saw the future and the end of Zorathia."

"If you read the scrolls, then you had this knowledge. Why not share it with us?" Yonan furrowed his brow.

"Would it have mattered? It has not to me, or to all the Elders and Priestesses past and present. We live our lives in the present, not worrying about the future, for we could not stop it." She sighed and smiled at them.

"When they saw Earth was doomed, they could have left and traveled to another planet?" Yonan asked.

"We lost the means for intergalactic travel after the ancient ones transported to Earth. Their vehicle imploded. They said it was like a bright light in the sky and never understood why it happened. Their futures were here, and they made the best of it they could. Which is why they built this utopian world."

"How terrible for them," Xenia said.

"I have a vague recollection of the story from when I was a child." Yonan said. "But if the future was known, why was the special gathering held to hear the message from the Supreme Creator? Was it made up to tell us what you already knew?" His voice was loud and terse.

"There is no need for anger here," Gayeena said.

"I agree. Please calm yourself," said Xenia, "We needed to be told, and one way was through Him."

"Well, you are much more understanding," he said to Xenia.

Gayeena's compassionate gaze turned to Yonan. "We did not make it up, as you say, for your benefit. The Supreme Creator chose that moment to share what will come. It was not me or the Elders. In fact, we did not know what the message would be. I was as surprised as everyone else."

"If we had known sooner, we could have traveled to a safer place on Earth."

Gayeena smiled again with her all-knowing expression. "It may have been possible, although sometimes, the future changes, particularly Earth. We knew about the shift, but to have the exact time, we would have had to spend a lot of time scrying the future and tracking our time. We live in the present. This is our way of life. It is too late to think about what we could or should have done."

"I see what you are saying, but am finding it difficult to accept." Yonan paused again and his eyes lit up. "Could we all travel to a time after the shift? Then we would not have to die."

"The physical bodies don't travel through the Gateway, only the astral bodies."

"I do not understand. We travel in our astral bodies to other places on the continent. How is this different?" It perplexed him. He noticed Xenia had been quiet, but she took his hand in hers to calm him. <Thank you, my heart.>

"Allow me to show you." Gayeena pushed a button on the wall above the first chair. "One sits in the device . . ." It made a whirring sound, and the ceiling opened. A pyramidal shaped hat, of sorts, descended, stopping over the chair. "And this piece goes on the head. The shape and type of power generated opens up a portal for the astral body to travel through."

Xenia exclaimed. "Fascinating. How do we get to the correct time and place?"

"Right. Good question," piped in Yonan, instantly understanding.

Gayeena glided over to a carved wooden door and opened it to reveal a room filled from floor to ceiling with shelves of ancient scrolls.

"They logged each time travel excursion with full details of the time frame, location, peoples, languages, and such." Gayeena retrieved a scroll, placing it on the center table. She unrolled it, careful not to damage the ancient papyrus.

"Once you see your future selves, you can come to these scrolls, find a similar time, and read about what they saw and experienced. It might help you understand your own experience."

Xenia and Yonan looked at the scroll in amazement. "This makes little sense to me," he said.

"It will, when you have seen the future in the crystal."

"Have you ever traveled forward in time?" Xenia asked Gayeena.

"No, but I have scried the future many times and read all the scrolls. However, nothing in the scrolls mentioned any attempts at changing the future. You want to ensure your future selves connect. I cannot guarantee you will succeed. There is no evidence they ever tried it before. You are the first who asked to try." She paused, giving them a stern expression. "You must keep what we are doing quiet. There are only a few devices. The Elders and I are discussing your experiment. We have not decided on how, or if, we will allow others to attempt it."

"We understand and we are grateful to you for helping us attempt it," Yonan said.

Xenia turned to Gayeena. "You mentioned languages. How would we understand other languages we've never heard before? I am concerned."

Gayeena chuckled, "Ah, it is simpler than you would imagine. Our telepathic abilities while in the astral body become more enhanced and cross over the limitation of language when going forward in time. At first, you will hear the foreign tongue, but your minds will automatically translate it."

Xenia looked doubtful. "I do not understand how it works."

"Your mind will connect with their minds, but on a higher level of consciousness, not the physical plane in which they think and talk. Do you understand?" Gayeena asked.

"Maybe. Does it make sense to you, Yonan?"

"Partly. It is complicated," he replied to Xenia.

Gayeena waved her hands over the couple. "It will all be clear to you when it happens. Be not concerned. Shall we begin with seeing your future selves?" She rolled the scroll and returned it to the shelf, then dimmed the light in the room.

"What do we need to do?" he asked.

Gayeena joined them at the table. "Which one of you will scry the crystal?" She raised a brow at each of them.

"Xenia should," Yonan said. "She is more sensitive than I."

"Not me." His wife shuddered with uncertainty and stepped back.

"You can do it. Let Gayeena guide you." He gave her a slight nudge toward the table.

Gayeena took her hands gently. "Let us calm ourselves by meditating together, concentrating our thoughts on your future lives beyond Zorathia. Now, place your hands over the crystal."

While closing her eyes, Xenia inhaled a slow deep breath and did as Gayeena bade her. The crystal pulsated with shimmering white light filling the room, becoming brighter and brighter. A vibrating high soprano-like voice reverberated around the room. Xenia opened her eyes and stared at the crystal. "There are images on the crystal's surface. It might be our continent, Zorathia. It is as if I am in the sky looking down. How strange it feels. It has gone dark . . . nothingness. I feel like I am moving."

"You are not moving, you are still." Yonan watched as her eyes fixated on the crystal. When he looked at the crystal, it was still. "You are doing it, Xenia. Keep going."

"Yes," Gayeena said, "stay relaxed. It is happening."

"Slowing down now . . . there is a light, and it is hot. I am inside a cave like the ones beneath our mountain. There is a large moving light in the center . . . it is a fire, and people wearing unusual clothing maybe made from animal skins. Some people are dancing, others sitting on the floor around the fire."

"How do they appear?" Gayeena asked.

"All are pale-skinned and the shape of their faces is like ours, with flat foreheads, and even, balanced features. Their hair is of different colors, not all black like ours. There are men and women with children. The men have hairy faces and . . . wait—"

"What? It is one of us?" he asked.

"Yes, it is me. Though she does not look like me, my soul essence recognizes the girl as me."

"Excellent," Gayeena said with a soft voice, not wanting to break her concentration.

"I am searching now to see the location of Yonan's future self. The vision is moving out of the cave to a distant place. You are there, but not close. You are with many other people, traveling toward where my future self is. I am sure we can get both of them to the same place." She stopped and closed her eyes, as if they were in pain.

The white glow from the crystal died down and Xenia almost collapsed, but Yonan caught her in his arms. "What is wrong with her?"

"She is fine," Gayeena said. "Seeing the future drains the physical energy."

"You did very well, my heart," he said, kissing her forehead.

"Very well. You must rest and recharge your own energy before you attempt to travel forward in time." Gayeena said. "If you wish, you may stay and go through the scrolls now."

"I am alright." Yet Xenia held onto the table to steady herself. "Let us research the scrolls while the vision is clear in my mind."

Gayeena moved to the door. "When you finish, push the button by the door to signal me and I will let you out. We will do the travel another day."

After Gayeena left, the couple searched through the scrolls for scenes similar to those she had viewed in the crystal.

"Here," Xenia pointed to the scroll she had been reading. Yonan looked over her shoulder.

"Following this calendar the ancient ones created, this entry is thousands of years in the future! Imagine that. They describe the people like the ones I saw. Intelligent, strong, and good people, it says. They are more developed than the natives in our time on the other islands, but not technologically."

"Very interesting."

"It is!" she said, beaming with excitement. "I can hardly wait to time travel."

At home, they talked into the night about the coming adventure until their eyes drew sleepy and they fell asleep entwined together.

CHAPTER SEVEN

Traveling Forward in Time

The day arrived when Xenia and Yonan would attempt astral time travel. They could not hide their nervousness and excitement. They hoped to land in the correct location and time.

Gayeena was waiting for them in the atheneum. "Ah, you are here. Prepared for your journey?" she asked, her mood encouraging as she glided about the room, readying the devices.

"Yes." The couple said in unison, sending tense sidelong glances to each other.

"I hear some doubt in your voices." She turned to them, her mind reaching into theirs. "You must be sure where you are going. I remember one Elder who on his first trip landed practically inside a volcano."

Xenia gasped.

"It was of no consequence. When you are in your astral body, it cannot hurt you."

"I see. What a relief." Xenia relaxed.

Yonan settled into his device with no problem, but Xenia could not get comfortable. "The chair does not feel right to me," she said to Gayeena.

"It is not designed for comfort. As soon as your astral body leaves, you will not notice. Please, both of you, take some deep breaths. We will not begin until you are ready and focused on your location." She placed Yonan's hand in Xenia's. "You will need to hold hands. This way, you will stay together until you reach your destination." Gayeena paced the room while speaking. She waved her graceful hands in the air.

"There are a few more things I need to explain to you. Zorathians can see each other's astral bodies, but humans cannot. However, in the future, there are some humans with expanded consciousness or higher soul vibrations. We believe they are Zorathians who have reincarnated into the future. They might see flashes of golden light from you, but will not understand what it means, particularly your future selves, because of your connection. They are susceptible to your suggestions, like whispering in their ear, so to speak. It is one way you might guide them to each other. You will use your telepathic abilities, like I mentioned before, to communicate."

"Alright," said Xenia, "It is clear." She gave Yonan's hand a light squeeze.

"How do we return to this exact time and place?" he asked.

"Your astral chords remain attached to your body. When you are ready to return, concentrate on this place, and you will come back."

"Sounds simple."

"That part is, getting to where you want to be is not. If you do not arrive in the right place, return here and start over. You are the only ones using these devices. But I must warn you." Her expression turned serious.

"Warn us?" Xenia perked up, tense again.

"Your bodies continue to live parallel with you. You will not return to this exact day. It is imperative you keep track of how much time has passed. We have an estimate of three moons until the Great Shift. It should give you plenty of time to accomplish your goal." She paused.

Xenia interjected, "You are scaring me."

Gayeena put up her hand, "If you do not return before the Shift occurs and your physical bodies die before you reenter them, you will be lost in the astral plane forever."

Exchanging shocked expressions, the couple gripped each other's hand, their eyes filled with fear. "What would it be like?" Xenia said.

Gayeena paused for a moment. "It would depend on where you are when the chord is cut and your bodies die. If you are still in the future, you would wander there endlessly neither alive there nor here, floating about. If it happens while you are transporting back here, you might be lost in the cosmos, or perhaps land in another time or place."

"This is serious," Yonan said.

"It is a risk and why you need to be aware of the passing of time. Now you know the potential danger, do you want some time to think about this before attempting to travel?"

Xenia's heart beat wildly and her body trembled.

"My heart, I will understand if you do not want to try this, what with the risks," Yonan said.

"Are you not scared?" she said.

"Concerned, yes, but not scared. I am confident we can keep track and return before the shift. How could we possibly need three moons to accomplish our goal?"

"To be lost in the astral plane forever . . ." She shuddered. "If you are sure, then I am." She gave him a reassuring smile.

"Good," Gayeena said. "Sit still and blink your eyes twice when you are ready and I will start the devices."

The couple settled back into the silver chairs with the strange hats lowering on to their heads, taking a few minutes to slow their breathing.

Yonan blinked his eyes—then Xenia—while they firmly clasped hands between the chairs.

Gayeena lowered the lights in the room until a soft glow emitted from the devices. "Now, Xenia, concentrate on the time and place where you first identified your future self. Yonan, you can tap into Xenia's thoughts and will have her vision of your destination. Understand?"

"Yes," he said.

The high priestess moved against the far side of the room, while the top of device headpieces whirred, spinning around and around, glowing. Xenia and Yohan's astral bodies lifted out of their physical selves, floating in the room above the chairs, and turned toward Gayeena. The astral bodies glowed a transparent golden light and the astral chords connected them to their physical bodies.

Gayeena was in a trance, her hands raised, her body glowing blue. "I am sending you my positive energy." A shape formed above the floor in front of Xenia and Yonan. "That is the Gateway." It looked like a hole in the middle of the room, its edges vibrating an intense white light with the center dark.

"Go into the Gateway. Continue to hold hands. Do not let go. I will wait here for a few hours. If you do not return right away, I will assume you have landed at your destination."

Gayeena's eyes followed the couple as they floated toward the Gateway and into the hole until they disappeared and the astral chord vanished. She knew the chord was still connected on another level. There was a loud pop, and the Gateway closed.

~ ~ ~

Xenia and Yonan floated through the Gateway. Once through, their astral bodies moved at a rapid speed toward a light which grew brighter and larger until they saw Earth below them. A different looking earth covered by large caps of ice. As they slowed and drew closer to the ground, Xenia pulled at her husband, speaking to him with her mind.

<Stop. Something is wrong.> Hovering above the ground she scanned the area. <I see a cave entrance. It is not the same one I recall, and there is too much ice everywhere. I think we have not gone far enough in time.>

<Do you sense your future self nearby?>

<No, I do not. We should return. Now.>

~ ~ ~

With another pop sound, the two returned to the atheneum where Gayeena waited, and they hovered above her.

"No good?" the high priestess asked the couple.

<We did not go far enough into the future. What did I do wrong?> Xenia asked Gayeena, while still in the astral body.

"You can try again. Stay where you are. The portal is still open. Concentrate on the vision you had in the crystal and visualize your future self, what she looks like, and communicate with her higher self or soul essence, if you will."

<I see her, yes, clearly.>

<I did not before, but I do now,> Yonan said, <I am ready. Are you, Xenia?>

<Yes, I am ready.>

"Move through the Gateway as you did before," Gayeena instructed.

Once again, the couple passed through and the gateway shut with a loud pop. Gayeena smiled.

PART TWO: PRE-HISTORIC CHAUVET, FRANCE

32,000 BCE

CHAPTER EIGHT

A Nomadic Gravettian Tribe

The biting cold hit Anyah's face the moment she stepped out of the animal-skin covered dwelling. Pushing her light brown hair inside the fur-lined hood, she darted her eyes about, making sure she was the only one out. It was early, before her grandmother and the other women had risen. She tugged the thick fur cape about her slight frame and tiptoed in fur-lined boots, careful not to make a sound. Fearful someone would discover her plans and stop her, she hurried out of the encampment and toward the valley. Yet, no sooner was she out of eyesight of the camp, than her beloved dogs found her and nipped at her heels.

"You two must be silent," she whispered, ruffing up the ear of the female, with long reddish-brown hair, she called Red, and hugged the male, with a thick white coat covered in black spots, she called Dig because of all the holes he dug. Making controlled quips, they wagged their tails, keeping close to Anyah.

It was hunting day. The men had left hours earlier. The hunt fascinated her, and she wished she could have joined them. Men hunted, women did not. But Anyah was not like the other women.

The three traveled along the river through the natural bridge, a massive archway carved from the mountain by the river millions of years before. On the other side, the hunters had gathered on the open range where the bison grazed. A flash of golden light appeared in the corner of Anyah's eye. When she turned, it disappeared. Though she was curious, she returned her attention to the hunt. Holding onto her dogs to keep them quiet, she hid in the tall grasses on the edge of the clearing, observing the men from her tribe surrounding one beast, with arrows poised and aimed. A rush of excitement flowed through her whenever she witnessed the downing of an animal. It meant a grand feast for their tribe, bones for tools, and skins for clothing and coverings for their dwellings. A necessary and dangerous part of life.

A cousin pranced about to gain the bison's attention, while the other hunters aligned before plunging their arrows into its side. Ten hunters to fell one bison. Down it went. The earth shuddered from its weight crashing to the ground. The other bison turned and charged away from the hunters, but another team waited on the opposite end of the valley. Their arrows were already in the air, landing into the beast's hide. Down it went. Two bison in one day. It was a significant victory, and Anyah wanted to yell and jump up and down to congratulate them, but she must stay quiet and remain hidden.

It would be hours before the men finished carving the animals to transport to their camp, where the women would dress the meat and dry the bones and skins. There would not only be much food, but much work.

With the dogs padding close behind her, Anyah ambled back to the camp, hoping to avoid seeing her grandmother, Neeyah. Another secret. Her first bleeding had come months earlier, and Anyah kept it to herself. She had prayed to never get the bleedings and was grateful she had reached the age of fifteen. Most of her friends' womanhood had occurred much earlier. It was difficult, since they lived and slept so close together. Her breasts grew faster than expected, and soon she could no longer cover up. As was customary, once of breeding age, they would pair her with a man in the tribe. She was not ready. The only power she had was delaying the inevitable. A sudden sadness deafened her excitement over the hunting. She dreaded being with someone she might not like.

As Anyah neared the camp, the aroma of roasted meats drifting in the air caused her stomach to rumble. There were many fires going at once, surrounded by the women of the tribe working at various tasks. As soon as she came to the first fire, she reached across the hot coals, yanking off a piece of roasting meat.

"Anyah! Where have you been?" Neeyah, her grandmother, said in an agitated tone.

Anyah cringed, dropping the meat on the ground. When she picked it up, she kept her eyes lowered. Her grandmother could tell when she lied. "I was searching for herbs," she muttered, shoving the meat into her mouth.

"Were you? Then where are they?" The older woman looked all around Anyah.

"Uh—" she gulped. "I dropped the basket in the river and the current pulled it away. Sorry. I will be more careful."

"How careless of you." Her grandmother scowled. "We need your help to prepare food for when the men return. They will be hungry."

Neeyah was a key member of the tribe and the oldest woman. She had earned her place years earlier while protecting baby Anyah from a snow leopard. The big cat's long claws had left deep scars down one side of her face from her forehead to her chin, covering an empty hollow where her right eye had been. As a reminder, she always wore a necklace made from the leopard's claws, threaded with fine leather lacing. The skin of the cat became the cape she had worn ever since. The leopard not only wounded Neeyah, it killed both of Anyah's parents, leaving the baby in her care. Though she lost sight in the one eye, she had vision as if with two, because her third eye had developed, providing her with second sight. Her abilities made her the tribe's wise-woman.

Following Neeyah through the encampment, Anyah observed the women huddled beneath their heavy capes and gathered around the deep fire pits, generating heat roasting the meats mounted on spits. She smiled at a woman busy piecing together a man's jacket of animal skins, with long sleeves and a hood. Anyah envied the skill, but her talents leaned elsewhere.

"Blessings to you, Anyah," said an elderly woman, while sewing intricately threaded patterns on the front of a woman's vest. As the granddaughter of the wise woman, they treated Anyah with special consideration.

"Thank you for your kindness, Avaya." Anyah showed the woman proper respect, but secretly she hated the special treatment.

Anyah joined Neeyah at the fire pit near their dwelling, removed her fur mittens, and warmed her hands. The old woman glowered. "Why are you moving so slow today? We need to talk later. I have some news." Her mood switched to a mischievous smile.

Anyah bit her lip. Had Neeyah found out her secret?

~ ~ ~

Xenia and Yonan watched young Anyah all day, hovering above her, until she returned to the camp. They stopped to observe the strange people of the future.

Yonan turned to Xenia. <They look similar to the natives of our time, though these people look more intelligent and have more skills.>

<Yes, they have evolved well, even without our technology. I like my future self, Anyah. She is fierce and determined to be an individual.>

<She may not benefit from such strength, my heart. The men in this civilization are the dominant gender. Where is mine? You said he was somewhere nearby.>

<Not here. He is with another tribe of people who will come to this area soon. They may have arrived. Perhaps you can search for him while I stay here with Anyah.>

Yonan agreed and floated away into the distance, high over the cliffs and toward the wide-open steppes, searching for his future self.

Xenia moved toward Anyah and Neeyah to observe the scene. And, as Gayeena had said, her telepathic abilities connected with the minds of those she wished to read, and she understood them instantly. Neeyah had the second sight, with the ability to see astral bodies. Xenia sensed this, immediately shielding her glowing light with her mind, and followed them into the enclosure.

~ ~ ~

As Neeyah entered their dwelling, she glimpsed a flash of golden light in the corner of her good left eye and turned in its direction. The light disappeared. Convinced it was the Great Protector watching over her and her people, she turned her attention to her granddaughter. "Come and sit with me." Neeyah motioned to the area covered with plush furs next to the hearth in the center of the dwelling. The smoke from the fire snaked through the opening in the roof.

Anyah removed her cape, hanging it on a hook on the wall covered with utensils and tools, clothing, headgear, and jewelry. She adjusted the woven leather headpiece before settling on the floor next to her grandmother. The same flash of golden light appeared in the corner of her eye she had seen earlier and she turned her head.

"Is something wrong?" Neeyah asked.

"It is the second time today I saw a golden light. But when I turn to look . . ."

"It is gone," her grandmother finished. "I've seen it too. You have the sight, like me," the old woman said, clasping her hands together with a joyous expression on her lined face.

"What does it mean, Grand-mère?"

"It is our Great Protector watching over us, is all."
Anyah shook her head. "I do not want the 'sight.' I want to be normal like everyone else," she said. "It is bad enough that people treat me differently because I am your granddaughter."

"Shame on you, Anyah. You have a great gift, do not shun it. It is a sign that things are coming to pass and meant to be, as with you, my dear. Your courses have begun. You tried to hide it, but you cannot hide from me."

Anyah hung her head. "I am not ready to be a woman in such a way. I want my life to continue as it is. Are you not happy with me?"

"My dear, dear, Anyah." Neeyah stroked the girl's face. "I love you with all of my heart. But life must continue, and we need to be sure our tribe lives on. The last great sickness took many of our women and children. It is yours and the other young women's obligation to our tribe to produce more offspring."

"I understand, Grand-mère, I . . . there is so much I want to do and to be."

"And what would you do? Run off to follow the hunt every day? You think I am not aware of where you go?"

"Then you must also understand how important it is to me. There must be something more to life greater than bearing children."

"It is your destiny, my child. I saw it in my vision. It will not be so terrible."

"But—"

"Stop. It has been decided. I have selected two men. You can choose the one you like best. Everyone in our tribe respects you. Whoever you choose will be good to you. Do not fear."

Tears filled Anyah's eyes, but she brushed them away in anger. "If I must, then I must."

"No tears. You should be happy."

It was disheartening that her grandmother had invalidated her feelings yet again. Neeyah always put the greater good first. Never mind what Anyah wanted. She straightened her shoulders, stifled a sob, and turned to the old woman. "When?"

"There is no great hurry. There will be a celebration to announce your readiness for marriage and engage with each man. You will have time to decide, but no longer than three moons." She wrapped her arms around Anyah and kissed her cheek. "Preparations are needed."

~ ~ ~

Although Yonan could not see what Xenia did in the crystal, in the astral plane, he was instinctively connected to his future self, or soul. Yonan allowed this connection to guide him while searching the vast terrain, flying low, on the lookout for a nomadic tribe. Over the next hill appeared a caravan of dozens of people and animals traveling toward the natural arch along the silt-filled river bed. Yonan increased his speed to reach them and scanned every male face, barely visible beneath the heavy fur hoods, until he recognized his future self, Rauk.

The man carried a heavy burden wrapped in skins and appeared older than Anyah. He took strong, assured steps across the rugged land. His bearded face held a sternness through his vivid blue eyes. Yonan was ecstatic, wanting to hurry back to Xenia to tell her. But first he needed to send some thoughts to this Rauk to ensure he would meet Xenia's future self.

Yonan hovered close to Rauk, sending his thoughts. <Keep moving in this direction until you reach the river. Settle on the wooded side below the ridge. There, you will find another tribe where you will meet your soulmate.>

The man stopped as though he was listening, then he called out to his leader and pointed towards the archway.

Yonan smiled, then took off to find his true mate, Xenia.

CHAPTER NINE
The Cave

Anyah left early again the next morning to visit the caves they had discovered soon after settling camp. Dig and Red followed along as usual, sniffing the air and ground, tails wagging. To get to the cave entrance, she followed along the river beyond their camp until she passed through the archway, then veered to the right toward the mountain cliffs. The cave entrance sat about mid-way up the mountainside. The wind whipped around her as she pulled her cape close with her fur mittens, protecting her hands from the cold. She quickened her step and Dig ran ahead on the narrow path along the mountain wall, but Red stayed close. When she reached the entrance, she stopped and listened. Dig let out a few barks and crouched down on the ground. Red ran to Dig's side and mimicked his pose.

"What is in there?" Anyah took a step, then paused again. "Is it a bear?" Standing next to the dogs, she pulled from inside her cape a carved bone with a pointed end and a long handle to use as a weapon, in case.

The sound of footsteps alerted the dogs, who barked and growled, using their bodies to shield their mistress. Anyah stiffened, immobile, until she saw a tall male figure moving towards them from inside the cave. He held a lighted torch made of wood and brush.

"Halt!" Anyah shouted. The figure continued moving until he appeared at the mouth of the entrance.

"I will not hurt you," he said in her language.

This surprised Anyah. She had met other tribesman on journeys whose speech she found difficult to understand.

The morning sun cast a warm light on him as he pulled back his hood and doused the light from the torch in the dirt.

Anyah did not relax, but her curiosity gave her bravery and she stood straight with her feet firmly planted, holding her weapon low without threat, but ready. "Who are you, and why are you in my cave?"

"Your cave?" He let out a loud, rich, and guttural laugh. "Please forgive me for trespassing." Making a mock bow, his sarcastic tone did not hide his twinkling blue eyes or diminish the broad smile on his full lips. He scratched his bearded face. "Who are you, might I ask?"

Anyah stepped back, eying him with caution. Though the dogs had quieted, their heads tilted with interest, not danger.

"I am, Anyah."

"I am, Rauk."

An awkward silence hung between them.

"My tribe is camped down the river. I come here often."

"Ah, and that is why you think this is your cave? My tribe arrived nearby early this morning and they are making camp. I am scouting the area."

"Is this your first visit here?"

Rauk took a few steps away from the entrance and crouched on his haunches. He snapped his fingers at the dogs and they responded by wagging their tails but keeping near Anyah.

Anyah scowled at her dogs. "Traitors," she mumbled under her breath.

"This is my first, not my tribe's. They say it has been many moons since then."

"I see. My dogs appear to like you. It is unusual for them to be friendly with strangers."

"I have dogs. They are at the camp with my family. What do you do here in the cave?"

"I enjoy the pictures on the cave walls. I've been practicing my own drawings." Anyah had told no one about her drawings, and she wondered why she told this stranger. Something drew her to him despite her wariness, and it was not his striking good looks.

"Yes, the drawings. They are amazing! I only observed a few before I heard your dogs. I would like to see your drawings."

"Just in the dirt." She let out an embarrassed laugh. "I am planning to try some on the walls today."

The news of her coming nuptials had upset Anyah, and all she wanted to do was draw and paint in the cave, the scenes she memorized of the men hunting. Meeting Rauk dispelled her anger. "Would you like to join me? You could hold the torch."

"I would."

He struck a flint to relight the torch and they entered the cave. The dogs ran on ahead. It smelled dank and musty as they toured the interior. Long spikes hung from the soaring height of the ceiling down to narrow points, which met spikes coming up from the floor of the cave resembling gigantic teeth which lined a natural walkway through the endless cavern.

"Over here, Rauk, we can light this fire pit for more light." Anyah motioned him to join her in the center of the huge front room, where the cold remains of a large fire pit beckoned to be fed.

"Your people do not live here in the cave?" Rauk struck his flint lighting rushes into a small fire and tossed it into the pit.

"No, it is too cold. We come here for celebrations and ceremonies." Anyah threw cave bear bones into the fire in the pit.

Wood was scarce on the steppes, and her people had learned bones were an excellent source for fuel. Anyah also discovered the charcoaled bones were perfect as tools for her drawings.

The flames rose higher. Sparks made spitting and popping sounds as they floated in the air. The two strangers drew close to the heat of the fire and warmed their stiff bodies. Dig and Red cuddled by the fire watching the flames dance and cast shadows on the walls.

Anyah let her cape drop to the floor and, pulling up the long sleeves of her deer-skin dress, she turned to gaze at the black charcoal drawing of a pack of lions running across the wall. It filled her with inspiration. She picked up a long slender stick of burned bone near the fire pit and, using her knife, whittled the end into a point.

"Are you going to use that to draw?"

Anyah nodded.

Rauk stood in front of the drawing of the lions. "These are astounding. I've seen nothing like it before. I wonder who made these marks?"

"It is a wonder. Those people haunt me in my dreams. What were they like? How did they learn to create these drawings? They seem so alive, do they not?" Anyah finished her whittling and stood in front of the blank wall opposite the lions, contemplating her first move.

Rauk moved over to stand next to her. "What will you draw, Anyah?"

His closeness made her nervous, and she stumbled over her words. "Uh, I . . . remembered something from when I was little. It was horrific and I have never forgotten it. I have nightmares reliving the scene."

"Tell me." His voice filled with interest as he sat on the cave floor.

With the stick of charcoal in her left hand, she made a broad stroke across the stone. While she drew, she told the story. "When I was much younger, my parents, Grand-mère, and their tribe were traveling to a new hunting ground when a powerful snowstorm made it impossible to see through all the whiteness. Separated from our caravan, we found shelter in a small cave . . ."

She stopped to make more strokes, forming the head of the leopard, taking care to draw the details of its snout, eyes, and teeth. "But we were not alone in the cave. As soon as Papa had created a fire, the leopard made itself known, and he pounced on Maman. Grand-mère shielded me with her body while Papa tried to save Maman, but the cat turned on him. Both dead, Grand-mère pulled out a long blade and stabbed the great cat mauling Papa. It struck out at her and clawed half of her face, but she did not stop. She stabbed it over and over, the blood splattering into the air."

Anya's hands shook slightly as she composed herself. "Grand-mère is the tribe's wise woman. She told me how to stop the nightmares. I must cast the leopard out of my mind onto to something else. Maybe, by recreating the leopard on this cave wall, I will cut the connection between it and my dreams." She picked up a container of ground red earth from the floor and with her fingers she rubbed the red color to create the leopard's spots.

She took a few steps back to examine her work and quivered from an overwhelming flood of emotion. Tears poured from her eyes as she cried uncontrollably until she dropped to her knees. Rauk rushed to her side, and Anyah leaned into his arms. His gentle touch comforted and calmed her until the shaking stopped and her breathing slowed. Their eyes locked in a knowing gaze. Flustered by her unabashed display, she withdrew and sat on the floor, her arms wrapped around her knees.

Undaunted by her sudden change of mood, Rauk gave her an understanding nod. "I sympathize with what you experienced, and I believe you have poured your angst into this emotionally charged drawing of such a ferocious beast."

"Thank you."

"I had a similar tragedy which gives me nightmares."

"Really? You have been so kind to listen to my woeful tale, please share your story."

"It was a hunting excursion, like any other. My brother and several of our tribesman had corralled a bison, surrounding him on all sides, targeting our spears . . . and the beast fell." He stood and paced the cave floor while talking, his hands waving animatedly about. "While we worked carving the animal, something spooked the other bison, and they stampeded, heading toward us. We scattered, running to get out of the bison's way. Clouds of dust filled the air and I could not see my brother." Rauk stopped, taking a deep breath.

Anyah's eyes widened, enthralled by Rauk's story.

"When the dust settled, I found my brother and several others trampled to death."

"How awful," Anyah said. "I am very sorry. When did it happen?"

"Last year. We were very close . . ." Rauk returned to sit next to Anyah, leaving a respectable amount of space between them.

"It is strange. I feel as though I've known you forever."

"I feel the same." He smiled.

Anyah returned the smile when a flicker of golden light appeared in the corner of her eye. She pivoted her head. "Did you see a golden light?"

"I did, but it is gone. I saw it yesterday on the trail traveling here."

"How curious, so did I. Grand-mère told me it is the Great

Protector watching over us. She says I have the 'sight' like her. I do not think so."

Rauk raised his brow. "It is a special gift. You are lucky. But I do not have it, so why would we see it today at the same moment?"

Anyah shrugged. "A good question for me to ask. That is, if she is not upset I have been away for so long. I must return to our camp. Grand-mère will be looking for me."

"Yes, I must complete my scouting before the sun sets."

They rose and Rauk dowsed the fire while Anyah put her drawing materials away in the leather bag and tied it to her belt. The dogs woke from their nap to run in circles around the two who were no longer strangers.

Rauk broke the silence. "Our tribe tells a story of how we are related to another tribe. They travel through this way. I wonder if it is your tribe?"

"Perhaps. It might explain why we have this connection. Maybe we have common ancestors?"

"It would be nice?" Rauk was beaming.

"It would." Anyah glowed.

CHAPTER TEN
The Celebration

Anyah danced down the path, laughing and jumping with the dogs as they hurried back to camp. Everything she viewed or smelled or heard had intensified. The colors of the sky, the smell of the cooking from their camp, and the yelps of her dogs filled her senses. She pulled her cape tight around her and slipped on the gloves, grinning ear to ear. It was Rauk. He brought her to life in a way she never realized existed, and she reveled in the newfound joy.

When she reached the camp, everyone was so busy no one noticed her until she heard a familiar voice.

"Anyah! Congratulations!" It was Mavelle, her closest friend, cooking at one of the open fire pits.

Anya stopped and turned around. "Hello, Mavelle. Why are you congratulating me?"

"Neeyah told me the joyful news of your coming nuptials." Mavelle pulled a ceramic container from the fire, setting it into a hole in the ground to keep its contents from cooling too fast. "This is for the celebration tonight, elk stew." She grinned.

"What? Grand-mère promised not to say anything yet." Anyah fought against showing her displeasure.

"You're upset?" Mavelle said.

"No, only surprised. Was not expecting a celebration tonight. She told me about her plans yesterday."

Mavelle embrace Anyah. "I am so happy for you. I hope to be

next. Did she tell you who the boys are?"

"No, not yet. Perhaps I will find out tonight. I must go speak to my grand-mère." Anyah ran to their dwelling, breathing hard. How could she? Anyah was furious. Grand-mère had promised to take it slow. Bursting into the dwelling, she found her grandmother seated on the floor with a pile of soft while rabbit skins in her lap.

Neeyah looked up from her project, surprised but happy. "Ah, there you are, Anyah. I was wondering where you had wandered off to again."

"You have been telling people I am to be married. You promised it would not happen right away." Her heart was pounding and the flush of anger rose to her face.

"I told you we needed to prepare. The celebration tonight is of your womanhood. The nuptials will be announced soon after."

"Well, Mavelle seems to think I am getting married." She threw herself onto the fur-covered floor, pulled off her cape, and crossed her arms in front in defiance.

"You will. I will not announce the date tonight. This is to introduce the men I selected, like I told you yesterday. Now you stop your pouting and help me get ready." Neeyah frowned at Anyah.

"Fine, only . . ." Why did her thoughts go to Rauk? His face filled her mind, but she pushed it away and noticed the pile of rabbit furs. "What are those for, Grand-mère?"

"For you, my dear. I will stitch these together for a fine collar to go under your cape. It will look beautiful, no?"

"It will be exquisite. *Merci.*"

"I will have it ready for the wedding, I promise." She held up the pieces and laid them around her own neck, stroking the white fur. "I had one like this when I was your age and married to your grand-père."

Anyah leaned across to touch the pelts. "I love how soft these are. Sorry for being difficult. I hoped my life as a single girl would last longer." She remembered the question she wanted to ask Neeyah about the golden light she and Rauk had seen simultaneously, but decided it was best to wait.

"Come outside and help with preparing the feast." Neeyah rose and pulled the covering aside from the opening of the dwelling.

Anyah heaved a sigh while pulling her cape back around her shoulders and followed Neeyah outside.

Later in the evening, the tribe assembled at the cave for the celebration. Several fires blazed and the cave interior glowed with the warmth from the tall flames. Anyah and Neeyah joined the other unmarried girls and elderly widows at one fire. Married women cared for all the little children at the one in the middle, and the men and boys clustered around another. The sounds of singing to the drums and flutes reverberated through the cavern.

Anyah and Mavelle huddled together, talking low in each other's ears. "Which ones, Anyah?" asked Mavelle with a glint in her eye.

Anyah shrugged her shoulders. "Grand-mère said she would announce their names tonight. There are few to choose from. The men are too old, too young, or already married." She glanced over at the men and boys with her head down, not wanting them to notice she was looking.

Mavelle was bolder and had no trouble looking directly.

"Stop, Mavelle. Do not stare at them." Anyah tugged at her friend's deerskin shift.

Mavelle laughed, her brown eyes crinkling. "One of them will have to be Jorah. He is the closest to your age, only four years your senior and your cousin. He is most suited. Do you not agree?"

"Perhaps, but he and I never agree on anything. I hope he is not a suitor." Anyah recalled Jorah teasing her relentlessly as a child and shuddered. "He barely acknowledges me these days. I cannot imagine being with him at all."

"Hush, your grand-mère is rising now."

Both girls quieted along with everyone else as Neeyah stepped reverently to the center of the room. She stood next to the tribe leader, Jeanu the Younger, an imposing figure of a man, tall with broad shoulders and a fierce stare that made Anyah cower whenever he was near.

"Tonight," said Jeanu in his booming voice, "we celebrate two honors. First, the success of our tribesmen on their hunt yesterday. Two bison were felled and we will have much meat for our stores for the coming winter." Roars of agreement from the men resounded. Jeanu turned to Neeyah and made a slight bow as she stepped forward.

"And for our women," said Neeyah, "we are most proud to announce my granddaughter, Anyah, has reached her womanhood." She nodded her head to Anyah, indicating she should stand.

Self-conscious at the attention, Anyah was still. Mavelle nudged her elbow, and the women began clapping in unison. Finally, Anyah stood looking around her at everyone's smiling faces, forcing a smile, then tried to sit, but Mavelle motioned for her to stay standing.

Neeyah continued, "And . . . we have selected Jorah and Meeks as her intended from whom she will choose her mate." More applause pounded through the air.

Shocked, her mouth hung open. Anyah looked at her grandmother, who beamed with pride. The two men stood next to Neeyah. Jorah was smiling. His brown eyes twinkled in the firelight, obviously happy about the situation, but Anyah could not contain her surprise and her knees wobbled.

When Meeks turned to her with his puffy eyes and swollen cheeks, Anyah almost retched, wondering how her grandmother chose him? A man who had four grown children and a protruding stomach his vest barely covered. His wife had died giving birth to a stillborn babe and though Anyah pitied him, being near him, let alone taking care of his children, was more than she could bear.

Neeyah motioned to Anyah to join her and the two men. She hesitated until Mavelle gave her a push. With one foot in front of the other, Anyah made her way through the people, shouting and clapping their hands, and took her place next to her grandmother. Unsmiling now, she nodded at Jorah and Meeks, hoping she might return to her place with the women, but the music began. Flutes and drums played a lively tune. Neeyah bounced with joy and grabbed Anyah's hand and thrust it toward Meeks and Jorah to start the traditional dance. Gradually, others followed, moving in a line around the fires, twirling and gyrating, their hands in the air and feet stepping to the rhythm of the drums. Anyah was not laughing or smiling. She was not feeling anything but dismay.

The music paused long enough for Anyah to escape the dancing and she hurried back to the women's circle, collapsing on the cave floor next to her grandmother, sending her daggers with her eyes.

"My dear," said Neeyah, "why are you looking at me that way? Are you tired? You looked very fine out there dancing." She patted Anyah's hand and kissed her cheek.

"Grand-mère, how could you?"

"Whatever do you mean?"

"Meeks?" she whispered in Neeyah's ear.

Neeyah gave Anyah an understanding gaze. "He specifically asked for you months ago, begging to be considered when you were of age. I could not deny him. It is customary. But I chose Jorah for you. He is your age and your cousin. You have things in common, yes?"

Anyah let out a huff. "What if I choose neither?"

"I will not listen to this. You are being childish." Neeyah looked away, then glanced back at her. "You have a few moons to decide. Become acquainted with them well. It is your duty."

A shadow passed over Anyah and she looked up to see Jorah's cheerful face.

"Anyah, I have a gift for you," he said, handing her a small leather pouch.

Hoping he had heard nothing she had said, a flood of warmth rose to her cheeks. "Thank you." She took the pouch and emptied it into her hand, a small carved ivory statuette in the shape of the female goddess with large breasts and wide hips. It hung from a fine leather strap. "It is beautifully made," Anyah said. She meant it. Jorah possessed great skill in carving.

He stooped, taking the necklace from her hand, and hung it around her neck. "It makes me happy you like it. Will you dance with me again?" He took her hand. She allowed him to guide her to where the others danced as a group when the music started up again.

Despite her reluctance, Jorah was an excellent dancer, and she enjoyed the rest of the evening. As long as she was with Jorah, Meeks stayed away.

CHAPTER ELEVEN

Rauk's Tribe

A roaring fire stirred in the pit where Rauk and the other men of his tribe gathered for the evening meal. The women clustered at a separate fire, chattering among themselves. The sun had set, and the firelight reflected on their faces.

Edmé, the tribe leader, and Rauk's uncle, stood with a cup in hand, raising it in the air. "To the success of our hunt today. Oo-ha!" The men shouted in agreement, raising their cups, "Oo-ha!" One by one, they retold the events of the day, some acting out with everyone cheering them on.

Eager to speak to his uncle about Anyah's tribe, Rauk pulled Edmé aside.

"Uncle, I discovered another tribe camped close to the great archway on the opposite side of the river."

"Tell me," Edmé said, moving them away from the fire to better hear each other.

"I have not yet gone to their camp, but I met a young woman from the tribe. Her grand-mère is the tribe's wise woman. You told me about another tribe that traveled through this way and was related to us. How so?"

Edmé scowled and stopped. "Hmm, long, long, ago, before I was born, my father and others in his age told me we once were part of a larger tribe. Something happened causing a split, and the two tribes parted, going their separate ways."

"What happened?"

"I was told enough to understand we should stay apart. Why? Do you think these people are the same tribe?"

Rauk paused, wondering about the powerful connection with Anyah. "I have no real reason to believe they are the tribe. How can I be sure?"

"I recall a few names my father shared with me who were involved in the split. Jeanu the Elder and a young girl who had the sight. Nayah, I think it was. She had a vision of something terrible, a warning. If they did not heed it, bad luck would come down on the tribe. No one believed her, because she was a child. But her family supported her vision."

"What was the vision?" Rauk considered what Anyah had told him about her grandmother being a wise woman.

"I do not remember details, only that it was a warning not to travel in a certain direction. It split the tribe between those who believed it and those who did not. Several families stayed at the encampment. Our family left."

"What happened, anything? I mean, did something bad happen?"

"Not that I recall. The story mentioned nothing bad had happened."

"The split was unnecessary?"

"Perhaps." Edmé turned to Rauk with concern in his eyes. "Why are you so interested in this story? I doubt this other tribe is the same. The coincidence is too great. What does it matter? From what I recall, the group that split was angry. The vision was not taken seriously. They probably hold a grudge. If you think they are the same, is best to stay away. We do not want any trouble." He gave Rauk a strong pat on his shoulder and returned to the fire with the others.

Rauk stood alone in the moonlight, despondent, wondering if he should heed Edmé's suggestion. He called Anyah's beautiful face and sensitive eyes to his mind. He would not forget her. There must be more to the story, and he wanted to find out. He would return and seek Anyah out at her camp, though a twinge of trepidation came over him. What if his uncle was right, and Anyah's tribe was the same one, once part of theirs? What if they met him with anger, or even violence?

CHAPTER TWELVE

Success or Failure

Two days had passed since Xenia and Yonan time-traveled. Their physical bodies would need to be replenished with water and food, so they returned to their time. As soon as they passed through the Gateway and into the travel room, the portal shut with a loud pop and their astral bodies automatically re-entered their bodies.

Xenia opened her eyes and looked down to see she was sitting in the device in her physical body, her mouth parched from thirst. She was grateful to be home. Turning to Yonan's chair, he opened his eyes and smiled at her. They were still holding hands and gave each other a gentle squeeze before releasing.

"Ah, it is good to be back," Yonan said to her as he eased out of the device and stretched his long body.

"It was an interesting experience and I think we were successful." Xenia stood and stretched, moving her stiff arms. Elated by Rauk and Anyah connecting, she was convinced deep feelings were forming between them.

"I agree!" He beamed with delight. "We may need to verify they continue the relationship."

"Yes, it is an excellent suggestion." Xenia hurried to the center table, to where the crystal glowed.

"Not right now," he chuckled. "I am hungry and thirsty. We can come back later." He pressed the button at the exit to alert Gayeena they had returned.

Xenia let out a small laugh and joined him at the door, embracing him, nuzzling his neck. "It is nice to touch you again."

They started at the sound of the lock, and the door opened. "Ah, you have returned. You are famished?" Gayeena said, standing aside to let them pass, and locked the door. "Was your journey a success?"

They followed Gayeena along the path back to the temple, telling her all about their experience and how they wanted to check up on their future selves. They agreed they would return the following day after they rested.

~ ~ ~

Xenia and Yonan returned to the travel room eager to see what the crystal would show, expecting to find continued success with Anyah and Rauk. Xenia settled her hands over the flat surface and meditated, fixing her mind on her future self, Anyah.

"I do not understand. It looks like Anyah is keeping company with another boy. Something is wrong." She moved backward in time to a scene with Neeyah and there was a conversation telling Anyah to stay away from Rauk.

"This cannot be!" She dropped her hands, and the crystal stopped vibrating and glowing.

"What is it?"

"We must go back. Anyah is not with Rauk."

CHAPTER THIRTEEN
New Love

Several days following the celebration, Anyah took her dogs to walk along the river. Full of anger at her grandmother, she pounded the air and screamed, "Why?" Tears streamed down her face. Red licked her hand and Dig bumped up against her, sensing her frustration. Anyah did not understand why Neeyah was pushing her into a marriage before she was ready. She thought of Jorah. He had changed. Her fingers fondled the pendant. She supposed over time she might learn to love him.

There it was again, a golden light in the corner of her eye. *What is it?* When she twisted her head to the right, it disappeared. One more thing to frustrate her. She climbed up on a large flat boulder on the river's edge and laid down gazing at the brilliant blue sky and billowy clouds. The wind blew stronger and colder near the water. She pulled her cape tighter. The dogs scrambled up the rock, struggling to find a flat safe spot to lie near her.

Snuggled against the warmth of the two dogs, she drifted into a semi-dream state. Images flashed before her closed eyes of places she had never seen before, until they slowed to a lush, green place with warm breezes and fragrant flowers all around, and a waterfall flowing into a lagoon surrounded by tall trees. Two golden-skinned youths appeared, a boy and a girl with long jet-black hair and wearing sheer tunics. They laughed and joked with each other as if they had known each other for years. Anyah wondered how it was possible, since she and Rauk had just met.

The dogs jerked from her, yipping, and broke the spell of her dream. She sat up to discover someone on the other side of the river waving to her.

"Anyah!" The man's deep voice vibrated across the rushing water.

Startled, her heart raced when she realized it was Rauk. Excited by his appearance, she smiled and waved. He pointed down river and made hand gestures that he would cross. She nodded and kept her eyes on him as he reached a shallow area. He plowed through the cold water, splashing it all around him, as if he could not wait to get to her.

She tried to hide her excitement at seeing him again lowering her eyes, peaking at him as he strode up to the boulder. "Hello, Rauk," she said, in a mere whisper, her voice suddenly tight and her stomach filled with a dozen butterflies fluttering wildly.

Rauk stood leaning on a carved wooden staff used for climbing.

Unable to hold back a broad smile, she asked, "Are you scouting today?" She shielded her eyes from the brightness of the sun that shone from behind him. Though his face was in shadow, his eyes still flashed their vivid blue.

"No, unless searching for you could be called scouting." He grinned at her, reaching over to scruff Dig's ears. Red jumped down from the boulder and up on Rauk's thigh, her tail wagging. "Oho, Red, yes, I will give you some attention." Rauk grabbed both Red's ears and gave them a gentle tug.

Anyah's face burned hot from his words, thrilled he had sought her out. She laughed at the dogs jumping up on Rauk as if he were an old friend. Maybe he was.

They strolled along the river, talking and tossing stones across the water, the dogs following along. Stopping to have a snack of dried meat and nuts from the bag Anyah carried, they settled on a grass-covered bank down river.

Rauk gave Anyah a thoughtful gaze. "I spoke to my tribe's leader, who is my uncle, Edmé the Younger. We talked about the possibility our tribes might be related."

"Did you?" She perked up. "Are we related?"

"Not exactly sure, but first tell me your grand-mère's name."

"My grand-mère? It is Neeyah. Why?"

"As I suspected. Edmé pronounced it Nayah, but it is the same."

"My grand-mère is part of the story about our tribes? I do not believe it. I thought it happened in the far distant past?" She sat up straight with a confused expression.

"According to Edmé, who was not yet born, Neeyah was but a small child. She had a vision of danger, but it was not taken seriously. Her family took offense, as I understand it, and along with many others, separated from the tribe."

"Really? I want to ask my grand-mère about this. It does not seem like a strong enough reason to split apart the tribe, does it?" She glanced at Rauk and he nodded in agreement.

"I wondered about that too. There may be more to the story, and my uncle does not know. Do not take it to heart. I am happy our tribes were once one. It is sad they separated. I would have known you sooner." He winked.

"There is something I must share with you. It happened after we met." Hidden beneath her cape, her hands fidgeted with the beading on her skirt, unsure whether it mattered what she was about to tell him. Being with Rauk stirred emotions she had not experienced with anyone, even Jorah. Emotions she hoped Rauk had, too.

Rauk gave her an expectant gaze and waited for her words.

"There was a big celebration. And to my surprise my grand-mère announced my womanhood to the tribe . . . and introduced my two intendeds." She stopped, afraid to look up.

He made a low grunt. "I see."

"But . . . I want neither of them." She peered at him through her lashes and his brow raised in—what was it—delight?

"Is it not customary you must choose from those selected for you?"

"That is the problem." She heaved a sigh and raised her eyes at him.

"Why do you not want them?" Rauk leaned forward, his gaze intent on hers. "Did something or someone affect your decision?"

Was he toying with her? She could not tell. "I, uh, I suppose something happened."

"What?"

"Must I say it? Can you not tell?"

"I dare not assume what you mean. I will tell you this," he said with an assured voice. "It makes me glad you do not want them." The fullness of his mouth spread into a broad, bright smile and his eyes sparkled more than ever. He held out his hand to her.

Anyah breathed again, as if she had stopped hours before. The flutters in her stomach had returned, and they were joyous. She took his hand, and they sat there gazing at each other for hours. The touch of his hand filled her with such happiness she did not want to let go.

"What do we do now?" Anyah asked, her heart filled with uncertainty.

"I think you should take me to meet your grand-mère." He got up.

"No! I must talk to her alone first. I did not tell her about you and this will come as quite a shock and a disruption in her plans. Let us meet at the cave tomorrow after the sun passes directly over. Please wait for me there."

With great reluctance, Rauk agreed, and they spent the rest of the afternoon together confirming their commitment to each other and reveling in the gloriousness of first love.

CHAPTER FOURTEEN
Neeyah's Past

Filled with love and optimism, Anyah and her dogs strolled leisurely to her tribe's camp. She absorbed the glory of her surroundings as if it were all new, daydreaming of life with Rauk, his powerful arms around her, protecting her, and loving her. "Is this really happening?" she wondered aloud, spinning around, her arms wide, unconcerned with the freezing cold air. She was delirious with happiness until she reached the camp. Everyone was busy with their daily tasks as usual. Overcome with sudden guilt for having whiled away the day doing whatever she pleased and being with Rauk, Anyah scurried through, her head down.

Outside her dwelling, Neeyah, and Mavelle and her mother sat side by side with a new pile of white rabbit skins they were about to scrape clean. On the fire spit was an enormous cauldron of steaming rabbit stew, Anyah's favorite. She stopped to inhale the delicious aroma, avoiding her grand-mère's gaze. "Sorry I am late returning, yet again, Grand-mère. Good day to you," she said to the others.

"You are making an unpleasant habit of lateness, and it is not good for your reputation." Neeyah tossed a dismayed look at Anyah.

Anyah bent over to her grandmother's ear. "I need to speak with you, if you please."

"Sit down and help with this. With two more helping hands, we will finish quickly, then we can speak." Neeyah pulled Anyah down to sit at her side, plopped two skins in her lap, and handed her a rib

81

to scrape the pelts.

Without a word, she hid her disappointment and joined them with the pelting. Fighting her desire to burst out with her news, Anyah waited until they completed the massive pile of skins and stretched the pelts to dry. They would piece the pelts together another day.

Relieved to be inside where it was warm, Anyah hung her cape on its hook and removed her boots to clean the soles.

"You were at the river today?"

Anyah nodded, not ready to tell all.

"Now." Neeyah settled on the fur covered floor, her aged hands calm in her lap. "You need to speak to me. I hope it is because you have been considering your choice of mate?"

Anyah took a place opposite her grandmother so they were on equal ground, which gave her strength to find the right words and achieve her desire. "It is about my choice, yes, but not what you may think." She took a deep breath to stay calm. "I choose neither Jorah nor Meeks."

"I do not understand. You must choose one or the other." Neeyah's expression was stern, but confused.

"I choose someone else. Someone I met recently. We want to be together." Anyah's muscles constricted, her stomach churning with fear of what her grandmother would say or do.

"Who could you have met I do not know?"

"His name is Rauk. I met him at the cave before the celebration. He is from another tribe camped on the other side of the river."

There was silence between them. A tense and uncomfortable silence.

"Why have you not mentioned him before? The men told me another tribe was in the area hunting nearby. But they had not made themselves known officially. You have kept this from me, why?"

Anyah feared the anger growing in Neeyah's voice. "I was going to tell you, but you were so excited about the celebration and with everything happening so fast, I did not think it mattered."

"How does it matter now? You just met this, Rauk."

"It matters, because we have an incredible connection. When we were together again today, it was . . . magical!" She almost giggled from the rush rising within, remembering what it was like being with Rauk.

Neeyah was skeptical and wary. "Tell me about his tribe. What have you learned about them? Why has a representative not come to announce their presence?"

Anyah burst with energy as she told her grandmother how they met and the story of their tribe being connected. "Is it true then?"

"True? You mean, did our people once belong to the tribe of Edmé the Elder? Yes, it is true. But Rauk, or even Edmé the Younger, does not know the actual story."

"I wondered if there was more, if you were the little girl who had the sight. Were you?"

"It was my very first vision, and I was half your age now. It terrified me. I did not understand how to explain my visions very well. My parents believed me, of course. Because I was so young, the rest of the tribe had their doubts. Especially Edmé the Elder. He tossed it aside. It meant nothing because it was a dream by a child."

Anyah reached out and placed her hand over Neeyah's. "You must have been very upset."

"It was not the upsetting part. I remember the vision of a terrible catastrophe if we continued on the route we traveled. Many perished. My parents were adamant we should not move forward. But Edmé the Elder demanded we push forward. A few days later, during a snowstorm, we were traveling along a narrow ridge on a cliff. The ground gave way, causing many people to tumble down the face of the cliff to their deaths, among them my maman."

"How horrible!" Anyah clutched her throat.

"When those remaining found a safe place to camp, my papa and Edmé the Elder got into a fistfight. That's when the tribe split apart. Many families who had lost loved ones in the tragedy followed my papa and we broke away going another direction, hoping never to see those tribesmen ever again." Her eyes went dark with anger. "I will never forgive those people for not believing in my vision and causing the death of Maman and all the others."

Tears spilled down Anyah's cheeks as she brushed them away. "What a horrifying experience for you and everyone. I am so sorry."

"My dearest Anyah, now you can understand my feelings about this Rauk and his tribe."

"Rauk had nothing to do with the past. It was before his time and mine, too. Must this hatred for the past keep the two of us apart? Are you telling me to give him up?"

Without a word, Neeyah's face turned stern, her eyes filled with her memories.

"Please, Grand-mère, meet with Rauk. See for yourself. He is good and kind and will protect me."

"And what, Anyah, go live with his tribe and leave me here alone? Because there is no way I will ever accept someone from that tribe into this one." She pulled her hand out of Anyah's and stood. "Never! He is not for you."

"If I must choose, I choose Rauk. Someone I actually care about."

With that, Anyah rose and ran out of the dwelling, passing Mavelle and her mother and all the rest of her tribesman, crying uncontrollably. She ran until far out of the camp and down to the river near the natural archway. The yelps of her dogs in the distance, calling to her, made her turn. Dig and Red ran down the embankment as fast as they could. When they reached her, Anyah threw her arms around the dogs, pushing her face into their fur, and cried. She was shivering, having forgotten her cape, and the sun was lowering in the sky. She was sure her heart was breaking.

"Anyah! Anyah!"

It was Mavelle, running toward her with Anyah's cape and boots. "You forgot these, my friend? You will freeze to death."

She wrapped the cape around her friend and helped put on her boots. Anyah stopped crying and sniffed. "I met someone. We want to be together, but Grand-mère refuses me. My heart hurts."

"Who? When? Why did you not tell me?"

Anyah told Mavelle everything about Rauk, then gave her a beseeching look. "You must think I've lost my mind."

"No," she said, her voice reassuring. "It all sounds exciting and romantic. However, I see your grand-mère's side. This Rauk is unknown to us. A stranger."

"That's just the thing. He is not, really. It turns out our two tribes were once one tribe."

"What? Impossible!"

"It is true. Grand-mère confirmed it. But there is an untold story behind her refusal, which I cannot tell you right now. She will have nothing to do with Rauk's tribe. If I defy her, she will cast me out. What am I to do?" Anyah began once more to cry.

Mavelle put her arm around her. "Dearest Anyah, I am so sorry. Do not fret. It might still work out."

"I hope you are right. Thank you for understanding."

"I will always support you, Anyah. You are like a sister. Come, let us return to camp."

CHAPTER FIFTEEN

Heart's Demands

Rauk stomped on the cave floor with his pacing, his brow furrowed. Anyah sat on the floor in front of the wall, staring at the snow leopard she had drawn the day they first met. Her eyes were red and puffy from crying nonstop.

"There must be a way to convince her. She will not see me?"

Anyah shook her head.

"All because of what happened before you and I were born. She holds a grudge so steadfast she will deny your happiness? Unbelievable!" He flailed his arms in the air, then stopped. "Then you must leave here and come with me. My tribe will accept you. We will be happy together." He pulled Anyah up from the floor into his arms.

"How can I leave without Grand-mère's approval? She will be alone without me. I am all she has left."

He cradled her face with his hands, searching her eyes. "Are you telling me you will give me up?" He choked out the words.

Sobbing uncontrollably, she nodded and buried her face in his chest, clinging to him with all her might. "I do not want to. But I must not leave her, either. How can I do this?" she wailed.

Rauk picked her up and carried her to the fire pit and placed her on his thick fur cape next to the warmth of the flames. She pulled him down with her until their legs and arms were entangled. Bound by love and desperation, their passion mounted into a burst of intensity, pain, and pleasure, mixed with their sorrow.

Days passed as the snail moved, and Rauk's tribe had traveled on. Anyah could not forget him. She forged through the motions of her life, numb and consumed with sadness. Neeyah acted as if nothing had happened. She did not mention Rauk, and neither did Anyah. Plans for the wedding with Jorah moved forward.

Anyah cringed whenever she came remotely close to Meeks. He showed his disappointment at being rejected by sending dagger-filled stares her way. No longer could Anya go wherever she wanted: to the cave, to draw and paint, or to spy on the hunts. She longed for Rauk's touch, kisses, and his scent.

She spent time with Jorah, becoming more familiar with each other, in order to transition into living together in marriage. He came by her dwelling to collect her for their walks. One day, only a few days before their wedding, they were strolling along the river. Anyah's thoughts wavered from Jorah to Rauk, and she stopped and turned to him.

"There is something different about me. Have you noticed?"

He hesitated, but could not deny it. "Yes, what has happened?"

"I am so sorry, but we cannot marry. You deserve an explanation . . . I just . . ."

She left him standing by the river with his mouth hung open, confused and hurt. Anyah ran back to her dwelling and was grateful Neeyah was not there. She packed some food and a skin of water into a bag. With her two dogs, she would search for Rauk's tribe. She knew the general direction they were to travel, and hoped to find it before she ran out of food and water.

Once she was out of sight of her own tribe's encampment, she stopped to assess what lay ahead—the steppes, a seemingly endless expanse of ice with wide patches of exposed ground. Winter was coming, and the sky warned of a pending storm. Forcing back a twinge of fear, she wished she was already in Rauk's warm embrace. Desire gave her strength as she marched on.

She found some shelter in a large hollowed out tree. Cuddling with her dogs, she slept until dawn. By midday, she found tracks and was sure they were Rauk's tribe. A wash of comfort flooded over her. She was not far behind.

The storm came with strong winds blowing the frozen snow from behind, pushing her forward. She tied the dogs on leather leashes, which she wrapped securely about her waist, and let them lead the way. Red and Dig pulled at her when fatigue set in. She could barely lift her boots in the snow as it deepened, it seemed, with every step.

When the storm passed, Rauk's caravan finally came into sight before nightfall. Instead of resting and waiting until morning, she and the dogs followed the light from their fires like a beacon of hope.

As she entered their camp, the men rose with their weapons poised until they realized it was only a young woman.

"I am Anyah, and I came for Rauk." Her body exhausted, she collapsed to the ground.

When she woke, she was inside a dwelling surrounded by the kind faces of women and a tall man standing at the entrance, watching.

"There you are," said the woman, holding a cloth on Anyah's forehead. "How do you feel?"

"Rauk? I am here to see Rauk."

"Yes, dear, we know. Just rest. You have traveled far."

"I am fine. I need to see him. He is here?" Anyah was anxious and rose from the soft bed of fur, but the kind woman gently pushed her down.

"Now, now, you must rest."

The man moved close to Anyah. "She is fine, Morah. I will speak to her now," he said in a gruff voice, his face moving into the light from the oil lamp.

Anyah looked up at him. "Is Rauk coming?"

"I am so very sorry you made this journey alone to find out Rauk is dead. He was killed in a hunting expedition, shortly after we made camp here."

"Dead? No, not possible. I came all this way to be with him. I left my tribe, my family." Anyah's head throbbed, and the room spun around as if she were falling into a great black hole.

"We are so sorry, dear," said the woman.

"It was strange," said the man. "Rauk stood stock still and would not get out of the way of the bison. It was as if he froze in place. The same thing happened to his brother. We shouted out to him to move and no one could get to him before the bison trampled him to death."

The words fell on Anyah's ears like boulders and stunned her to silence, not knowing what to say. No tears came. She was sure her heart had broken in two.

Once she had regained her health and strength, she and the dogs headed back to her tribe. Edmé the Younger insisted two of his men must accompany her.

Neeyah was grateful to the other tribesmen for bringing Anyah safely home, but she could not find the words to ease her granddaughter's pain. Her actions had driven Anyah away, and she bore the blame for Rauk's tragedy. Over time, they forgave each other.

Jorah sought Anyah out and courted her during the following weeks, despite her despair and depression. Anyah grew to trust Jorah and one day, while walking along the river as she had done with Rauk, she told Jorah about the man she had loved and lost.

"I heard about this man." Jorah's voice was barely a whisper.

"How?" Anyah stopped and turned Jorah around to look at her. "What have you heard?"

"There have been rumors around the camp. I was waiting for you to tell me. I was told he killed himself at the loss of you. Is it true?"

Anyah burst into tears, turning her back to him. Her body racked with sobs. "Maybe. No one is sure exactly why . . . But yes, he died."

Jorah put his arms around her. "I am so sorry, dearest Anyah. Let me help you get past your loss."

He was so gentle and kind, Anyah could not bear it. How could she tell him all of it?

"What can I do?" he urged.

She pulled from his embrace and faced him. "You will not want to help me once I tell you the whole truth."

"Of course, I will. I care for you. I love you."

"You cannot love me! I am carrying Rauk's child." There, she'd said it, and though she was afraid, she looked him in the eyes, expecting a look of disgust. Instead, his face showed a loving expression and a smile of complete acceptance.

"I have suspected this is so. It does not matter, for I will give this child all the love it deserves. Because two people who loved each other conceived it. I only hope someday you will come to love me in return." He opened his arms wide, and Anyah fell into his embrace with surprise and relief.

"I am so grateful for your friendship and love. I will try to be a good wife to you, for you deserve my respect, and I hope love, too."

They married right away with the entire tribe, celebrating and receiving Neeyah's blessing. When Rauk's tribe passed through the great archway again, Neeyah reconciled with Edmé the Younger and the two tribes became one, agreeing to share in the hunting and trade.

Anyah gave birth to a strong and healthy boy, and Jorah insisted they name him Rauk. Anyah was grateful to Jorah, and eventually, she grew to love him as a husband and a father to her child.

A few years later, Neeyah joined the Great Protector in the life beyond, leaving Anyah as the tribe's wise woman. Anyah settled in to a happy and full life, embracing her destiny wholeheartedly. She used her gift to guide their people, and with Jorah, she begat many children as her grand-mère had wanted. In her new role, she made it acceptable for women to join in the hunt if they chose . . . including herself.

CHAPTER SIXTEEN

Failure

When the time travelers returned, the sconce's white glow softly lit the room. Settled in his body, Yohan squeezed Xenia's hand, letting her know he was there, and let go.

"I sure hope we were successful," Xenia said as soon as she opened her eyes.

"We were. How do you feel?"

"Tired and a little thirsty. You?"

"I am not as weak as before. We were not gone as long. Gayeena must have left this for us." He pointed to the small table set with cups and a pitcher of water, including fruit and nuts on a plate. "Shall I turn up the lights?"

Xenia took the cup Yonan handed her. "Not yet. I want to look into the future to see the results. I was so pleased Anyah and Rauk were together again at the river. They looked happy."

"Definitely happy. I agree you should look into our future before we go home. I do not think I could sleep otherwise."

Xenia finished eating some berries and took her place at the table in front of the scrying crystal. Yonan took a long gulp of water and stood next to her.

Her hands over the crystal and meditating on the point in time they had left, she said, "I see them and they are parting. I will move forward a little . . . they are together again at the cave . . . oh dear." Xenia did not like what she saw, her optimism quickly giving way to disappointment.

"What is it?" Yonan tried to view the crystal, but the vision was not visible to him.

"Just a minute . . ." She stared into the surface of the crystal, adjusting her hands slightly as the images sped forward in time, and then she stopped. Her face told Yonan what he had suspected.

"I guess it did not work?" Yonan said.

"This is so frustrating. The original vision still happened, even though our future selves came together."

"What was the problem?"

"It was me . . . I mean Anyah. They fell in love, like we wanted, but her grandmother would not allow Anyah and Rauk to marry. Something about a rift between the two tribes and she was still angry about it. At first, Anyah could not leave her grandmother, though when she changed her mind, it was too late and Rauk was killed in a hunt."

Yonan gave a forlorn sigh.

"We failed." Tears welled up in Xenia's eyes. "I am afraid we will never get our future selves together for the long term."

Yonan took her hand and guided her to sit with him on the curved bench against the wall. "We did not fail. Through our efforts, they found each other and fell in love. Your future self is still you, loyal and always wanting to do the right thing. Remember, they can choose which way to go or what decisions to make, even with our urging and gentle suggestions."

Xenia laid her head on his shoulder. "I suppose you are right. Shall we try again?"

"Are you up to it?"

"Yes, I want to find where the next lifetime is and who we will be."

The couple returned to the crystal, and Xenia began her search. Once in trance, she watched the image move across the planet through time as the Earth changed, the melting of the ice caps and more green spots appeared, the movement slowed and zoomed into a place crowded with many villages, with people dressed in thick trousers and overcoats, wearing round wide-brimmed hats pointed at the top. Her mind picked up on a language unknown to her. A tonal form of speech. She followed the image to a royal palace, she assumed, from all the gold and elaborate white carvings and bright colors of red and gold. There she found Yonan's future self in a place tending to trays of silkworms, feeding them mulberry leaves. But he was a woman and among many other women tending to dozens of trays of worms.

"Yonan, you are tending silkworms."

"Fascinating. Someone in the future discovers them."

"It must be you who takes the knowledge to the future. But you are a young woman among many women working with the worms."

"I am? Are you there?"

Xenia continued to follow the vision in the crystal and found herself. "Yes, I am standing next to you working together with the worms."

"I am in a place full of women?"

"We are both women."

"Not the arrangement we are seeking, though."

"They are already together for whatever relationship they find. There is nothing we need to do, anyway. I will continue forward."

Several minutes passed. Yonan tapped his foot.

"Stop that, Yonan. You are disturbing my concentration . . . all right, I have come upon another place. It is hot and dry. There are vast barren lands of sand with large cities of stone filled with many people. I sense my future self and also your future self are present within the same structure."

"How convenient. What kind of structure?"

"It is enormous, made of stone. Tall columns with spacious halls and rooms so huge the people are like ants. There are many people in this building, most appear to be servants . . . Wait . . . I sense myself. Let me get closer." Xenia zooms in on a slight-built girl in a procession with other women, all dressed in the same white gowns that touched the floor. "She looks much like you and me, but smaller, shorter. I think she is a servant, as there are others dressed exactly the same."

"Do you sense where my future self is?" Yonan's impatience was irritating her.

"Give me a chance. I am trying to understand what I am seeing to research it in the scrolls."

"Sorry, I want to see the future. When I tap into your thoughts while you are scrying, your mind blocks me out, just like Gayeena."

"It must be a protection thing. I sense you, your future self." Xenia was drawn away from the girl, and moving through the halls to the other side of the great structure to another enormous room, where a group of men, wearing long robes made of fine white cloth, clustered around a table full of scrolls and maps. One was a boy, but it was obvious he held an important position judging how the others treated him with respect. Behind him and to the side was an older man, who she sensed was protecting the boy. "Aha! I found you."

"This is wonderful. Our future selves are in the same building? What luck! Can you tell if they know each other?"

"No. You appear to be a guard of sorts to a very important person." She stopped and dropped her hands. "I cannot do anymore today. I am extremely tired now. I will come back tomorrow to research the scrolls for any information the ancient ones may have written about."

"It should be a lot easier to get them together and stay. I hope." Yonan embraced her. "You did very well."

"Let us rest today. Should we tell Gayeena about our plans to try again?"

"I will take care of that. Let us return home now. We have another exciting journey ahead of us after we attend the End-of-Life Ceremony."

CHAPTER SEVENTEEN
Farewells

"I cannot do it. Please do not make me go," said Xenia, her eyes red from crying as she lay in their bed curled up in a ball.

Yonan rolled over, spooning her back, his hand stroking her shoulder. "I know, my heart. I do not relish watching our dearest friends and family dying right before our very eyes, but this is our last opportunity to say goodbye."

"I understand your two aunts wanting to go early, and Seema and Tahn, too. But to watch it is another thing. Why are Gayeena and the Elders making the ceremony public?"

"We do not have to go. It is for those who want to be there, and why it is public. We told Seema, Tahn, and my aunts we would be there. But if you want me to tell them we will not go, I will do it."

"No. I am behaving like a child today, defiant. My whole being wants to fight this thing." She turned over to face him.

"I do, too. But we are doing the only thing we can. Support others and ensure our future selves find each other." He kissed her cheek.

Xenia wrapped her arms around him and squeezed with all of her might.

"Ow, you are extra strong today." He smiled and kissed her again, deeply with passion, and she reciprocated, tangling her limbs with his, and taking in his hardness.

A few hours later, they were on the way to the beach where the ceremony would be held at the amphitheater built into the hill. It could accommodate hundreds of people. When Xenia and Yonan arrived, Seema and Tahn were already on the staging area with eighteen others who were to end their lives. Yonan recognized his two aunts up there as well. A pang of sadness shot through him.

Xenia held her breath when their friends appeared on the stage. She pulled Yonan to the side. "I cannot watch," she said in a hushed voice close to his ear so others passing by could not hear.

"It will be fine, my heart. Take my hand and close your eyes if you must. Our being here is homage to our dearest friends."

She took his hand and sank into his shoulder, tears falling down her cheeks.

They chose seats next to Yonan's father. Family was important to the Zorathians, but once they lived hundreds of years, the family connection lessened. The coming of the Great Shift was now drawing everyone closer together as they came to terms with their coming deaths.

"My son, it is good to see you. I was planning to visit you soon. You have friends up there today?" he motioned to the staging area.

"Yes, father, our best friends, Seema and Tahn."

"Ah, I know them. Your late mother's sisters are up there," his father said and pointed to the stage.

"I noticed. It will be strange without them," Yonan said, as his thoughts were of his mother, who died decades earlier from an unknown illness she caught from the island people. Nothing the Zorathian physicians did could save her. It was a rare instance.

"I am actually looking forward to passing on. I hope to find your mother in a future life." Yonan's father said.

Yonan cringed from feelings of guilt. He gave Xenia a strained look. <I want to tell him.>

She shook her head.

Yonan gave her an understanding nod and turned back to his father. "I really hope you do, Father," he said, with a loving smile.

The four Elders, two women, and two men, appeared on the stage wearing their official purple silk caftans. Gayeena glided across, stood in front of them, and said prayers over everyone on stage, wishing them well in their future lives. The Elders followed behind. Each held a draught for the twenty to drink, and then they sat down in the lotus position on cushions. Behind each person was a delegate who sat waiting to catch them once the poison in the draught took effect.

The congregation meditated, sending positive energies to the departing. One by one, as the poison took its permanent sleep-inducing effect, they drooped into the arms of the delegates behind them and their bodies were carried off the stage and placed on the pyre, readied on the beach.

Xenia took in a sharp breath when their friends were carried away. Yonan tried not to appear distressed when they removed his aunts. He regretted not visiting them to say farewell in person. All in attendance shed many tears with prayers of love. Once the stage was cleared, the congregation followed in a procession to the beach to watch the lighting of the pyre.

"This is unbearable," Xenia cried into his shoulder.

"The pyre will burn for at least six hours before they have reduced all the bodies to ashes. We can come back to see the last step when they send the ashes to sea in a boat set afire to sink off the coast."

"Yes, it is the least we can do."

The air filled with the overpowering stench of burning bodies, forcing many of the congregation to leave early, including Xenia, Yonan, and his father.

PART THREE: EGYPT
48 BCE

CHAPTER EIGHTEEN
The Palace

It was dusk. The torchlight danced across the polished marble floors as the sound of flapping from her sandaled feet echoed throughout the great hall. It was Iras's first experience serving as handmaiden to Queen Cleopatra VII, who co-ruled with her brother and husband, Ptolemy XIII. She feared they would punish her for arriving late. The former handmaiden had fallen ill, and Charmion, the Queen's closest advisor, requested Iras to serve as a replacement. As she scurried down the corridor to the Queen's private chambers, she wondered why they had not filled the opening with an existing maid. But the thought faded as soon as she reached the entrance, flanked by two Nubian guards who thrust their spears across the door. She stopped short.

"Who goes?" one guard asked.

"I am Iras, new handmaiden to Her Majesty, Queen Cleopatra." She attempted a brave face, showing the bracelet identifying her as royal servant.

"You are late." The guard on the left side of the door said and fell at ease. The other guard opened the door, allowing Iras to enter. She took light steps into the immense room. The ceiling soared so high she could barely make out the colors and patterns painted on it, though every wall was ablaze with lighted sconces filling the space with bright light. On the other side of the room was a dais near the terrace, which held a magnificent view of Alexandria. Two maids stood motionless with their heads bowed. The Queen was bathing in the shallow pool behind the sheer curtains.

Charmion stood nearby, tall and stately, a well-bred Greek, dressed in a sheer white linen gown topped with an elaborate gold and lapis collar showing her high position. She motioned Iras to join them.

Iras hurried up the two short steps to the dais. Charmion whispered instructions to her, then stepped back to observe while Iras worked.

The Queen clapped her hands. One maid held a towel and the other maid held a tray of fragrant oils. Both hurried through the opening in the curtain. Iras followed to assist Cleopatra out of the pool.

"Ah, you must be Iras," said Cleopatra. "Thanks be to Isis. You are much needed." Speaking in Egyptian, her seductive voice glided over Iras's ears like soft butter. Iras had been told the Queen spoke Egyptian—unlike most Ptolemies—but the fluency surprised her.

"It is an honor to serve you. Would you like me to anoint you with perfumed oil?"

Cleopatra looked Ira up and down and frowned, turning to Charmion, "Make sure she is appropriately dressed by tomorrow." To Iras, "Jasmine with a touch of water lily, before my skin dries."

Iras nodded, her face red, wishing she had worn a simple white gown like the others, instead of her thick homespun shift. A maid held out the tray of oils, and Iras deftly blended the two oils in a small bowl and turned to her mistress, who was holding her arms out ready. She massaged a generous amount of the oil on the Queen's pale olive skin to hold in the moisture, keeping it soft. Iras noticed her mistress's dimpled and wrinkled skin, thinking she must have been in the water for hours. Yet, when she finished, it glistened from the oils, and the floral fragrance surrounded them.

"You have a fine touch, Iras."

"I am pleased you approve," Iras replied, stepping back, as two of the maids patted the queen dry with thick absorbent towels woven from the cotton grown on the fertile lands along the Nile. The third maid brought out a linen robe so sheer it was almost transparent. She and Iras wrapped it around Cleopatra, securing the waist with a finely tooled golden belt with a chain and tassel on the end. She slipped into golden sandals and stepped down from the dais, taking a seat at a dressing table upon which were several wigs propped on stands. Without a word, she pointed to the black wig of long, thick coils. Iras placed it on her shaved head, the length resting right below her shoulders, and added a golden headband with a serpent twisted around the front.

Stepping back to admire the total effect, Iras was in awe of the power emanating from such a tiny woman, whose beauty came from her confidence, wit, and the way she moved and spoke. She pressed her hands together before her and bowed.

Cleopatra leaned forward to gaze at her reflection in the highly polished copper hand mirror.

"Shall I hold it for you, Your Majesty?" Iras reached for the mirror and held it for her mistress as she touched up her eyeliner and green shadow.

"That will be all. Iras, you may go, but keep close by when I am ready to retire."

"Your Majesty." Iras crossed her arms in front of her and bowed low. She was about to take her leave when the door opened and a man entered, dressed in a type of soldier's attire, with a metal breastplate and helmet, who sought Charmion's attention.

The advisor hurried to the entrance and took something from the man.

"Your Majesty, an urgent message from your sister, Arsinoe," she said, thrusting out her hand, which held a small scroll.

Cleopatra took the scroll, unrolling quickly, and read it.

"Shall he send a reply?" Charmion asked, indicating the man waiting at the door.

Iras assumed the man must be someone of great importance to be allowed inside the Queen's apartment.

"No need. I will go to her now. You may lead. Iras, my fan."

Iras did not know where anything was. As she glanced around the room she was grateful when a maid offered an elegant white ostrich feather fan. She mouthed a thank you to the maid, who blinked in surprise at her appreciation, apparently not used to being treated so kindly.

As Iras gave the fan to the Queen, a sudden flash of golden light appeared in the corner of her eye. She twisted to see where it came from, but it was gone.

"Is something wrong?" Cleopatra asked, looking in the direction Iras had turned.

"I thought I saw something, but it is gone now." She moved out of the Queen's way, and glanced over at the man who stared at her, his eyes intent, and the hint of a smile passed over his lips. There was something familiar about him, though she did not know any Macedonians personally, other than the Queen. She could not put her finger on it, but he unnerved her.

Cleopatra snapped her fingers at the man and he stood at attention, opening the door to lead the way. "Wait here until I return," she said to Iras, as she sauntered out and down the hall, followed by Charmion.

Iras was alone with the two maids. "My name is Iras." They were Egyptian, like her, as were most of the lower-level servants in the palace. The Greek Macedonians had ruled Egypt for three centuries, and usually the close inner circles of the royals were Greek, too. "Who was the man who was here? A soldier?"

The girls giggled. "He is the bodyguard to Ptolemy, his name is Kyros. He is a member of Ptolemy's inner circle. A very important man. I am Satia," she said, "and she is Semat," pointing to the other maid.

"I hope we will become friends while working together."

Semat beamed. "I would like that very much. The handmaiden who became ill was not friendly with us. She was Greek and looked down upon Egyptian servants."

~ ~ ~

The next day, the Queen sent Iras to the lower levels to collect an amphora of her favorite sweet red wine she imported from Greece. Security measures were common to protect the royals from assassination attempts, even though they guarded the wine well. Lit sconces set far apart created an eerie light in the dim corridors. Iras jumped when a rat passed over her foot. She quickened her steps until she reached the door to the chamber. The guards did not move to open the door.

"I am the Queen's handmaiden, Iras, sent to fetch her wine." She held up her arm, showing them the bracelet.

Without a response, the guards opened the door and let her into the brightly lit room. Dozens of clay jars sat on wood stands in rows so far back she should barely see them. Several male workers preparing and storing the wine gave her a brief nod. "May we help you?" said a man who wore a bracelet with the Ptolemy symbol and other marks, showing he was of a high rank.

"My lady, the Queen, wishes me to fetch her favorite wine, the one with honey, mint, and cinnamon bark flavors." Iras stood tall, her shoulders squared, implying she was of superior status as handmaiden to their illustrious Queen.

"This way," said the man, and she followed.

The room was filled with rows of large ceramic amphorae of varying sizes, some as tall as five feet high, where workers were busy syphoning wine into smaller vessels. He directed her to the Queen's private reserve room containing her favorite wines shipped from Greece. The man went to a row he explained stored the specific wine the Queen requested, retrieved a two-gallon amphora and handed it to her. It was much heavier than she expected.

"Will you need assistance in taking this to Her Majesty?"

"No, I can manage." Iras struggled until she balanced the inverted teardrop shape to her body and she wrapped her arms around it.

"Will you always be the servant to come for the Queen's wine?" the man asked.

Iras assumed it would be the case, though no one had told her. She was yet to receive instructions as to her full duties. "Yes," she replied, and left.

When the Queen's wine was depleted, Iras would go to fetch the wine. It was on one of those assignments that she sensed someone following her while she journeyed through the dimly lit corridors of the underground. She was not afraid, but cautious. On the other days, no one else had moved through those corridors, intended as secret passageways for a select few persons.

She stopped. The sound of heavy steps grew louder, and she turned. "Who is there?"

From around the corner appeared a familiar face. It was Kyros, the bodyguard she had met a few days earlier in the Queen's chambers. "Are you following me?"

Kyros did not stop. He marched up to her near the sconce. The light shone on his helmet, casting a shadow on his face. In the semi-darkness, Iras sensed the same familiarity as before.

"Not intentionally. Please forgive me if I made you uncomfortable. There was a strange golden light coming from this passageway. I followed it, not you. I am surprised to find you here."

"What golden light. I have not seen one, at least not today."

"Today? What do you mean?"

"It was the other night when you came into the Queen's chambers. There was a golden flash of light in the corner of my eye. Was it like that?"

"No, this light moved ahead of me, as if it were guiding me down this corridor. It would disappear, then reappear. It is gone, now that I found you."

He grinned at her, a broad gleaming smile sending shivers down Iras's back. She could not hide the smile spreading across her face. Kyros looked pleased, yet shuffled from one foot to the other as though he was uncomfortable. The long flaps of metal surrounding his knee-length tunic clinked together with his movement.

"You are Gabiniani, yes?"

"Many royal guards are. Why do you ask?"

"You remind me of some of my family who are descended from the famous Egyptian warriors."

"Interesting. And now you are a servant to Queen Cleopatra, my liege's wife and sister. You are new?"

"Only recently I began serving the Queen. I am most honored and support her wholeheartedly."

"As you should."

"I must complete my task, or she will wonder where I've gone."

"Of course. Allow me to linger here a moment to be sure you arrive there safely."

It was comforting to know he was watching out for her, though she could not fathom why he would bother with a lowly servant. Perhaps it was because she was a servant to the Queen, and he was a guard for Ptolemy. She hurried on to the wine room.

The next few days, Iras found Kyros in the corridors when she arrived, waiting for her, insisting he accompany her. During those brief periods, they shared similar stories of their families, and were sure they were not connected. Iras looked forward to her task each day to fetch the Queen's wine, until one day, Kyros was not there. Wondering why, she tried to put him out of her mind, unsuccessfully. *What happened? Was he found out and told not to go to the underground?* Did someone discover she had been spending time with the King's bodyguard?

After she collected another amphora of wine, she started back through the corridor and neared the end to ascend the stairs to the upper levels. Kyros came rushing down the steps. He pulled her aside and put his finger to her lips. His touch burned through her with feelings she had never experienced before.

"Is something wrong?" she said.

He removed his helmet and set in on one step and turned to her with a stern expression. "Yes, very wrong. I cannot meet you here anymore. I am sorry." He put his hand on her arm and she shuddered from his touch, fear rising from deep within.

"You no longer wish to be with me?" Her face fell with disappointment, wondering if it was something she had said or done.

"That is not the reason. I very much want to be with you. I should not be telling you this, but . . . I am concerned for your safety."

"My safety?" She took a step back.

"You and the Queen. You cannot divulge it was me who told you. Tell her you overhead some whisperings. Promise me."

"I promise." Apprehension filled her.

"Ptolemy's advisors and Arsinoe are planning to push out Queen Cleopatra. They want Arsinoe and Ptolemy to rule Egypt."

"This news will devastate her," she whispered, her voice faltering. "What should I tell her?"

"Urge her, along with all her staff, to flee as soon as possible, or there may be bloodshed."

Kyros took the container from her shaking hands placing it on the floor leaning it against the wall, then pulled her into an embrace. Iras did not resist letting her body press against him. This is what she had wanted since the first day she set her eyes on him. He bent his head and kissed her deeply, his hands moving over her firm body. Iras moaned with desire. "What will happen to you?"

He loosened his hold on her and paused, "I am the King's guard, I must protect him, too. It is my calling."

"If the Queen escapes and I go with her, I will never see you again?" Tears welled up, and she choked on the words.

"It is possible. I cannot read the future, only what is happening now. I must leave you here and return to my post. But hurry to the Queen to warn her. It will happen soon." He kissed her again with such intensity it overwhelmed him. Stumbling backward, he grabbed his helmet and rushed up the stairs two steps at a time.

Her knees about to give way, Iras backed against the wall and wrapped her arms around herself, breathless and inflamed with passion—and scared to death. Once she regained her composure, she picked up the amphora and hurried up the steps to the throne room where Queen Cleopatra was waiting for the wine. She wondered if she would ever see him again.

CHAPTER NINETEEN

Treachery

Iras moved as fast as she could while carrying the heavy amphora to the throne room. Cleopatra paced the floor while Charmion rattled on, her voice edgy. Their serious expressions told Iras to keep quiet until there was a moment to share what she had learned from Kyros.

Iras set the amphora of wine into the wood rack on the table, and broke the clay seal. Satia helped to pour the wine into a bowl and as was the Greek custom, Iras diluted the wine with clear water, mixing well before ladling into the golden goblets on a golden tray.

"Wait—" Charmion said. "Call in the taster." She cast a concerned look at the Queen.

"Yes, with the information we have today, from now on, even the sealed wine will be tasted."

Iras and Satia poured wine into a small clay cup and a servant entered the hall. She was given the cup to drink.

Cleopatra stopped pacing and glanced at the taster. When enough time had passed and the taster was still alive without symptoms, Iras presented the goblets to the Queen. She grabbed one and downed nearly the whole thing in one gulp and wiped her mouth with her wrist. She tipped the goblet at Iras, signaling she needed more.

"What took you so long?" she said.

Iras bowed her head. "Please forgive my lateness—" She was about to tell her news, but stopped herself.

Charmion took the other goblet and sipped from it. "I must tell you, my Queen, there are rumors. He is up to no good." Her face paled.

Iras wondered if Charmion knew. Should she speak? Not sure whether to interrupt or stay silent, she turned away and stumbled, her sandal caught on the hem of her long skirt, sending the tray out of her grasp crashing to the floor. Its metallic sound reverberated through the hall. Mortified, Iras quickly picked up the tray, afraid to look at either Charmion or the Queen.

"What is the matter with you?" Charmion said with irritation.

"My apologies, it is about what you were saying . . ."

"Tell me." Cleopatra said.

"Well, it confirms what I overheard some guards whispering about." She didn't want to divulge that it was Kyros who told her.

"What did you hear, Iras? Tell me."

"Arsinoe and Ptolemy's advisers are plotting against you. They want you out." There, she said it. Would they want to know which guards? Where she heard it? How would she answer? She could barely breathe.

"I told you I am not making it up. Arsinoe is involved," Charmion said to Cleopatra. "It is imperative we get out of the palace before they plan to act. We must act first."

"Yes, I agree," Cleopatra said. Stamping her foot and swirling around, her gown fluttered. "I noticed Arsinoe acting peculiarly when she called me to her chambers. She must have been trying to get information from me. Ptolemy is not smart enough to devise this plan on his own, or even want it. He is but a boy and does not know what he is doing. Go, both of you, and gather the others. Start packing and arranging our transportation. I need to figure out where we can go that will be safe to plan our response."

Iras and Charmion hurried out of the throne room, through the halls, and up the stairs to the Queen's chambers on the upper level. Iras said nothing while Charmion cursed under her breath.

They worked well into the night gathering the Queen's belongings and items they would need on the journey for however long they would be gone, assuming they would return. By the time Iras laid upon her pallet with the others in the Queen's chambers, she could not sleep, tossing from the anxiety of the flight from Alexandria.

None of them, except for Cleopatra, knew the destination, lest information on their departure leak to Ptolemy's advisors. Perhaps even the captain of her barge would not know until they were all aboard.

Physically exhausted and full of fear, Kyros's face came to mind—and his touch, that lit a passion in her, she knew would not be satisfied. Would she ever see him again? With Egypt's co-rulers at odds, the likelihood diminished with each waking hour until her eyes finally closed and sleep swept over her. The morning came as soon as she shut her eyes. The room was bustling with activity.

"Iras, rise now, we must hurry," said Satia, as she rolled up her pallet and threw it in a large reed basket. "Put yours in here."

Iras followed suit and placed her pallet in the basket. She did what she could to help, though everyone seemed disoriented with the urgency and fear. The Queen entered her chambers dressed for travel. Ashamed for having overslept, Iras whispered apologies to Satia and Semat. The Queen's guards ushered Cleopatra, Charmion, Iras and the rest of the entourage to the secret passageways beneath the palace leading to the docks where her royal barge sat waiting. The Queen's belongings and supplies were delivered to the barge by the time they arrived at the dock.

Everyone boarded as quickly as possible and settled the Queen on the dais, when two chariots pulled by powerful and fast steeds drew up at the bank. Two of Ptolemy's royal guards marched up the gangplank and onto the barge, pushing their way past the servants up to Queen Cleopatra. She did not look surprised.

"Your Majesty, we were to deliver this edict to you personally, before you left," said the first guard to step forward with his hand stretched out holding a scroll.

Charmion took the scroll and handed it to Cleopatra. She sat up straight, holding the scroll in her hands. It had her brother's seal.

"What does it say?" asked Charmion.

"As we suspected. Ptolemy's advisors stripped me of my authority and title. You may go." She ordered the messenger and turned to Charmion. "We must hurry. I have an army to raise to reclaim my throne!"

CHAPTER TWENTY

No Longer a Secret

When Xenia and Yonan opened their eyes after settling on the devices, they looked around and discovered they were not alone in the room. Every device was occupied. Xenia started to speak when Yonan raised his hand, motioning her to keep quiet and follow him. He pressed the button at the door, signaling they had returned. Soon, Gayeena opened the door to let them out and shut the door quietly.

"You must have been surprised by so many others in the room when you returned. Come with me and I will explain." They returned to her private quarters at the Temple and she poured cups of cool, clear water for each of them.

Xenia gulped the water to quench her thirst, for they had been away this last time for nearly three days. Yonan did the same and reached for the fruit on a platter Gayeena offered them, taking a seat on the long cushion sofa.

"It was right after you two returned to Egypt, correct?"

They nodded.

"Two couples came to me asking about their future lives and told me Seema had mentioned it to them."

"Seema?" Xenia faltered. Were they wrong to tell Seema? She looked at Yonan.

"Yes, High Priestess," Yonan said, "we told Seema and Tahn it was possible to time travel to future lives. But they weren't interested. They were our dearest friends, and we had to share this information.

I hope we didn't make a terrible mistake."

"Not a mistake, it was unexpected, is all. Several people came in the last few days. Most of them only wanted to learn about their future lives. Those using the devices wanted to do what you two are attempting. With this new turn of events, I must schedule the use of the devices now. You understand."

Dismayed by the news, Xenia frowned. "I understand, but we are having trouble accomplishing our goal. We must be doing something wrong. I am worried we will not have enough time if we must share. However, I am happy others are doing this, really I am."

"I am sure you are, Xenia. What is the problem the two of you are facing? Have you not found your future selves?"

"We found them with no problem. We helped them get together and fall in love. But . . ."

"Good News," Gayeena smiled. "But what?"

"The first lifetime, Xenia's future self, chose not to be with my future self, because of her loyalty to family," Yonan said.

"Then she changed her mind and traveled to be with him finding out he had died in an accident." Xenia struggled to keep from bursting into tears.

"An unfortunate turn," Gayeena said. "And then you traveled to another lifetime, in Egypt. What is happening there?"

"We came back to discuss our next steps, if there are any. It looks futile to me," Yonan said.

"They found each other and were connecting. We were optimistic they were falling in love. Something happened politically, and it will separate them. My future self is a maid to a queen who must flee the country to save herself, and her staff must go with her," Xenia said.

"We need to use the crystal to check on their progress before we decide what to do. However, the crystal is no longer in the room," Yonan said to Gayeena.

"I agree, you need to do another scrying. We moved the crystal to a quiet place with no disturbances. Go to the small room at the side of the Temple. I think it is empty right now."

"Thank you, High Priestess," Xenia sighed.

They took more water and the plate of food with them to where the crystal had been moved. A peaceful room used for private contemplation away from the main temple area. The colors were soothing, soft green walls and a fountain with water tumbling over pebbles making a light tinkling sound. Narrow windows made of the same crushed crystals as the other windows allowed enough soft light. More relaxed, Xenia found the crystal mounted on a pedestal against the far wall.

"Do you want to rest before trying it? We've had a lot to take in. There is no need to rush," said Yonan.

"This room is restful, and the water has replenished my thirst. I would like to try." Taking in several long breaths with her eyes closed, she concentrated on the future Egyptian lifetime, and on Iras, wondering where she had gone and whether she was with the Queen? *Are they safe?* Her connection to Iras was strong, as she placed her hands over the crystal and opened her eyes, waiting for the vision sure to come.

"I see them . . . the Queen, Iras, and her handmaidens, including her adviser, Charmion. They are traveling away on a barge east through the delta, toward a place called Syria . . . I will move forward in time to where they go . . ." Xenia followed the vision. "I found her again. It is about a year later, must be around 48 BCE. Iras is still with Cleopatra camped on the border and there are men in uniforms. They are preparing to battle Ptolemy's forces, and Cleopatra is hoping to return to Egypt. This is good."

"Then Kyros must still be in Egypt," Yonan directed.

Xenia pushed the vision searching to Kyros. "He is in the palace in Alexandria . . . you, I mean Kyros, is there with Ptolemy, but it is not clear to me what is happening." She allowed the vision to dissipate and took a seat on a padded bench. "I am tired and not sure what to think about the vision. I am confused."

Yonan sat next to her, sliding his arm around her shoulder, and leaned his forehead against hers. "We need rest. Tomorrow we will travel to the Egyptian time and all will be revealed."

CHAPTER TWENTY-ONE

Caesar to the Rescue

Hoping to reunite Iras and Kyros, they decided it was best to separate. Xenia to find Iras, while Yonan sought Kyros at the palace in Alexandria.

Yonan headed directly to Ptolemy's chambers, but they were empty. He scanned the rest of the palace, finding Kyros in the strategy room on the lower level. All the advisers, Arsinoe, the general and Kyros, and Ptolemy were shouting, their voices falling over each other. The intense energy in the room made Yonan move back to observe, unsure of what was happening.

"Quiet!" Shouted the chief adviser, "We will accomplish nothing if we do not keep our heads." The room grew still.

"Caesar's army is closing in," said Arsinoe. "We must leave the palace now!"

"No, I will not give up. You told me I am Pharaoh," cried the young Ptolemy. "I want to fight him." He pounded his small fist on the table.

"Take him out of here until we have decided," the chief adviser directed Kyros. "He does not understand the situation. Arsinoe, you can stay if you wish."

"If I do not understand, then teach me," Ptolemy scowled, folding his arms.

"We do not have the time. We are in crisis."

"I will come with you, Ptolemy," Arsinoe said.

Kyros took Ptolemy's arm and gently guided him out of the room. The boy resisted.

In the corridor, the young Pharaoh stood pouting. "How dare you!" he spat. "You are to do as I bid you." He turned on his sister. "And you, too!"

"Your advisors know what is best for you. They are the experts. You must keep quiet," said Arsinoe.

Kyros turned to the boy. "Highness, I am to guard you and keep you safe. When the chief adviser tells me to take you away, he rules on your safety."

"I want to be involved. This is my life and my reign." The boy king stomped his foot and strode down the hall.

"I will take care of him. You can return to the strategy session," Kyros said.

Arsinoe nodded in agreement.

As Yonan watched the scene, he could read her thoughts. She knew the end was near.

Kyros pursued Ptolemy, hastening to catch up with him. He was concerned for the boy's safety, as well as his own. Losing the palace to Julius Caesar was inevitable, and they must hurry. Longing for news of Iras, he was at least assured of her safety, since she was with Cleopatra, though he had little hope he would ever be with her again. His heart pounded at the thought of her. Why fall in love only to lose each other so soon? There was no sense to make of it.

~ ~ ~

Xenia arrived at Cleopatra's camp on the Syrian coast near the Egyptian border. There were dozens of tents with troops primed for the Queen's next move against Ptolemy at Pelusium. Xenia did not comprehend the concept of war, though she had read about it in the scrolls. She was there only to be sure Iras was safe and somehow could be together with Kyros, though she realized it was as futile as Yonan believed.

Cleopatra's tent contained all the amenities and comforts deemed customary except an endless supply of servants. Iras and the other two maids dragged their bodies from exhaustion and fear. Not used to the battles and throngs of men surrounding them, they kept to themselves, venturing out of the tent only when necessary.

Iras lamented that they may never return to the palace. Every day, she thought of Kyros, especially at night. He was alive because Ptolemy was alive. Her ears would strain for his name whenever there were conversations about Alexandria.

She smoothed the linen of her skirt with her hands, hoping it would help. Being out in the desert, she had only the one outfit with no way to clean anything. Water was at a premium, and was one amenity they did not have in large supply. At least they covered the sand with many carpets for the sand and dust laid on everything. She glanced at her Queen, lounging on the one divan brought for her bed. Katia stood behind, waving a large palm branch. The fans were not in the luggage. It seemed to serve well enough, at least the Queen did not complain.

Charmion burst into the tent, out of breath. "Your Majesty, we have news. Julius Caesar has come from Rome and he captured the palace, sending Ptolemy fleeing Alexandria with his army."

"Julius Caesar himself? This could be my answer. I will go to him for his support of my cause."

"The palace is surrounded. How will you reach to him?"

"I am Cleopatra. I will find a way."

Iras shuddered when she heard Ptolemy had gone into hiding. Kyros would be with him. She wondered where they had gone and if Kyros was safe. Cleopatra ordered Iras to stay behind at the camp with the other servants. There was nothing she could do but wait.

~ ~ ~

By the time Iras and the other maids returned to Alexandria weeks later, she found Queen Cleopatra the guest of Julius Caesar in her own palace. Caesar had sided with the beautiful queen and his powerful Roman army fought against Ptolemy, sending him out of the city into exile. For the next year, Caesar and Cleopatra shuttered themselves within the palace walls while battling Ptolemy's forces.

Iras and the other handmaids continued to serve their Queen, though Iras worried about Kyros, keeping her fears to herself. In the Queen's chamber, she was about to offer wine to her mistress when Julius Caesar entered, unannounced as usual. The lack of formality irritated Iras, but their level of intimacy was not her concern. The story of how Cleopatra had breached the palace walls rolled up in a carpet to gain Caesar's support was by then known to everyone. She laughed secretly at her Queen's cunning and power of seduction to get what she needed and wanted. How Iras wished she had such power. But it was not to be. She was lucky to be alive.

"My darling Cleopatra, you are as ravishing as always," Caesar said, taking Cleopatra's hand as he kneeled beside her divan.

Such an old man for the young Queen, Iras thought, but handsome all the same.

"I have good news," he said. "We defeated Ptolemy's forces at the Battle of the Nile and we've received word Ptolemy drowned while crossing the river, attempting to escape with the rest of his army. It is over."

Cleopatra jumped up. "How wonderful, my love!"

Iras nearly crumpled as she reached for the nearest chair. If Ptolemy is dead, then so must be Kyros. Her heart broke for him and her loss.

CHAPTER TWENTY-TWO

A New Strategy

When Xenia awoke in the device, she burst into tears. Another attempt to be together for a long lifetime in the future was foiled. The frustration of having failed a second time overcame her. She stifled a sob when Yonan gave her hand a gentle squeeze, letting her know he was awake.

"My heart, please do not cry," he said quietly, trying not to disturb the couples in the other devices.

"We will never complete our plan." Xenia looked around the room and stifled her sobs.

One couple awakened and waved cheerfully at Xenia and Yonan. Xenia forced a smile. Yonan had already signaled for Gayeena to open the door. There were still two other couples in their devices. The door opened, and they all filed out, following the high priestess to the small room where the scrying crystal awaited. Once there, the woman jumped about excitedly.

"We cannot wait to share our success!" she said with glee.

"Congratulations!" Gayeena said, "Do you wish to tell us about your achievement? You do not have to. What happens is your own private story."

The man chimed in, "We need not keep it a secret. We are thrilled and want to share it with you."

Xenia wanted to be happy for them, but they had only been trying a short while and it bothered her they had achieved their goal before she and Yonan. The woman burst with enthusiasm as she recalled their experience finding their future selves in a place called India during a time where a pale-skinned culture ruled over the country. She told how her future self was to be married, but through their intervention, connected with the future self of her husband, and they married instead.

"It is wonderful," said the woman, with her husband looking pleased.

Xenia cast a disappointed look at Yonan.

Yonan asked, "Is that all you need to know? Do you not want to see into your future to check up on them, make sure they are still together? We have found things do not always work out."

The woman replied, "We understand there is no guarantee our future selves will live long and happy lives. Lives are very different in the future and in different places. Our goal was to find them and get them together, and we did."

Despite knowing the couple's goal was not exactly the same as hers, Xenia experienced envy for the first time in her long life. She thought Yonan would be satisfied by finding their future selves twice and wanted to be together. But he was frustrated. Xenia worried they might never achieve the goal he had set out for them. How would she tell him she thought his expectations could be beyond their reach?

After the other couple left the room, Xenia read the crystal again, searching more other future lives. This time she found one in a place called England. Xenia had learned from the scrolls about the Roman calendar and how they kept track of time differently than Zorathians. The next lifetime was in the 1500s and was once again in service to a queen. Xenia scanned her future self's life to find out if she would ever marry. She did not. Instead, that self remained in royal service, but died unexpectedly from food poisoning before she turned twenty. Yonan's future self was an earl who found a wife late in his life. Their paths never crossed.

Well, their paths will cross this time.

Determined to get things right by understanding more about the world they would visit, Xenia and Yonan researched the scrolls and found references made to the same time period. According to the scroll, during that time, kings and queens would approve arranged marriages for their staff in the privy sanctums, and for high-ranking courtiers. They took the chance and planned to manipulate King Henry VIII and his wife, Catherine of Aragon, into selecting an appropriate marriage between their future selves, and, of course, make sure they met first to establish their soul connection.

Xenia was a Maid of Honor, named Bessie, in service to Queen Catherine, and Yonan was an earl who must get Henry's approval. It was a challenging task, but Xenia agreed with Yonan that they might make it work. And, to make it work, Yonan must get the earl to court in order to find and meet Bessie. They were sure it would all work out this next time.

PART FOUR: ENGLAND

1531 CE

CHAPTER TWENTY-THREE
A Maid of Honor

Yonan found the earl at his estate in the country north of London, busy managing his affairs. He sat in a grand library hunched over a large ornately carved desk, without a thought of finding a bride. Yonan whispered into the earl's ear, he could solve his loneliness by finding a love to share his life.

The earl stopped reading and gazed out the window at his lands and realized how lonely he had been since his father passed away. Perhaps seeking a bride might be the answer.

Upon hearing the earl's thoughts, Yonan sent him whisperings of urgency to encourage him to make haste to London, where he would be sure to find a bride.

The earl shuffled through the piles of papers on his desk and came across a summons from the king to attend a special banquet to be held soon. He had forgotten about it, but knowing he could not ignore such a summons, he called his servants to prepare for a journey—hoping he would arrive in time, since his estate was days away by horseback.

~ ~ ~

It was early, and the light had not yet shone through the glass-paned windows. Bessie sat up with a start, her golden locks tumbling from her nightcap. "Mary! Where are you?" she called to her servant, whose pallet across the room was empty. Bessie rose from her bed, as

Mary entered with Spotty, Bessie's spaniel, padding behind her.

"There you are. Hurry, and help me dress."

"Yes, mistress," said Mary, a young girl with protruding eyes and a thin mouth, as she scurried about the room gathering Bessie's clothing. Dressing her mistress was tedious, with many clothing parts to assemble and stitch together, but much less than what the Queen's ladies faced each day.

A pretty, eighteen-year-old girl with fair-skin and green eyes, Bessie loved her queen and had served as Maid of Honor for the past two years. She had received the appointment on the recommendation of Elizabeth Scrope, Countess of Oxford, a Lady in Waiting who knew her family well. Her parents were of the gentry class and hoped the Queen would find a suitable marriage match for their daughter, though there was no word yet about any arrangement. Bessie wanted marriage, but not while in service. Most of the Ladies in Waiting were married career women.

Dressed, and her hair properly covered with a gabled bonnet, she peeked in the mirror for one last look, pleased her bright blue eyes did not have unsightly bags. The Queen was very particular in her ladies' appearance. She left Mary to her daily chores, kissed the top of Spotty's head, and headed down the hall. Two other Maids of Honor came around the corner and joined her.

"Good morning, Bessie," said the two ladies in unison, and giggled.

"Good morning," Bessie said, tilting her head to each.

The three hurried down the wide hall toward the Queen's chambers. Their backs board straight, heads held high with hands clasped in front, while their full skirts made swishing sounds. When they arrived in the Queen's sitting room, there were several other Maids of Honor, and four of the key Ladies in Waiting already seated, chatting in whispered voices.

Lady Oxford waved the three young girls in. "You are just in time. We heard some startling news about the King and Queen."

Joining the ladies in the circle, she listened intently while they shared the rumors.

"The annulment is going through and His Majesty plans to marry Anne Boleyn as soon as possible," Liza, a Maid of Honor, said.

"After six long years, we knew this would happen eventually," another whispered. "Does Her Grace know?"

"I'm sure of it. The King visited last night, and I heard raised voices and the Queen sounded distraught. Have you seen Her Grace this morning?" asked Lady Oxford.

"Not yet," said another.

The door to the Queen's bedchamber opened, and the ladies stood and curtsied, making way for Queen Catherine in her velvet morning robe, as she greeted them with a forced smile on the way to the dining room. They said nothing about the King's visit during the meal, only pleasantries and the weather, though it was obvious to the ladies something was terribly wrong.

Once they finished their meal, the Queen returned to her bedchamber to be dressed for the day. Though Bessie was not a lady of the bedchamber, they allowed her to observe. Should it ever come, she would be promoted to the position. She suspected a promotion would be highly unlikely.

It was a great privilege to dress the Queen. A time-consuming task which comprised cleansing her body before helping her on with the undergarments—various pieces of support clothing, the bundle around her waist, and the hooped skirt she introduced when she first arrived in England. It took at least three ladies to lift the black brocade kirtle over her head and tie it in place over the hoop, the thick brocade and embroidery making the voluminous skirt and four-foot train extra heavy.

Bessie lamented of all the additional funding the Queen had recently added to the Great Wardrobe in hopes she would be more attractive to the King, to lure him away from Anne Boleyn. If it was true he was remarrying, Bessie worried what would become of the Queen, and of her own personal situation.

Once the Queen's attire was in perfect place, the ladies stood back to admire her in the elegant gown. Tiny seed pearls encrusted the bodice and sleeves and an elaborate headpiece covered her head with a wisp of her graying auburn hair peeking out above the forehead, and a black veil pinned at the back. She was at her best for the banquet honoring their guest, the Ambassador from the Holy Roman Empire, Eustace Chapuys.

The Queen called her ladies into the privy chamber, taking a seat in her favorite wing-backed chair surrounded by them, some on the floor, others seated on stools close by. Her back straight and hands clasped tight in her lap, she kept her face solemn.

The silence was deafening.

"My ladies," Queen Catherine said, breaking the silence, "You may have heard some rumors. I wanted to be the one to tell you what is true . . . and what is false. What is true is that His Majesty has been awarded the annulment. He plans to marry the whore." She always called Anne Boleyn "the whore," never her name, and she spat it out with a vengeance. Even though Anne was one of her Ladies in Waiting, Anne was rarely present anymore because the King kept her close to him.

Confirmation from the Queen's own lips stunned her ladies.

"What is false is, he thinks I will accept it . . . I will never accept the annulment and have my daughter, Mary, called bastard. I am the

Queen and he cannot do this!" Her knuckles had turned white from clenching her hands so tight. Still, the Queen did not show her distress. Only her voice trembled.

The ladies let out shocked gasps and worried glances even though they knew it would happen no matter what the Queen wanted.

"Your Grace, this is unconscionable. No, he should not do it," Anne Stafford, Countess of Huntington said.

Liza clutched her chest. "None of this is right. My heart bleeds for you, Madame."

Catherine nodded in appreciation. "Your support is much needed, but we shall all put on a unified front and attend the banquet tonight, behaving as if nothing has or will happen. Do you all understand?"

Bessie and the other ladies all agreed, promising to act normal, but it would not be easy. They spent the rest of the day with their heads down in needlework and embroidery or reading aloud to the Queen until it was time for the banquet.

CHAPTER TWENTY-FOUR

A Flirtation

The banquet hall was ablaze with light from every sconce on columns and walls, including the immense chandeliers hanging overhead. They shimmered, casting rays on the silver and gold goblets and plates gleaming on the tables decorated with elaborately embroidered runners over table drapes touching the floor.

Awaiting the King and Queen, the lords and ladies preened in their finest court attire, sumptuous velvets and satin brocades in the approved colors of their stations. The trumpets sounded and King Henry arrived bedecked in a purple velvet doublet trimmed in gold. He strode down the aisle and stood before the dais, waiting for his queen. When Queen Catherine entered, it was with great aplomb, followed by her Ladies in Waiting and then the Maids of Honor, all wearing black satin brocade and draped in strands of pearls to emulate their Queen, adorned heavily in her best jewels. Bessie trailed behind.

Henry bowed, taking his wife's hand as he always had and kissed it. Catherine curtsied and stepped onto the dais, taking her seat. The King sat next to her, with Anne Boleyn on his other side, dressed in a vibrant green—a bold statement showing how she differed from the Queen's other ladies. The importance of Anne sitting at the head table was not lost on the Queen, her ladies, or the rest of those in attendance. Granted, others sat at the table. On Anne's other side was the Duke of Norfolk, who seemed quite attentive to her. Queen

Catherine was holding her own, deep in conversation with Ambassador Chapuys. At the King's command, the musicians played a melancholy tune during the meal.

Bessie sat at one of the long tables with the other Maids of Honor, dozens of them, all chattering with gossip about one thing or another, keeping quiet about the recent news of the King and their Queen. Servants strutted into the hall carrying massive trays of roast game and pheasant.

Despite how the King was treating her beloved Queen, Bessie could not help but admire his appearance. At thirty-five years of age, he was in his prime and showing off his gregarious nature in public. He stood impressive, athletic, and handsome. Still, her heart hurt at the humiliation the Queen had sustained while the King flaunted the Boleyn fiend. Pushing aside those thoughts, she focused on the coming dancing after the meal. She loved to dance and hoped someone would ask for her hand. She gazed around the room and noticed someone she had not seen before standing off in the corner.

Leaning in to Jane, next to her, she spoke low. "Do you know who the man in the corner is? I do not recognize him."

"Him? He's the newest Earl of Warthingham. His father recently passed away. He has a pleasing face, does he not?"

"I suppose, but his air is one of . . . well . . . superiority?" She wrinkled her nose with disdain.

Jane laughed. "What does it matter? He is rich and looking for a bride."

Bessie could sense him staring at her, when a flash of golden light appeared in the corner of her eye. Assuming it was a reflection from all the golden goblets and charger plates on the table, she thought little of it.

She purposefully ignored him and scanned the rest of the room for other dance partners. There was always the old Duke of Haversham, who was pushing fifty. His dancing was fair enough. Or she considered Hubert, also eyeing her from across the room, a young page of the King's chambers. Definitely not marriage material, but as a dancing partner . . . *He'll do.*

Later, after they cleared the tables, dancing music began in a sprightly tune from the flutes, harp, horns, and rebecs. The younger maids-of-honor giggled and smiled openly, hoping to be asked to dance by anyone.

Yonan hovered over the earl. He knew this was his chance and sent whisperings to the Earl of Warthingham's ear, drawing his attention toward Bessie.

The earl gazed at the young woman with fresh interest.

At the same time, the Queen vaguely listened to the Ambassador droning on in boring conversation while noticing the earl crossing the room to invite Bessie to dance. The Queen observed the two intently.

Bessie shied away at first, but the earl insisted, taking her hand and guiding her out to the dance floor. She could not understand why she followed and did not refuse. His expression was impossible, his piercing sea-blue eyes, and those infuriatingly white teeth. She'd never seen such white teeth on an Englishman before. To inflame her even more, his dancing was impeccable. Not a step out of place. They turned and weaved in and out of the other couples in line until they met again and took hands, turning forward facing the King and Queen. The Queen nodded at Bessie and smiled, which surprised her. Bessie smiled back with a nod.

The music ended. She curtsied, and the earl bowed.

"My thanks, may I have your name, please?" he asked.

"Uh, B-Bessie," she blurted, feeling a rush to her cheeks, and hurried off to join the ladies without waiting for his reply.

"Bessie, you looked divine out there dancing," said Cecile. "You have a flush on your cheeks, too. Is it from the dancing, or because of the earl?"

"He is a fine dancer," Jane said, casting her a wink.

"Maybe, but he is infuriating."

"Why do you say that? You looked like you enjoyed the dance."

"The dance, yes. Him, I dare not even say." Bessie turned, glancing around the room. *Where did he disappear to?*

"If you say so, Bessie. But somehow, I don't believe you," Jane cackled.

Later, in her room, as Mary helped Bessie out of her clothes, the earl came to mind. Why did he irk her? And yet, she could not stop thinking about him.

"Thank you, Mary, you get some rest until the morrow."

"G'night to you, mistress," the servant replied, and prepared herself for bed, curling up on her pallet on the floor.

As Bessie relaxed, she caught the same glint of golden light in the corner of her eye, but was drifting off to sleep.

~ ~ ~

While Bessie dreamed, Xenia hovered above her, planting memories in her mind of a far-off place in a much colder climate, running wild with strange animals and a man she loved. She sent memories of Zorathia, where everything was in perfect balance, and memories of Yonan, who was the same as the earl. Xenia watched as Bessie smiled in her sleep.

~ ~ ~

The Earl of Warthingham could not get Bessie out of his head. No matter what his occupation of the day, his thoughts returned to her. He came to court to find a wife, but to find someone so quickly was unexpected. He submitted a request for an audience with the Queen to discuss his interest in Bessie and waited impatiently for her reply. Several days passed. He assumed his audience had been denied until a messenger arrived with a note from the Queen with her seal. He tore it open and was delighted to find an appointment for the following day.

Dressed in the required black velvet court suit with a white ruffled collar, John Sidney, the Third Earl of Warthingham, waited in the anteroom to the Queen's reception hall. When the doors opened and he entered, the guard announced and led him down a carpeted path to where Catherine sat on her throne, impeccably dressed in black and adorned in her favorite pearls.

Not intimidated, though it was the earl's first audience with the Queen, he bowed deeply to his knees.

Catherine scrutinized him with squinted eyes. "You may rise, Lord Warthingham. I understand you wish to speak to me about one of my Maids of Honor, Elizabeth Cheney."

"Yes, Your Highness. Cheney? Is she a relation to Sir Thomas Cheney?" he asked, making polite conversation. Of course, he'd asked around to learn all he could about this captivating young woman before he requested this audience with the Queen.

"I believe a cousin," Catherine replied. "She is a gentlewoman, not of royal birth, but is well read, and possesses typical skills required of a maid-of-honor. Though she has only been with me for two years, I've grown fond of her and seek a suitable marriage arrangement."

"My father passed on this last year. We have a formidable estate and I plan to spend much time in the country, not at court, and hope to find a bride who would appreciate country living."

"I'm sorry to hear of his passing. I hadn't met him personally, though I know he was well-respected."

John smiled, "Thank you, it is well to know." He paused a moment, trying to be thoughtful and patient, but he could not. "I respectfully ask for Bessie's hand, and if she would be suitable for county life and willing to leave the court. Of course, with Your Highness's and His Majesty's approval."

"Hmm," Catherine murmured, as she eyed him closely. "You would be a suitable match, and giving up court life wouldn't matter to her. A good marriage was always the eventual plan by her parents when she was put into service with me. A formal request for approval from the King is required. Until then, I can promise nothing. We should wait for the two of you to meet until we receive the King's reply."

"Of course, I am ever so grateful for Your Highness's help in this matter." He bowed low and stepped backwards several steps.

"You have my permission to withdraw," Queen Catherine said with a slight wave of her hand.

Lord Warthingham left the throne room feeling elated, hopeful he had accomplished his goal and everything would work out perfectly.

CHAPTER TWENTY-FIVE

The Queen's Distress

While in residence at Windsor Castle, the King and the "whore" rode off on horseback, but had not returned. The Queen wrote a letter to the King. Uncommonly irritable and anxious, the Queen awaited a reply. When she received a letter, she excused herself to her bedchamber to read it in private.

The ladies sat busy with various activities, embroidery, cards, and reading, attempting to appear as though everything were normal. Not long after the letter arrived, a messenger demanded presence with the Queen, but she sent word from her bedchamber that she would not receive him. He left a rolled document. It was all extremely unusual.

A long while passed before the Queen called her ladies into her privy chamber. She looked distraught, her eyes red-rimmed and puffy, but she held stoic amid what they knew to be disturbing news. The ladies sat around her. Maria de Salinas, her favorite, held the Queen's hand while the others waited for her to speak.

"My ladies," Queen Catherine said, breaking the silence, then bursting into more tears. "The King has written me a letter demanding I never . . . write . . . to him again," she choked. "I am never to see him . . . again!"

Bessie and all the ladies held their breath, expecting more was still to come.

"And to add further insult . . . the edict I received are orders to vacate these rooms at Windsor and remove myself from court." She paused, taking in a deep breath, and sighed. "We are to move to Moor Castle within the month. I am no longer welcome at court."

"Not welcome?" cried Lady Huntington.

The ladies all talked over each other, expressing their shock and concern for their queen, and casting worried glances at each other.

"What does this mean for all of us?" asked Bessie.

"It means I must reduce my household. A few of you will be reassigned. I must do so. The apartments at Moor are much smaller than these."

"I am sorry, Your Grace," said Lady Oxford. "You shouldn't be subjected to this insult."

Bessie was quiet, stunned by the news and sure she would be one lady reassigned since she had served less than the others. "Madame, pardon me," she said, "but what exactly does reassign mean?"

The Queen gave her a sympathetic look. "Unfortunately, it would mean being placed in service elsewhere, or possibly a marriage match."

Bessie hid her elation with a slight frown. She secretly hoped for marriage, which would give her the option of leaving service for good. But how would she get the Queen to find her a marriage match? Startled by a golden light to her left, she turned her head, but it disappeared, and she wondered what it was for only a moment, for her attention pulled back to the Queen.

Catherine pulled herself together, and Maria dabbed the Queen's eyes with a handkerchief. Everyone was still waiting for her to give some direction. Bessie noticed the Queen had a strange expression on her face. She acted as if she were listening to something.

"Is something amiss?" Bessie asked.

"No, some thoughts came to mind I had forgotten about." She waved her hand for the others to leave her and Bessie alone, and they threw a few questioning glances Bessie's way as they left.

Motioning to Bessie she should sit beside her, Queen Catherine took a deep breath. "I had been waiting for a response from the King before telling you. It came a couple of days ago, but his absence has consumed me to discuss it with you until now. She put her hand to her eyes to brush away more tears."

"Your Grace, please, how may I aid you?" Bessie felt helpless as she took a stool next to the Queen's chair, her gown spread out surrounding her.

"You will not be moving to Moor Castle with us."

"Are you letting me go?" Bessie feared the answer, feeling her own tears welling up, though she held herself firm.

"Not exactly. I've received an offer for your hand. I sent notice to the King for his approval. The King always liked you, Bessie, and he sends you his best in your marriage to the Earl of Warthingham."

Stunned, Bessie cried out, "Oh, no!"

"I beg your pardon," Catherine said with a shocked expression. "It is decided and is an excellent match. I promised your parents I would find such a match for you in time. I am offended by your response, especially when I've just been cast out myself with no hope for my future."

"Your Grace, please forgive me. Of course, I am grateful for what you have done. I was surprised. It was unexpected." Mortified that she insulted the Queen, Bessie's face turned bright red.

Catherine patted Bessie's hand. "There is a good girl. Now, please send in the ladies. We have much to do. We will notify you when the formal meeting is arranged between you and the earl." The Queen's face fell back into her distress.

Bessie rose and nearly ran from the room to let the ladies in. When she saw Elizabeth, the Countess of Oxford, she pulled her aside. "My Lady, the Queen informed me I am to be wed as soon as possible to the Earl of Warthingham!"

"What splendid news, especially now with all the changes. At least you will not be left with no place to go. I am happy for you."

"Thank you."

"You don't look happy. What is wrong?"

"It's nothing. I will miss you and everyone else. These past two years have been very special to me." She managed a sincere smile, for she would miss them and the Queen.

"Please let me know if there is anything I can do to help, when I am not at the Queen's disposal. Keep me apprised of your progress with the marriage." She embraced Bessie, and they followed the other ladies into the Queen's privy chamber for instructions.

CHAPTER TWENTY-SIX

First Meeting

Bessie could not believe the speed at which her marriage arrangement had moved forward. As the Queen told her, a formal meeting was scheduled between her and the earl. She was nervous. What would she say to him? Did they have anything in common? Or did it matter? She wanted her mother to be there, but the timing of events was out of her control and her parents could not attend the wedding at Windsor. They lived in a county closer to the earl's estate and planned to meet after Bessie was settled. The wedding would happen in less than a fortnight and her mind was spinning with helping with the Queen's move.

The income from the Queen was spent on gowns required for her service. She had nothing to wear as the wife of an earl. But when she learned the Earl provided funding for a wedding dress and for an adequate wardrobe as his new wife, she was furious with herself for being pleased. She did not want to like him.

The night before her meeting with the earl, she tossed and turned in her bed, and Spotty, taking up half the bed, did not help. Finally, she rolled over, her arm around her dog, and fell to sleep.

Mary woke her with a cheerful smile. "Awake, Mistress, this is the day you meet your husband." She giggled like the child she was, and gathered together the gown for the meeting.

Bessie rubbed her eyes and pulled herself up to sit on the edge of the bed. The winter morning light shed little warmth upon her. "I'm thirsty. My throat is dry, and I'm exhausted."

"Here miss." Mary handed her a cup of hot tea.

"Hmm, thank you, I really needed this," she said, sipping the tea and watching Mary place her best satin shoes next to the chair in the corner of her room. "Mary, I will ask the earl if I may take you with me."

Mary's eyes bulged with surprise. "I would very much like to continue serving you."

"Good. You have been a great service to me. I hate to think what I would do without you." She smiled, finished her tea and stretched. "Has Spotty been taken for a walk yet?"

"Yes, mistress, before I woke you. There were snow flurries. Spotty had fun trying to catch them."

"Sorry I missed it. Now, Spotty, you sit still while Mary dresses me. We have someone important to meet with today." She scratched behind Spotty's ears. "Yes, you will meet him, too. I must know if you approve."

By the time she dressed and had her morning meal, it was almost time for the meeting. The Queen had assigned the Countess of Oxford, as chaperone, and to introduce Bessie to the earl. She arrived on time to Bessie's chambers to collect her.

"Lady Oxford, I am so glad you are here. I had hoped my parents would be here, but they will not. I appreciate your presence today," Bessie gushed.

"I am happy to be here for you, my dear. You are splendid with your golden hair shining, and you chose the right gown. The blue brocade with gold trim shows your coloring beautifully."

Bessie bent down to pick up Spotty. "He's coming with us. I hope you don't mind. It's very important to me they get along with each other. Not that it would change anything, but it would give me peace of mind."

"Well . . . fine, but you won't carry him, will you?"

Bessie put Spotty down and laughed. "No, of course not. I'm so nervous."

"And so you should be, but I hear good things about the earl. He is not someone for you to fear. Let us go, or we will be late."

They had set the meeting place in a private room. Spotty tagged along on his gold-washed leash behind the two ladies. The earl was already there in a black suit, looking admirable with broad shoulders and billowy sleeves, and quite shapely, hosed legs.

A sudden fluttering in her stomach made her skip a step and her hands were clammy. What was the matter with her? When the two women entered, the earl made a deep bow, and the women curtsied.

"Your lordship, I am the Countess of Oxford, Lady in Waiting to the Queen. May I present to you, Mistress Elizabeth Cheney, your intended." She turned to Bessie. "And this is his lordship, John Sidney, Earl of Warthingham."

Bessie stepped closer, offering her hand, and he took it lightly, kissing the top of it. She lowered her head to hide the warmth rising to her face, glancing up at him through her lashes. She had forgotten how tall he was.

"I remember," he said.

"And this is my dog, Spotty." She tugged on the leash, and Spotty turned to look at the earl. "Say hello to his lordship, Spotty."

The little dog stopped short and tilted his head.

"Hello, Spotty," said the earl, as he bent over and held out his hand.

Spotty sniffed the proffered hand and gave it a small lick, wagging his tail.

"He likes you," Bessie said, relieved.

"Well," said the countess, "I will take the seat in the corner, with

Spotty." With Spotty's leash in hand, pulling the dog away from the couple, she looked back at them with a smile.

"Please—" The earl motioned to a long, padded bench against the wall furthest from the countess, hoping for some amount of privacy for their conversation.

Bessie took a seat, shaking from nervousness, not sure what to expect from the meeting since no one had told her much about the marriage.

"First, please call me Lord Warthingham around other people, but you may call me John in private. As you may know, after we are married, I will call you Lady Warthingham or her ladyship when others are present. In private, I would prefer to call you Bess. Bessie is, well . . ." He paused, as if searching for the right words. "Well, Bessie is not suitable for a wife." He cleared his throat and turned his gaze direct to hers.

"It is alright with me, Lord . . . I mean, John, I much like Bess. It is more mature." She made an embarrassed laugh at his formality, and she wondered if he was always that way.

He did not sit on the bench with her, but continued to talk while pacing back and forth. "I was fortunate to have an audience with the King, however brief, to request a leave of absence from court for the first year of our marriage, and he gave his approval. There is much to accomplish at the estate in Warthingham." He stopped and turned to her.

Bessie was giving him her full attention, trying to grasp everything he was telling her. It was so much to take in.

"I was told you would be open to country life, not seeking a career in service."

Bessie perked up, realizing he was expecting a response. "That is correct. I don't wish to be a career Maid of Honor, or Lady in

Waiting, to anyone. Country life is most appealing as I come from a country family, and I miss it."

John sighed with relief. "Good, good, however, we must return to court after the first year, at least for a while."

"I understand."

Finally, John sat beside her, leaving as much space as the bench would allow, what with her full skirt taking up much of it. His face turned serious, "We don't know each other at all, and the marriage is rushed, not allowing us time to become acquainted . . ." He paused again. "I want you to know, I hope we will grow in fondness for each other, and maybe, perhaps, feel love. For that is my wish, and I hope you wish it too. Having observed my family and those in my class, arranged marriages can be quite difficult. I do not want the same for us."

Surprised by his admonition, Bessie drew back. She had not even considered the prospect of love. Her parents told her an advantageous marriage was more important than love. She was only hoping for a suitable match financially. With John, she might have love.

"Have I offended you in some way?" he asked, concerned.

"No, I'm sorry, I, I hope for the same, John." He was not as she had imagined him to be. She had an affinity for him, but knew not where it came from so suddenly. The recent dreams came to mind, and she wondered why she was thinking of them.

"I'm relieved you agree. Our new life together will be easier. Since I must return to the estate soon, the marriage ceremony will be held tomorrow in the chapel here at Windsor, and we will depart the day following. Warthingham is several days' journey. Do not worry about your wardrobe. Bring what you have and once we arrive at Warthingham Hall, we will provide you with anything you need. I assume you have no substantial belongings?"

"No."

"Then you should have enough time to complete any personal matters or farewells you wish."

"Thank you, John, for all your considerations. I look forward to tomorrow." She gave him her most sincere smile possible. "May I bring with me my maid, Mary, and my dog, Spotty?"

"Your dog?" He chuckled. "You may, and your maid as well," he replied.

She became relaxed with him by the time John waved the countess over to collect her. Much to Bessie's delight, Spotty took to John right away, which was an excellent sign. Her future would change a great deal and she was both excited and wary, for she knew nothing of managing the household of an estate.

CHAPTER TWENTY-SEVEN
A Wedding

Elizabeth, Lady Oxford, and Anne, Lady Huntington, met with Bessie the morning of the wedding. They explained to her the expectations as a new bride and lady of such a household. It was overwhelming to Bessie and she tried not to cry. How would she manage?

"My dear, Bessie," said Elizabeth, "don't fret. There will be plenty of help when you get there."

"I agree," said Anne. "I remember when I was first married to the earl. I was very young and all alone, too. Your parents will meet you at his estate, will they not?"

Bessie gazed at the two ladies. "Yes, my parents wrote they will meet me at the estate within a fortnight. It has been a year since I saw them last. They regretted not being here, but the estate is closer to them, and I am grateful to be living nearby." She dabbed her eyes with a handkerchief and straightened up. "I'm ready now. I appreciate your help, really I do."

"There's a good girl. I mean, you are no longer a girl, are you?" said Elizabeth. "You've grown into a mature young woman and now you will be a countess. Hold yourself up and always think of appearances, no matter what you feel. It is what we all do."

Bessie was wearing the new wedding gown of gold and ivory brocade with the veil the ladies had made for her, and together they left her room and hastened to St. George's Chapel. There, two Maids of Honor, Cecile and Liza, were waiting. Bessie burst with happiness at the sight of them.

"The Queen gave us permission to attend. We didn't want to miss it," said Cecile, handing Bessie a small bouquet. "These are for you." She curtsied. "You will soon be a countess, Lady Warthingham." She giggled.

"And this is for you from all the others." Liza gave Bessie a little drawstring bag. Inside was a necklace of seed pearls.

"Thank you." Bessie was about to burst into tears again when Elizabeth ushered them inside. The maids sat up front.

It seemed silly to her they would be married in St. George's with so few in attendance, but it was an informal ceremony, not like the royal weddings she had attended here with the full Catholic Mass. The priest waited patiently while John stood tall, looking proud. Heat from her blush colored her cheeks. The lilting music from a harpist echoed in the chamber.

John's manservant served as his witness, and there were two others sitting in the front row. *Who are they?* Bessie wondered, since they were not introduced to her.

Stepping lightly down the long aisle until she reached John, Bessie wanted to pinch herself. It was all unreal to her. The words coming from the priest's lips sounded like they were from a tunnel, and her own voice was strange. When she turned to look at John, her heart stopped for a second. He suddenly looked familiar, as if she had known him for eons. How could it be? It was wonderful, and joy filled her heart, eager for her new life to begin.

The ceremony was over. The signatures placed in the church register, and they said their farewells. She honestly would miss them, Queen Catherine's ladies, but Bessie looked forward to her future.

They were off on the long journey to Warthingham Hall, on

horseback. Bundled in thick furs against the cold air, Bessie loved to ride, and though John offered to provide either a carriage or a litter, she preferred to ride alongside him. It was to take five or six days to travel to make the journey, but Bessie was used to long travel serving the Queen, since the court moved around several times during her two-year service. They spent the evenings at inns along the route, and their first night John procured two rooms for them. Though they were married, he said they would not have their first night together on the road. Bessie was relieved to hear it. Consummating the marriage so soon almost brought on the heaves.

They spent their time getting to know each other, sharing about their childhoods, his family, her life at court.

Arrival at Warthingham Hall was a pleasant surprise for Bessie. Although it was called a hall, it had once served as a castle, defending the surrounding area. Wide lawns flanked the drive up to the estate. John assured her in the spring, the gardens would keep her occupied if nothing else. He did not lie. Bessie adored gardens, and was also anxious to explore the four-story castle keep, which John told her presented breathtaking views of the countryside.

"John, I am amazed at the beauty and size of this estate. Shame on you for not preparing me for this." She winked, teasing him. Secretly, her sense of inadequacy nearly overcame her, but she held herself steady as they reached the entrance where they dismounted.

"Please forgive me, my dear, for my thoughtlessness. I suppose growing up and living here all my twenty-five years, I am used to it. I should not have assumed you would know what my estate would be like."

"I promise you I will work hard to be worthy as your wife and the mistress of this grand estate." The words came easily, but Bessie had her doubts and worried she had taken on more than she was able.

CHAPTER TWENTY-EIGHT
Preserving the Past

Filled with confidence for their success, Xenia and Yonan returned to their time.

Xenia took the day to rejuvenate her energy and lounged on the corner sofa in the sitting room at home. She gazed around the room at her paintings, depressed her art would be lost forever. She rose and moved to stand before each one, recalling the day she had painted the scene. A gorgeous sunny day on the coastline. Their favorite place, the waterfall and lagoon. The others all brought tears to her eyes and a lump in her throat. At once, she got an idea and took down all the paintings, rolled them up together, and tied ribbons around the bundle of twelve works of art.

When Yonan came in the front door, he was curious. "What are you doing with your paintings? It looks odd without your beautiful work on the walls."

"I'm taking them to the Elders. There must be a way to preserve them somehow. Someday people will discover our continent, or by some miracle it will rise again above the water level, and future humans will find them." She gave him a desperate look.

"I agree. A good idea and I will accompany you, and after, we should check in with the builders on the beach and find out if there is anything we can do to help."

"I have been focused on our personal project. I should have been there to help more often. I wonder how much they have constructed of the three ships."

The Elders had administrative offices in the center of the village. Yonan sent them a telepathic message that he and Xenia were on their way to speak to them about something important. He received a reply they were there.

As were most of the buildings in the Zorathian community, the administration building was round. All the elders had workspaces comprising sitting areas instead of desks and chairs, with a central meeting place for small groups. The ambience was calm and introspective, with soft green and blue-gray walls. When Xenia and Yonan arrived, the Elders were waiting for them in the central area.

"Ah, it is good of you to come. Gayeena mentioned to us you have been attempting time travel. We hope it is going well. Please sit down," directed Elder Samin. "What is it you wish to speak to us about?"

Xenia handed him the package of rolled paintings. "These are twelve of my very best silk paintings of Zorathia. I am hoping there is a way to preserve them or put them in a safe place, just in case in the future they might be discovered."

"Your work is exceptional, Xenia, and they would be a fine testament to our culture. We have something for this purpose." He opened a large closet and returned holding a long metal tube. "Our forefathers brought hundreds of these from their planet, made of a metal not found on Earth. We are planning to store as many of the scrolls as possible in these to preserve them, too."

Xenia beamed at Elder Samin. "Wonderful! I'm so happy I brought these to you. I can rest easy knowing they are safe, and will pray they will be found in the future."

An assistant helped unroll the paintings, admiring Xenia's work. "We will store them in the underground caverns. The containers have a special seal we hope will keep water out indefinitely, and the metal is nearly indestructible."

Yonan examined the tubes closely. "I did not know these were here. It seems there has been a great deal of information kept from us. Why?"

Elder Samin gave him a questioning look. "Why? It was not intended as a secret. We did not need them until now."

"Gayeena has said much the same thing." Yonan wondered if that was the real reason, but kept his thoughts to himself.

He and Xenia thanked Elder Samin, and they left, headed to the beach, where three ships were in varying stages of construction, with one further along than the others and nearing completion. Xenia gave a forlorn sidelong glance at her husband. "I expected they would have completed the first ship by now. We might have taken on too much in the short time we have left."

"I agree. It is concerning."

Elder Ziros waved to Xenia and Yonan and they all gathered together near the larger ship. It was over a hundred feet long, with fourteen rows of oars, and three decks with masts for sails taller than they had ever built before. It was impressive, but unfinished.

They all greeted each other by clasping wrists.

"Elder Ziros, let me first apologize for not being here more often to help." Yonan offered.

"It is all well and good, Yonan. Glad both of you came today to observe our progress. It is slow, I know. This is all new ground. I found in the scroll archives mention of larger ships seen in the future by a people called Romans. I tried to implement some of the notes on our ships."

"You are doing a fine job, Elder Ziros," Xenia said. "What can we help with today?"

Ziros waved his hands. "We have enough people helping. There is a more pressing problem. Our schedule is daunting, to say the least. Three-hundred Zorathians have signed up to journey the oceans on these vessels. We won't complete all three ships in time. We will need travel time to find the higher ground, which Gayeena has been working to identify, and our map makers to plot a course."

"You could complete one and send a first group out," Yonan said.

"It does not seem fair, but it has become a moral issue and a desperate attempt which could still end in failure," he said, speaking under his breath, looking around, not wanting the workers to overhear.

"We understand," Xenia said.

The couple insisted on staying and helping as much as they could. Xenia had more skill in working with tools and wood than Yonan. The sun set and the workers returned to their homes.

"I would like to look at Bessie's future with the earl, before we go home. I mean, to make sure it is the success we think it was."

"It has been a long day. Are you sure you are not tired?"

She shook her head, and the two left the beach and went up the mountain to the temple. The path was busier than usual. As the Great Shift neared, more people were visiting the temple for centering and praying for inner peace.

CHAPTER TWENTY-NINE
Married Life

Life at Warthingham Hall was more than Bessie could ever have dreamed. Upon John's insistence, her parents stayed for a very long and much needed stay before returning to their own simpler life at their manor.

It was as Elizabeth and Anne had said. She had plenty of help to settle into life as a countess. The servants loved Lord Warthingham and their admiration for him overflowed onto her as his new bride.

During her first six months, she learned so much, and became more accustomed to her new life. Her initial doubt at her ability to fulfill her duties as the wife of an earl had dissipated and she and John had grown quite close. They chatted about many topics. She truly was interested in everything he did, as it was such a new existence for her. Her fondness for him grew quickly.

She had arranged a special dinner and outfitted herself in one of her newest gowns of deep purple with a square neckline and a bodice richly embroidered in gold thread.

"You look absolutely beautiful, my Bess," said John.

"Tonight is special, and I wanted to look my very best for you."

"And why, pray tell, is tonight so special?"

"Before I tell you, there is a question I've been meaning to ask ever since the day we met for the first time alone at Windsor Castle. Why me?"

"What do you mean?"

"Why did you choose me, when you could have chosen any girl, or woman, at court?"

He smiled a knowing smile. "Because as soon as I set eyes on you, I knew. There was no question in my mind you were the one for me."

"You mean at the banquet? How did you know?"

"I'm not sure. There was a golden flash of something, from somewhere, and at that exact moment, I had a special sensation, deep in my core . . . we were meant to be together."

Bessie gaped at him, "At that moment? But you didn't know if I was available, or if the Queen or the King would give their approval?"

"I knew it would all work out, as if it were some omen, or divine intervention. I am deliriously happy you are here by my side as my wife. And you? Are you happy?"

She hastened down the long dining table to sit next to him and took his hand in hers. "I never imagined I could be this happy, and hearing you tell me these words makes me even more so. And now, I have something very special to tell you, too."

"And what is it, my dear?" He looked deep into her eyes, full of love and admiration.

"I am with child." Her face glowed with joy.

"A child? Already? How delightful, perfect, wonderful." He leaned over and kissed her deeply.

After dinner, they retired extra early to celebrate their love and the coming child.

~ ~ ~

Their first-year anniversary was nearing and Bessie was almost seven months pregnant. Everything appeared to be normal until one day Bessie took ill. At first, they thought it was related to the unborn child, but was a massive headache and she retired to her bed for rest and recovery.

"John! John, my head. The pain. It's unbearable!" Bessie tossed and turned in their bed, writhing in pain.

"Yes, my dear Bess, I am here, I am here." John wiped her fevered brow with a cool cloth.

"Your lordship," said Mary, "Is there no physician in the area, like they have for the palace?"

"Other than the local barber who handles toothaches and certain surgical tasks, there is a woman in the village who helps with herbs and such."

"Shall I go to her for help?"

"Yes, Mary, please go as fast as you can," John urged. Turning his attention back to Bessie, he stroked her hair and face. "Mary will get you something to ease your pain. Just hold on, my love."

When Mary returned with only a small bag of herbs, she explained, "The wise woman told me these herbs are to be made into a tea and given to her ladyship in small doses, up to three times a day until her headache is reduced, if not gone."

"Well then . . . make haste to prepare the tea! Bring it here forthwith," John ordered, sending Mary out of the room swiftly, for she had never heard him speak so loudly.

"John, please, your voice hurts my head," Bessie murmured.

"Forgive me, my love. Slowness sparks my agitation. Soon we will have a soothing tea for you to ease your pain."

"Thank you, dear John."

John sat vigil at Bessie's bedside all night. He sent for the midwife to be sure the unborn child was safe. He gave Bessie some of the tea and she calmed.

The midwife arrived and examined Bessie. "My lord, the child seems to be fine, and her ladyship's headache has improved, she says."

"Yes, we've been giving her an herbal tea for the pain."

"If it is helping, good. I will come back in a couple of days to check on her."

"Thank you for coming." A servant showed the midwife out and John returned to Bessie's side. "My love, are you feeling better?"

"A bit. It comes and goes now, but the light from the window is too bright. Can you have someone cover it with a drape?"

"I will, here drink some more of this tea."

John was beside himself with worry. The following day, Bessie was still complaining of the pounding in her head, and any sounds made it worse. He gave her more tea. But the following morning, he could not rouse her from her sleep.

"Bess, wake up, my love."

She did not move. She was limp. John checked for a heartbeat, and it was weak, so he continued shaking her—but nothing.

When the midwife arrived, as she had promised, John was sitting in the chair next to Bessie's bed, his head in his hands, sobbing.

"Dear God, what has happened, my lord? Let me examine her."

John put up his hand. "There is nothing you can do. She's gone."

"What? Let me check the child." But after a few minutes, the midwife hung her head.

John rose, moving mechanically to the window, and pulled the drape aside, letting the sunlight stream in, casting a strange lightness on the otherwise dour mood.

Mary came in to the room and ran to Bessie's bedside. "My lady!" When she saw Bessie's face laying there still and pale, she fell to her knees and burst into tears. "How could this happen?"

"She was very lethargic and said she had strange dreams last night, but she said the pain was much better. She asked for more of the tea. I couldn't rouse her this morning. And now she is gone."

"My Lord, the wise woman said to only give her the tea up to three times a day. How much did she drink?" Mary struggled to her feet.

"She kept asking for more. It was helping. I couldn't deny her. And now, Bessie is gone, and the child too."

Later, Mary returned from the village and found Bessie was already prepared for visitation. She pulled Lord Warthingham aside.

"My lord, I went to speak to the woman who gave me the herb. She is very upset her ladyship was given so much of the tea. The herb is powerful enough that in large doses it can sometimes cause death. My lady must have been very susceptible, the wise woman said. I am so sorry. I should have been watching the dosage." Tears spilled from her red-rimmed eyes.

Lord Warthingham's face was ashen. "My God, it's my fault. I recall you mentioning small doses, but it was helping, so I kept giving her more! How will I ever live with this?"

"It was not intentional, my lord. No one will blame you. I swore the wise woman to secrecy and I won't divulge the error, for I feel to blame as well."

The two huddled together in their grief until the mourners and visitors arrived.

~ ~ ~

"No!" Xenia dropped her hands away from the crystal and buried her face in them.

Yonan reached for her. "What has happened, my heart?"

She looked at Yonan with a tear-stained face. "Bessie, she died, and she was pregnant! And you—I mean her husband, Lord

Warthingham, blamed himself, though it was an accident. I looked later in his life, and he still married the same woman I had first seen in my scrying."

"How do you die, Xenia?"

"She was sick, and they gave her too much of a dangerous herb. My heart grieves. I really wanted things to work out for them. They were married barely a year, and she still died young."

"She died young before we intervened."

"Yes. What does this mean?"

"I'm not sure, my heart. It is shocking. Despite our efforts to change the course of her life, she still died of a similar cause."

"And the earl—you—still married the other woman."

"It is disappointing and not the long life together we hoped for."

Feeling discouraged, and with their device scheduled for another couple, they had to wait to travel again. Less than two months left till the Great Shift. They went to Gayeena to express their concerns.

"Xenia, do not grieve for Bessie. It is possible she was meant to die young and there was no preventing it. I suggest you try moving your scrying further into the future."

"What difference would it make, High Priestess?" Xenia asked.

"I recall people lived longer—and there may be safer places to live—perhaps where they do not reside in a royal household."

"Thank you for your encouragement and suggestions," Yonan said.

"I want the two of you to succeed in your desires. Go, I bid you well." Gayeena said a small prayer of success over them and left.

Xenia searched the future for a lifetime without royal involvement and where their future selves could be freer. Using the calendar from the England time period, she moved forward several hundred more years to another continent, many times the size of Zorathia.

"I found us again! We are living in the same time period and appear to be traveling toward the same area in the middle of the continent. It is the mid-1800s. My future self is a young girl, about eighteen years of age, traveling with her family. Your future self is a young man about twenty who is traveling with his mother. She resembles the indigenous natives near Zorathia in her coloring. But you have blond hair, blue eyes and white skin. I cannot explain it."

As she had done for the England period, Xenia scanned forward in the girl's life. "In the girl's future, she will marry a much older man at the demand of her aunt. She will bear a stillborn child and suffer from depression and grief, committing suicide while still young. When I scan the boy's future self, he also dies young while traveling with his tribe." Xenia took her hands from the crystal and sat on the couch to rest, motioning Yonan to join her.

"Yonan, we should try to get the two to meet before the girl reaches her destination, or she will end up married to the wrong man who will cause her great unhappiness."

"Do not fret, my heart. I will be sure my future self gets to the same place as yours for them to make the proper soul connection."

PART FIVE: THE CONFLUENCE, SOUTHERN IOWA TERRITORY

1833 CE

CHAPTER THIRTY

The Fur Trader's Family

In the Des Moines-Mississippi confluence, the Sauk, Meskwaki, and Whites had lived peacefully together for ten years. It was a safe place for a mixture of races and cultures to co-exist. When the Black Hawk War ended in 1832, the Sauk and Meskwaki were banished to Kansas. However, there were some who refused to go to Kansas and ventured north to hide.

The August weather was mild but humid, and late in the day, when the fur trader Lascaux arrived at the trading post on horseback. Lascaux was born to French immigrants and, along with English, spoke French and Meskawki. Despite the grim history between the Meskawki and the French in the 1700s, Lascaux had overcome those differences, and the Meskwaki accepted him as another White man. Keme, his son, a young boy of six, followed close behind on his pony. Keme took after his mother, a Meskwaki, in his looks, with his dark hair and eyes, and brown skin. His long black hair hung loosely about his shoulders. Both wore buckskin and calf-high moccasins. They brushed off the dust from the trail and daily hunting.

Several other customers were leaving as the man and the boy marched up the steps and into the store. A young man of about sixteen, who stood behind the counter, eyed Lascaux and Keme curiously as they entered.

"You new?" Lascaux asked the young man.

"Uh, yes, sir. What can I get for you today?" he replied politely, before turning a hard look on Keme.

Keme ignored the clerk and went over to look at the boots in the corner.

Lascaux rubbed his neck, tired from the long day, and scanned the shelves behind the counter. "Let me have some flour, 'bout five pounds, lard, and some coffee," he said, but the clerk was paying no attention.

"Hey," he shouted at the boy he'd been watching the whole time. "What are you doing back there? I don't want you stealing anything and I get blamed for it."

Keme turned and gave his father an innocent look.

"Don't you talk to my son like that!" Lascaux growled.

"Your son? You mean you and an Injun had him?"

Lascaux reach across the counter and grabbed the boy's shirt, pulling his face within an inch of his own. "Never talk like that around me. Do you understand?"

"Easy, Lascaux," said a man who had entered the back door. "Jimmy, you too." The store owner, an older man, stood behind the counter next to Jimmy, waiting for Lascaux to cool down.

Lascaux loosened his grip on the boy. "You just watch it, you hear me?" he demanded, and then he let his hand drop.

The boy shuddered and huddled against the shelves behind him.

"Sorry, Lascaux, he's new and still doesn't understand the arrangement around here, you know, between everyone. I needed help and he and his family had settled near here off the confluence."

"Fine, fine, but he needs to learn some manners. Don't appreciate being treated in such a way. My son is an honest boy. He doesn't steal, and neither do his mother's people.

"I know, Lascaux, I appreciate your business and we've been friends for a while now." He turned to the boy. "Go into the storeroom and count out the new shipment."

"Yes, sir," said the boy, his head hung low. "Sorry, sir. Won't happen again."

"Damn right it won't." Lascaux spit.

"You hear what happened with the treaty?" the store owner asked, ignoring Lascaux's comment.

"Yep, we'll be going north, now the confluence is being disbanded. A real shame, though, we liked it here. But Leoti's family is moving north, too."

"Well, I'll miss ya, Lascaux, you been a real good customer. I wish y'all the best of luck. Now, what can I get for ya today?"

~ ~ ~

Under the shade of the tall trees, Leoti crept along the stream searching for berries in the bushes, and herbs up along the slopes, supplies for their trip north to new lands. The sky was overcast and the air chilly, yet she was warm, for she wore the traditional Meskwaki garments made from deerskins. Lascaux did not mind what she wore, though some women who married White men tried to fit in and would wear the White woman's clothing, not Leoti. Her long black hair gleamed when the filtered light hit it just right, and her serene oval face was the color of golden honey with rich full lips. When Lascaux saw her the first time, he knew she was for him and she also knew, and followed him willingly.

Her basket full, Leoti rose, stretching her back from bending over for such a long time. She looked out across the stream and saw a strange golden light, and then it moved. She inched as close as possible to the edge of the stream without getting wet. The glowing light moved in her direction. She gasped, nearly dropping the basket. There were two shapes of glowing light resembling figures. Afraid, she turned and ran away from the stream, screaming for Lascaux. She knew he was not there, but he was her first thought for protection. Leoti kept running until she reached their cabin and shut the door, pulling the wood latch down across the inside. She closed the shutters on the windows and peeked out through the cracks. There was no sign of the glowing figures, yet she shuddered with fear.

Moments later, the sound of hoofbeats alerted her that Lascaux and her son Keme had arrived. She unlatched the door and ran straight into her husband's arms.

"Whoa, there, Leoti, what the hell's wrong?" Lascaux asked.

"Mother, why are you shaking?" Keme asked in Meskwaki.

"Let's get inside. It's getting dark now." Lascaux urged them into the cabin.

"I saw something strange. It frightened me," she said.

"Why don't you sit and calm down? Tell me what you saw."

Keme brought in their supplies and the skins from their hunt of the day and set them down to listen to his mother's earnest voice.

"They were glowing with golden light and coming straight at me," she said, her hands still shaking.

"Who were coming for you? Glowing light? What do you mean?" Lascaux gave her a strange look.

"I was down by the stream and on the other side in the distance I first saw a light, then it moved toward me and it turned into two forms, floating above the ground."

Lascaux handed her a flask of water and she sipped from it.

"What were these forms?" he asked.

Keme sat at the table next to his mother. "Were they spirits?"

"Now, I don't want to hear anything about spirits, you understand?" Lascaux tensed.

Leoti's eyes were wet. "Could they be spirits?"

"You know how I feel about magic and spiritual stuff, Leoti. What your people believe is all fine and dandy, but it's not for me," Lascaux said.

"I've seen nothing like this before. I don't know what they were. They frightened me," she said.

"Mother, the Shaman might know." Keme patted Leoti's hand to comfort her.

"Yeah, might be a good idea. And ask why you saw them. It spooks me, Leoti. You never told me you had that kind of magic in you."

"I don't, or never did before. I am not sure what is happening to me."

"You go on tomorrow," said Lascaux. "Your people will move soon. We must vacate this cabin, anyway. In the meantime, I'm hungry as a bear. What's for supper?"

~ ~ ~

<Why is she running away?> asked Yonan. <Did she see us?>

<Yes, she did. She must have a higher vibration, and we forgot to set our astral bodies to invisible. Maybe she is a reincarnated Zorathian. Yet, I'm not getting a sense she has the gift of second sight, like Gayeena said some humans have.>

<Hopefully we did not frighten her too much. Who is she?> Yonan asked.

<She is the mother of Blue Fox, your future self, but she looks younger than she was when I saw her in the crystal. It is unclear. Also, this place does not look familiar.>

<We should follow her?>

<Yes.>

They moved over the densely wooded area and sought the

woman out as they floated over the land.

<There she is.> Xenia pointed below. <She is going inside the wooden structure.>

<There is a man and a young boy on horses riding up. Let's get closer.> Yonan moved to the cabin and read the minds of those talking inside. <She is upset about seeing us. Who is the boy with them? He looks like Leoti, not the man.>

Xenia peered through the open door. <He is their first son, your brother, but he is very young. You are not here, I mean the other boy. We are in the wrong time. Something went wrong. I am not sure what happened. We must go back and retry getting to the right time. You have not been born yet.>

~ ~ ~

By the next day, Lascaux had thought a lot about what Leoti had told him. He was more spooked than he let on with her, because he needed time to sort it all out in his head. Lascaux respected the Meskwaki, but he wanted nothing to do with religion, and that included the spiritual beliefs of the tribes he had run across. The idea his wife would have any of those inklings or magical abilities gave him the willies, and possibly even their son had it, too.

When Leoti and Keme returned from their visit to her family's camp, he had already decided.

"Leoti," he said, "what did your people tell you?"

"They did not know what it was. It didn't sound familiar to any of them. The only possibility is it might have been some ancient spirit."

"But why did you see it?" Lascaux was not comfortable about the situation.

"The Shaman said I could have the 'sight,' though I've had

nothing like it happen to me before and I doubt I ever will again. I am sure of it, my husband."

Lascaux sat there, mulling over what she had told him. His mind was made up. He could not stay with her if she had this sight. "I'm sorry, Leoti, and Keme, I can't do this."

"What 'this' do you mean?" she asked.

"I can't live with the thought you might have more of these episodes."

"But, husband, even if it happens again, it is not my fault. I am not making it happen."

"I know, but I can't help how I am. My aversion to this sort of thing just makes it so dang hard for me to accept. I'm leaving."

"Again? How many times must you run away when things do not suit you?"

"Papa, you are going somewhere?" asked young Keme.

"Not tonight, son, but tomorrow, you go to your people and I will travel south."

"No!" cried Leoti, "You will abandon us, me, your wife of seven years and your son?"

"I'm sorry. It must be this way. I fear this 'sight' and would grow to hate you for it. I don't want that to happen and neither would you."

"This is the last time, Lascaux. If you leave tomorrow, we will not be here if you decide to return. Tonight, you sleep on the floor."

Keme wrapped his arms about Lascaux, begging him to stay. The man would not change his mind. The next morning, it was as he said. He loaded up his gear and headed south from their cabin, leaving them to go to her family alone.

CHAPTER THIRTY-ONE

Miscalculation

As soon as Xenia and Yonan returned to Zorathia, they hurried to the scrying crystal. "I need to redo the search in this time period. We ended up twenty years earlier. Not sure how it happened. I will go to the time where Emaline and Blue Fox will be in the same area north of where we were today."

Placing her hands over the crystal, Xenia went into her mental state to connect with the future. "I am there now. It is an older version of Leoti and an older Keme. This is odd. I do not see Blue Fox." She moved forward and backward in time. "I do not see Lascaux either."

Yonan looked equally puzzled. "Perhaps you need to go further back to when we were there. Look there again, if you can pick up when we left."

"Yes, I am moving back in time to the day after we were there . . ."

A few minutes pass. Yonan tapped his foot impatiently.

"He left!"

"What?"

"He could not deal with her vision. It terrified him to the point he got on his horse and left Leoti and his son. I do not believe this. How could he?"

"Where did he go?"

"South. That explains why Blue Fox was not in the future. He and Leoti never had a second son, because Lascaux deserted them.

This is our fault!" Xenia dropped her hands and sat down. "What should we do?"

Yonan paced. "We have to go back and try to keep him from leaving."

~ ~ ~

Returning to the cabin before Lascaux left, and first making sure their astral bodies were invisible, Xenia tried to send Lascaux urgings to stay with Leoti, but his mind was too strong for her. Yonan tried as well.

This is bad, Xenia thought to herself, before communicating to Yonan. <I feel terrible Leoti and Keme were abandoned. We must follow him and keep trying until he returns to Leoti.>

<We will follow and I will convince him his fears are unfounded and his love for Leoti is stronger.>

<And if we cannot convince him?> Doubt had been clouding her mind ever since the failure in England.

<We will not give up.>

<I am not confident this time. He seemed certain he was doing the right thing.>

<We will change his mind. My not being born in this time period is a change to the future we did not plan.>

<You are right, we must keep trying.>

The couple found Lascaux on a road leading toward the river. They landed on his direct path before he would reach the ferry crossing and waited.

<It is a very beautiful country here,> Xenia said. She gazed across the landscape, admiring the lush, rolling, green hills. Homesteaders had cultivated parts, and their fields stretched out beneath the brilliant blue sky with its scattered clouds.

<I agree. This would be a wonderful place to live. I can only assume the northern parts are equally beautiful.>

Xenia turned. <He is here. You need to be the voice he hears. Be sure to send him some visions of his future without Leoti and his son. To make him miss them.>

<I will remind him how much they love him and rely on his strength.>

<Yes, go, now,> she said, and watched him as he floated over the land toward Lascaux.

~ ~ ~

When Lascaux reached the river, he saw a flash of golden light in the corner of his eye and turned his head to the side to see what it was, but it vanished. He felt a shiver down his back. *Is this what Leoti saw?* He stopped and dismounted, leading his horse toward the ferry—a huge flatboat built to haul a wagon, its team, and equipment. Mostly, the travel was from Illinois to Iowa. Since he would travel to Illinois, there were fewer passengers.

The ferry was unloading a large haul of pioneers. Lascaux moved aside to wait until they finished and the ferryman was ready to take the ferry back across the river. He found a spot along the riverbank, tied his horse to a bush nearby, and planted himself under the shade of a tree. The view across the Mississippi was astounding. He thought as much, every time he made this trek, though it had been years since he had last crossed the river, before he met Leoti and they had Keme.

His mind filled with thoughts of his family and he felt a tightness in his chest. He missed them and questioned his impulsive decision to run out on them. The golden light came again, and when he turned his head to the right, he could have sworn he saw Leoti walking toward him. He shook his head, rubbed his eyes, and looked again. It was not Leoti, but a White woman going off in the brush, he guessed to relieve herself. But the vision of his wife rocked him to his core.

Lascaux tried to think about where he was going and what he would do with his life going forward, but he could not. All he could think about was Keme growing up without him to teach him how to be a man, and he thought of Leoti and her beautiful smile.

He sat there a long time, thinking, as the sun continued to move lower in the sky, until he looked over at the ferryman and realized he was no longer there. *Dang it!* He had daydreamed away the crossing. The ferry was half-way across the river by then. He swore several colorful words and stood up, not sure what to do. Should he wait until the ferry came back?

He mulled over the visions and the strange golden light, and concluded the magic he feared could come in many forms. He wasn't afraid of what he had seen—curious, maybe. Feelings of guilt for his behavior at abandoning his family overcame him. He realized he could not live without Leoti and his son.

Like the dog with his tail between his legs, Lascaux mounted his horse and turned back toward their cabin to beg Leoti for her forgiveness. He would tell her of his own visions and they would have a merry laugh about it, he hoped.

CHAPTER THIRTY-TWO

Blue and Keme

Four years later, Leoti gave birth to another son, and they named him W"pekwi Wâkoshęha. It had not been easy for her to allow Lascaux back when he had returned from the river. She almost refused his protestations of love and promises. But something told her she should believe him and give him another chance. It turned out to be different and another baby boy came into their lives. There had been no other episodes of her seeing any strange golden light beings and Lascaux kept his promise to never leave again.

Like his father, the second son had yellow hair, blue eyes, and a fair complexion. His father called him the English name, Blue Fox, or Blue for short, because of his eyes and having Fox Indian blood like his mother. Blue was strikingly different from his brother and mother, and though the Meskwaki accepted him as their own, in the towns and at the trading posts, he would get strange stares from the White settlers, especially when the two brothers were together.

Lascaux taught his boys to speak English and the ways of the White man. Their mother taught them the Meskwaki language and their ways to understand who they were, "People of the Red Earth."

Lascaux chose to live with his wife and sons away from the White man. He did not want to live with the Meskwaki either. They lived between the two worlds, dipping into each one as needed for him and his fur trading and for Leoti, for her family.

The boys thrived growing into strong young men. Blue had

reached his eighteenth year. Keme, twenty-four, had since married a Meskwaki woman and lived with her in the village, but continued to trap and hunt with his brother and father.

It was late fall. The three men were in the deep woods checking the traps and had spread out.

"Keme," Blue called out.

"I am here, brother, no need to shout." His dark eyes twinkled, a raccoon in his grasp as he strode up to his brother from behind.

Blue spun around. "Have you seen father? He has not returned. I thought he went east."

"I have not seen him. I'm sure he will be around soon."

The sound of a gunshot startled them. "It could be father, a warning signal?"

"It came from over there." Keme pointed to the east. The two ran off in search of their father.

"Blue, Keme, over here," shouted Lascaux.

When the brothers arrived at the scene, they found Lascaux lying on the ground next to a dead fox.

"Father, what happened?" Blue asked as he rushed to Lascaux's side.

"Damn fox attacked me while I was busy opening a trap. Finally fought him off and shot him," he said, while gripping his left arm with his hand.

"It bit you?" asked Keme. "Let me see."

"I'm fine, I tell you. Go get the badger out of the trap, will you?" Lascaux directed.

Blue examined the dead fox. "I think he's rabid."

"You sure?" Lascaux studied the animal. "You might be right."

"That's not good. People die from rabid animal bites," Blue said, concerned for his father.

Lascaux shrugged it off. "The bite isn't bad. I'll be fine."

Keme brought over the dead badger from the trap and placed it in the bag with the rabbits. "The fox is rabid? Father, this is serious. The Meskwaki Shaman may help."

"I'm telling both of you I am fine. Let's get these animals home and skinned."

Two weeks had passed when Lascaux developed a fever and he started having pain in his arm around the bite. "Please husband," said Leoti, "let us take you to our medicine man. He might be able to help."

But Lascaux refused, convinced it was something else and he would be fine in a couple of days. By then, he could not sleep, and when his family tried to get him help, he became angry.

Leoti motioned Keme to follow her outside. "Go to the medicine man and tell him what is happening to Lascaux. I am sure he will come."

"Yes, Mother." Keme left and returned later with the medicine man, who was also the ceremonial chief of the band of Meskwaki.

He nodded to Leoti, saying nothing, and went directly to Lascaux on the bed. He examined the animal bite and shook his head sadly. Still, he said nothing. From his bag, he retrieved some feathers, little pouches of powders, and a gourd rattle. By this time, Lascaux was completely irrational, shouting obscenities at everyone and claiming there was a wild animal inside the cabin. Lascaux tried to get out of the bed.

At the direction of the medicine man, Keme and Blue tied their father to the bed to keep him from thrashing while the medicine man performed his rituals. Soon, Lascaux calmed down and his sons joined their mother outside, giving them privacy in hopes the medicine man's healing rituals would help.

When the medicine man finished, he went outside, spoke quietly to Leoti, then left.

"What did he say, Mother?" asked Blue.

"He did all he could. Your father's illness has taken over his body and his mind. He only could ease the mind, but the body is dying. Come, my sons, and bid farewell to your father."

The boys and Leoti surrounded Lascaux's bed, holding hands and singing Meskwaki songs to send him to other life. The dying man raised his hand to stop them and tried to speak.

"What is it, my husband?" asked Leoti, kneeling by his side.

His voice was ragged and a mere whisper, "I know I didn't show you how much I cared for you, but please know, I loved you with all my heart." He turned to the boys. "And both of you need to care for your mother. She is a good and kind woman and deserves your honor and respect." And he drew his last breath.

CHAPTER THIRTY-THREE
A Fortune Teller

It was 1857, and Iowa had since become a state. A group of Meskwaki made an unusual purchase of land from the White man and established a settlement in Tama County. Keme, his wife, and children had already moved months earlier to join the settlement.

Leoti and Blue had stayed behind to complete a deal with some settlers for their plot of land and the cabin before heading north in the spring. On the way, they stopped at a small trading post for Blue to trade pelts for food.

Blue dismounted his horse and tied the rein to the hitching post. "You go on son, I will wait out here," Leoti said, as she dismounted and went to sit on the porch in front, closing her eyes for a brief rest.

Inside, there were other customers, and the owner at the counter was busy. Blue browsed the items on the shelves and tables. Someone was staring, and he turned to a strange-looking woman standing in the corner. She was short, with long wavy dark hair, with light skin and dark brooding eyes. She wore a colorful shawl with a long fringe and lots of shiny jewelry that tinkled when she moved. Her eyes held an odd expression as she came toward him. She put her hand on his, sending shivers up his arm. Her body tremored, as if she was shivering. Her eyes fluttered and rolled back into her sockets. She spoke with a deep voice, thickly accented and unfamiliar to Blue.

"You will find a great love in the beautiful White woman who captures your heart . . . but the happiness will be at great risk." When her eyes became normal, Blue did not know what to say, but she spoke again. "My son, did I speak to you?" she asked.

"Yes, don't you remember?" He was unsure what she meant.

She patted his hand and tilted her head. "Sometimes I do, sometimes not. I hope it was not anything disturbing." She smiled.

"Uh, not really. You said I would find a great love with a beautiful woman. Nothing disturbing about it." He laughed, uncomfortable with the unusual conversation.

"Ah, good, good, I wish you all the happiness then." She turned to leave, but Blue stopped her.

"Wait, you also said something about the happiness would be at great risk. What did you mean?"

"I don't know. These words are not mine. They speak through me."

"You mean, like from the Great Spirits?"

"Perhaps. I am sorry I cannot be more help to clarify the message. Hopefully, in the future, when you meet the woman, it will all come together."

"I hope it does too. Thank you. Are you traveling through here to somewhere north?" he asked.

"No, my family is going west, to California. Have you heard of it?"

"Yes, but I am going north. Good luck to you on your journeys."

"And good luck to you," said the woman, as she sauntered away from him, joining a man who looked similar to her, all dressed in black with a colorful sash and a scarf tied around his head.

The man behind the counter was available, and Blue went up to him. "Do you know who that woman was?"

"You mean the Gypsies," he said with an accent.

"Gypsies? Who are they and where are they from?"

"Ha, they are from nowhere—nomads, travelers from Eastern Europe. I remember them when I grew up in Italy," said the man.

"Did she ask you for money?"

"No, she didn't."

"Good. What do you need today?"

"I have some pelts to trade."

After Blue conducted his business, he joined his mother outside. When they resumed their journey down the road on their horses, he told her about the strange woman.

"She sounds like a dark spirit. You should not listen to strangers who try to tell your future." His mother shook a finger at him.

"Have you ever met anyone like her who told your future?"

"Not like her, but once a Shaman told me, I would marry outside my kind, but he was of our people, not a stranger."

"The woman said I would find a great love with a beautiful woman."

"I hope it happens, my son." Leoti smiled.

"Wouldn't it be somethin'?" Blue thought of the Gypsy woman and hoped she was telling the truth. He would like to marry someday, but was not ready yet.

CHAPTER THIRTY-FOUR

The Smythe's Journey

The wheels of the wagon turned over and over along the uneven path as the Smythe's traveled on their journey to Iowa from Ohio. They had separated from the wagon train some time ago to veer south. Emaline and her sister Lucy trudged on foot alongside while their pregnant mother, Charlotte, lay inside. Their father, Darwin, drove the team of four horses pulling the overburdened wagon.

Exhausted, and with her feet aching from the constant walking, Emaline longed for rest, and to escape from the drudgery. She pulled her bonnet down over her hazel eyes to shield them from the sun overhead, peeking through the flurry of white clouds. Across the plains, the river was visible, lined thick with trees and shrubs along the bank.

"Ahead, Papa. The river!" Emaline hailed.

"Yes, I see it too," shouted Lucy, as she hugged her sister Emaline. "I never thought we would reach it, did you?" She laughed, her crystal voice tinkling in the air.

"We will rest as soon as we cross the river," Darwin promised his daughters.

The long days since leaving Dayton, Ohio, seemed endless. The move to Iowa had not been a unanimous decision. Emaline's father owned a general store, but it was not doing well, and when his sister wrote that her husband had died unexpectedly, he decided to move his family to help her run the large farm.

The girls threw fits of dismay, refusing to go along. They loved their school and had many friends they did not wish to leave. Yet the decision was made, despite Charlotte being pregnant. Emaline worried about her mother even though Charlotte had told her she was happy about the new baby. She was older, and the pregnancy was not as easy as when she had her first two daughters.

Now the river, and the promise of much needed rest, beckoned closer. Darwin was a trailblazer, not wanting to camp unless he took advantage of as much daylight as possible. Knowing Iowa was across the river motivated him to push forward.

"Mama, we are at the river," exclaimed Emaline when she climbed into the wagon.

"That is good, my dear," said Charlotte. Her face was pale, with strands of hair stuck to her damp forehead. As she tried to rise from the cot, the enormous bulge of her belly caused her to gripe. "Oh, I am having early cramps."

"You aren't going into labor, are you?" asked Lucy.

"No, it was the motion of the wagon. I was holding on too hard to keep from falling off the cot. I am fine. Do not worry." She gave a wan smile, but neither of the girls believed her.

They remembered the problems their mother had with her last pregnancy. It did not go well, and they doubted this one would either.

"Papa said we'll set up camp and rest for a day or two once we cross the river. You just stay put," said Emaline.

Darwin purchased the passage on the ferry for their wagon, team, and four passengers. They trudged on, despite the fatigue. Their destination nearing with every step kept them on the path and their eyes glued to the opposite bank—Iowa.

Once across the Mississippi, Darwin searched for a place to pull the wagon up to level ground and unhitched the team, while the girls unloaded the things they would need for cooking until later when he would put up the temporary tents.

The girls helped their mama out of the wagon and settled her on a stool alongside the wagon.

Emaline dug through her belongings to find her sketchbook and pencils. "Mama, would it be alright if I take a walk and do a little sketching? I promise I'll be back to help finish up with the meal preparations."

"As long as you return within the half hour. The sun will set soon and I want you in camp before dark. We don't know what's out here in the wilds. But while you are down there, bring back a bucket of fresh water. Lucy will help me, and then she can take a break when you return."

"I won't be gone long, thank you." Emaline picked up a wooden bucket, put her drawing tools in a bag, and slung it across her shoulder, then walked toward a stream that branched off from the river.

It was quiet, and the trees created a shroud of cool darkness. She stepped carefully along the stream until she found a smooth, dry place. After first filling the bucket with the crystal-clear water, she settled herself down and breathed in the air, relaxing in the rare moment of privacy. Removing her bonnet, she unpinned her light brown hair, letting it fall below her shoulder and flipping it out to air her hot scalp. When she pulled up her skirts to adjust her stockings, she wished she had time to remove her black leather boots to cool her feet.

Emaline thought she saw a flash of golden light. When she turned to see where it was coming from, she noticed a young man wearing buckskin breeches and moccasins on the other side of the stream. He did not see her, and used a spear to catch fish. At first, he appeared to be an Indian, but he had long blond hair and fair skin, though tanned. How odd, she thought. Emaline could not stop staring at him until he looked up and spotted her. Mortified that he'd seen her exposed limbs, she quickly pushed her dress down and lowered her eyes, pretending she did not see him. He stood and stared at her.

Finally, she raised her eyes and nodded to acknowledge his presence, grateful he was on the other side of the stream. There was something uncommonly familiar about him, and it confused her. She had never seen a man like him. She had gone to an all-girl school and the only boys she knew were through the church and only from a distance. Her father was very strict about who she socialized with, and he prohibited boys.

His constant staring was upsetting, making her want to leave. But before she could, the golden light returned. The flashes of light muddled her sight, and instead of the stream she saw a vision of a cave, and there were strange-looking people huddled around a large fire. She saw a woman drawing on the wall of the cave and knew instinctively the woman was herself. When the vision passed, she looked across the stream and the young man had left.

Emaline had never experienced anything like it in her life and did not know what to think of it. She definitely could not tell anyone in her family. They would think something was terribly wrong with her, or crazy.

She gathered up her drawing materials and got up to leave. She looked all around, but the man was gone. That was as strange as the golden light and the vision of the cave. Disappointed she had done little drawing, she headed back to their camp to assist her mother and Lucy with the meal.

CHAPTER THIRTY-FIVE
The Meskwaki Village

When the young woman lost interest, or was daydreaming of other things, Blue headed away from the stream. She seemed familiar, though he knew he had never laid eyes on her before. He continued hunting fish along the water's edge, and carried his catch back to camp where his mother, Leoti, tended the fire. He held up the dozen trout proudly.

"You got a good catch today, Blue," Leoti said.

"Yes, it was a good day fishing," he replied, and handed her the fish. "The tracks of the others are several days ahead and they will have reached the village by now."

"It will be good to be with my family again. What little is left of them," Leoti lamented.

"I have longed to be with others of our people, Mother. We have lived apart from them for too long. Though I miss our father."

"I miss him too. It was his desire for all of us to live apart from my people."

They continued their journey until they reached the village. Keme and his wife welcomed Blue and Leoti wholeheartedly, offering them shelter in the wickiup, which housed several families with plenty of room for two more people.

Keme told Blue the Meskwaki had established amiable relationships with the local settlers, and some of them paid wages to young Meskwaki men who wanted to work on the farms.

Keme and Blue sat at the fire outside of the wikiup. "Tomorrow, you go with me to the big farmhouse where I work. The foreman will hire you. You will see. He is a good man and pays fair wages."

"I have not done White man's farming."

"Neither had I. It is simple work to learn. I will show you and our other brothers who work there, too. There are other farms where our men work."

"I appreciate your help, Brother."

"We work at the White man's farm during the summer, and when winter comes, we all journey to the forest to hunt, returning in the spring. It is a good life."

Blue went with Keme to the farm, and just as his brother had said, the foreman hired him on that very day.

CHAPTER THIRTY-SIX
The Farmstead

They stopped again outside the large town of Cedar Rapids, to replenish their stores. Once rested the Smythe's headed west toward the Toledo Township in Tama County. Aunt Josephine's husband had settled on two-hundred and fifty acres, fifteen years before, and was the largest parcel of land in the area of other well-to-do farmers.

Emaline gasped with pleasure when they descended a hill and the farm was in view. A two-story, frame house with a veranda that surrounded two sides of the structure, with fields of corn and wheat as far as the eye could see. *How wonderful to live in a place such*, she thought.

The mercantile her father had owned was of adequate size, but the family lived in the accommodations on the second floor of the store. When the wagon pulled up in front of the house, the whole family gaped in awe at the impressive structure.

"Darwin, my brother!" Josephine ran down the steps of the front porch and threw her arms about her brother. "It's been years, but you are much the same. I'm relieved you have arrived."

"I am relieved as well, Josephine, and here is my family." He re-introduced his wife and the girls.

"Oh, my goodness," said Josephine. "Why wasn't I told you were with child?"

"Thank you, Jo. Good to see you after all these years." Charlotte clutched her belly and bent over.

"Let me help you." Josephine took Charlotte by the arm and assisted her up the steps and into the house. The girls followed.

A farmhand took care of the horses and Darwin took advantage of having the help and made his way inside, too.

When Emaline entered the house, she was in awe of all the elegant furnishings. She thought only people in the city had homes like it. "How beautiful your home is, Aunt Josephine," she said.

"Thank you, my dear. Please, call me Aunt Jo. I must admit the new Victorian furniture styles are my favorite. They were shipped from New York and arrived shortly before my husband passed away."

Emaline sat on the burgundy brocade upholstered settee, but realized her clothes were too dirty to sit on such elegance and got up. "I'm sorry, my clothes. I should change."

Josephine wrinkled her brows and brushed off the seat, though there wasn't any dirt visible. "I'll show you to your rooms. I'll have the housekeeper send up some hot water for you all to wash—and change into something clean."

Charlotte took refuge on the settee instead. "I'm afraid I won't make it up the stairs soon. I'm not feeling very well."

"Mama, can I get you some water?" Emaline asked.

"I've ordered some tea for you all and some sandwiches are being prepared as I speak. I'll hurry the cook along." Josephine left the room toward the kitchen.

Darwin pulled on his suspenders and rocked back on his heels as he gazed around the room. "Such extravagance, don't you agree, Charlotte?"

Charlotte groaned, "Darwin, I'm not well."

He went immediately to her. "Is it the child? Let's get you upstairs and onto a bed."

"I can't climb the stairs, my darling. I'm sorry."

"I will carry you." Without hesitation, he lifted her up into his arms. "Josephine! Which room is ours?"

A young maid appeared in the parlor. "Please follow me, sir," she said.

Emaline and Lucy hurried behind their father and the maid up the stairs. In no time, Charlotte was resting on a large double bed in the most beautifully decorated room Emaline had ever seen. Everything was in yellow, the floral wallpaper, the matching bedspread on the yellow canopied bedstead. Even the rug.

"What a lovely room," Charlotte managed from her lips before she passed out.

"She's delirious. Is there a doctor nearby?" Darwin asked Josephine when she entered the bedroom carrying a tray of tea.

"Is she sick?" she asked.

"No, the child. She lost the last one and had two other miscarriages. I'm concerned this one is not going well." Darwin's voice strained with worry.

"I'll send someone for the doctor. He is in the township and it will take a while for him to get here. I believe there is a midwife, too."

Emaline and Lucy helped get their mother undressed and washed her down with the fresh hot water the maid carried up from the kitchen. They hoped their mother would awaken, but she lay still on the bed, her breathing slow and shallow.

"Papa. Come sit by Mama. She'll want you here when she wakes up."

"Yes, yes," he said, and took the seat Emaline vacated for him next to the bed.

Hours passed and still no doctor. Charlotte came to for a moment, then fell back into unconsciousness. The sisters brought in their mother's belongings from the wagon and kept themselves busy putting her things in order in the room—all the while worried about her condition, and their new brother or sister.

As the afternoon turned into evening and the darkness fell upon the house, they left Papa sitting vigil and went downstairs to the dining room where a supper had been set on the sideboard. It was late when the doctor arrived and Josephine took him directly to the bedroom where their mother lay.

"I am scared," said Emaline. "Will she lose this child, too?"

"Maybe, Sister, I hope not. She wants this child so much." Lucy reached across the table and squeezed Emaline's hand.

"I can't take this any longer. I'm going up."

The sisters ran up the stairs to the bedroom. Aunt Jo stood in the doorway.

"Don't go in, my dears. It is not a pretty sight."

"We are going in," said Lucy.

The girls pushed past Josephine despite her resistance. When they entered the room, they stopped short. It was a gory sight indeed. The pristine white sheets were now dark red. The doctor stood next to the bed, his head hung low and his hands covered in their mama's blood.

"No!" shouted Emaline, collapsing on the nearest chair. Lucy stood motionless in shocked silence.

"Get those girls out of here, now!" shouted the doctor.

Josephine pulled the girls out of the room and pushed them into a bedroom, quickly lighting a lamp. "Please stay in here until we come and get you." She left, shutting the door behind her.

"God please, not again," Emaline cried.

"Oh Mama," cried Lucy.

They huddled together, shuddering with sobs, waiting for someone to come for them.

About an hour later, Aunt Jo opened the door. "You can come in now." She escorted the girls down the hall to their parents' room where their papa was standing at the foot of the bed. The doctor was packing up his case.

The bed had been all cleaned up. The stained sheets replaced with clean white sheets, and their mother was quietly sleeping.

"Mama?" Emaline edged closer to the bed. Her mother looked so pale. "Is she alright?" She turned to her papa and took a step back.

"Papa? What is wrong?"

His face was ashen, tears streaming down his cheeks. He clenched his hands on the footboard. "She's gone, my dearest daughters."

Emaline and Lucy looked at him in disbelief and to their mother. She lay motionless, her hands laid across her chest as they do with the dead.

"It's not true, she is not dead!" Emaline said as she stroked her mother's hair. "Wake up Mama."

Lucy clutched the sheets. "Mama?"

"I'm sorry I could not help her," said the doctor. "She had hemorrhaged by the time I arrived. The child . . . stillborn." He bid his leave and left.

The room was stuffy with the smell of blood hanging in the air. The lamps flickered in the night's dimness. No one said a word more, all was as still as the woman who lay in the bed.

CHAPTER THIRTY-SEVEN

Settling In

Two months passed, with summer upon them, and a somber stillness hung over the farm and everyone on it. Darwin had withdrawn into the business of the farm with Josephine by his side. Together, they tried to make sense of the paperwork left behind by her late husband, Amos. Lucy and Emaline mourned the loss of their mother and their infant sibling while orienting themselves to a new life on a farm.

"How are you this morning?" Lucy said as she entered the dining room.

Emaline had spoken barely a word in the past two weeks, even to her father. "I'm fine, you?" She sat at the table waiting for the cook to bring in the breakfast. Having meals prepared for them was something new, but easy to get used to.

"Fine?" Lucy plopped down at the table and rested her chin on her hands, her brown eyes staring at Emaline across from her. "I don't think you are fine, though."

Emaline shrugged.

The cook came in and busily filled the chafing dishes on the sideboard. "Can I get you anything else?" she asked.

The two girls shook their heads.

The cook turned and stomped out of the room.

"What an odd woman," Lucy said.

"I can only imagine what she must have gone through. All the changes. First Uncle Amos dies, then all of us show up, only to have two more deaths. No one talking." Emaline gazed out the window of the dining room.

"I suppose so." Lucy went to help herself to sausage, boiled eggs, and corn bread. "What are you going to do today?" She returned to the table and spread the perfectly ironed white linen napkin on her lap.

Emaline sighed. "Perhaps I'll do some sketching around the farm. Aunt Jo mentioned something about a sewing circle coming here. Some women from the church. She is expecting both of us to be in attendance."

"So soon? You know how much I hate needlework."

Emaline broke into a smile for the first time since their mother passed. "It's a shame. Because your work is truly beautiful."

"Well, you remember what Mama used to say. 'If you're going to do something, do it well.'" Lucy brushed away a tear.

Emaline rose and went to the sideboard, taking some corn bread and sausages on her plate, then returned to her seat.

"Is that all you're going to eat? You'll waste away," Lucy said.

"I haven't been hungry since . . ."

"I know . . . and I've had the exact opposite experience. I've never been so hungry." Lucy went back to the sideboard for more sausage and fried potatoes.

Aunt Jo entered carrying a sewing basket. "Good morning, my dears. As soon as you've finished your breakfast, I want to show you the projects I've set aside for you to work on when the ladies arrive this afternoon."

Emaline grimaced and shot a sidelong glance at Lucy, who looked as badly as she felt.

"Such faces." Aunt Jo said with dismay. "Now these ladies have been eager to meet both of you."

"Must we, Aunt Jo? We really aren't up to socializing yet," Emaline said.

"You girls need to find an occupation. I know you have suffered a great loss. So, have I. But idle hands are the Devil's workshop, as they say." She set the basket at the end of the table. "This is an introduction to the local ladies' society, such as it is. The county population is a few thousand, but everyone is spread out wide. I've invited those who live the closest."

"Well, if we must," Emaline said.

"Yes, Aunt Jo," Lucy said, with a frown.

"They are expecting to get to know both of you. They will be here at two o'clock. Put on your best faces and your Sunday best dresses and proper hosiery. No aprons. And polish your shoes for once."

After breakfast, Aunt Jo went over the projects for the afternoon.

The two girls practically ran out the front door, stopping on the veranda.

Emaline said under her breath, "How dare she? Mama is barely cold in her grave and Aunt Jo wants us to socialize."

"What can we do? The ladies are coming."

They looked around to be sure Aunt Jo was out of earshot.

"Aunt Jo is getting on my nerves," said Emaline.

"Mine too. Who does she think she is? She's never even had children, and now she wants to act like our mother." Lucy sat down in one of the rocking chairs on the porch.

"Have you spoken to Papa recently?"

"Not outside of supper, which as you know, is like pulling teeth. He's very sad and has buried himself in the operation of this farm. I guess it is a good thing. It takes his mind off Mama."

"Yeah, I suppose so. Well, I guess we should go get changed and show some interest in those sewing projects before the ladies arrive. There's no way we can get out of it, is there?" Emaline asked.

"Nope," Lucy said, as she got up and went back into the house, followed by Emaline.

CHAPTER THIRTY-EIGHT

The Connection

The sun shined brighter, the air was warmer, and the wind blew softer. Emaline woke up feeling energized for the first time since her mama died and she wanted to do some sketching. She changed from her nightdress to a summer corset and chemise, slipping into a long-sleeved blouse and a long skirt over one petticoat. Grabbing her drawing materials in a bag, she rushed down to get a quick breakfast while the food was still hot. Lucy wasn't interested in tagging along, so Emaline went outside in search of Papa.

He stood out by the barn with the foreman deep in discussion.

"Papa, do you mind if I follow you around for a while?" she asked, her sketchbook and pencils in hand.

"Of course, I don't mind. Just keep out of the way."

Yet it wasn't long before she grew bored and took to observing the field workers. When they first arrived on the farm, she learned the local Meskwaki tribesmen worked the fields for pay during the summer months, and then left in the winter to hunt. It was such an unusual arrangement. One they had never seen in Ohio.

She found a spot in the shade of a large tree near the backside of the barn. Retrieving her drawing tools and small drawing board, she sketched. Her teachers had encouraged Emaline to pursue her drawing. One of her teachers had an art background and gave her some lessons. She particularly enjoyed drawing people.

Several workers came in from the far fields. Among them was the young man she saw along the stream when her family had camped. Bewitched by the coincidence, her heart pounded from memories she knew not from where, but she pushed the feeling aside to focus on her drawing.

The blond man approached her. "You look familiar," he said. "You were at the stream, drawing then, too. Wasn't it?" he asked.

Emaline looked up at him. Those eyes, she thought. "It is you? What are you doing here?"

"I work here. Some of my tribesmen work here, too."

"Tribesmen?" How could he be a tribesman, what with those brilliant blue eyes and blond hair?

"My name is Blue, short for Blue Fox. We are Meskwaki." He smiled.

"Blue Fox? Sounds like an Indian name. You speak English so well."

"It is my English name. My mother is Meskwaki and my late father was French. He taught us English."

"Forgive me for being so insensitive. I've not met any Meskwaki, or any other Indians before. My name is Emaline."

"You are Master Smythe's daughter. I heard he had two. I saw your wagon arrive with your family, your mother and sister?"

"Yes, my sister's name is Lucy."

"I am so sorry about your mother. Of course, we all heard about the tragedy. It must be very difficult for you, moving here and losing her so soon."

His compassion surprised her. "Thank you. What a strange coincidence we are both here, having seen each other at the stream." Though he was fair-skinned, the sun had given him a golden tan.

"May I see what you are drawing?"

"You may." She turned her drawing board around for him.

"You are very good. You really captured the men while at work. They almost look like they are moving on the paper. How do you do that?"

"I don't know. I suppose it comes naturally to me, though I had some instruction from one teacher. I want to be an artist someday. But living here, I doubt it will happen. We used to live in a big city in Ohio."

"An artist *someday*? I think you are one now. Though I have seen little art in my life. Sometimes, in the general store, they have magazines with pictures on the covers, drawings. You could do that."

"An illustrator? I had not considered it. Perhaps."

"Why not?"

Blue was so enthused, Emaline almost believed him.

"Hey, I have an idea. You could come to my village and draw the women and children while they work and play. That would be more interesting than these men working in the field."

"I would love to see your village and draw. It would have to be when I can get away or when you are not working."

"Hey, Blue. Get back to work." The foreman shouted from the field.

"Do not worry. I will find a way." He gave her a wink and strode off to return to his labors.

Blue mesmerized Emaline, and it wasn't only his eyes. The interest he had in her drawing inspired her. She hoped somehow, she could go to his village. But she doubted her father, and certainly not Aunt Jo, would allow it.

There it was again, in the corner of her eye, a strange flash of golden light, but this time there were no strange visions. Later, she thought about Blue Fox, and as she hoped she would see him again, a sudden joy flooded her being. A feeling she hadn't had since her mama was alive.

CHAPTER THIRTY-NINE
Prejudice

That evening in the parlor, Emaline and Lucy were dutifully working on their needlework while their papa had his head buried in a newspaper.

Josephine screwed her face into a pinched look. "Darwin, who is the young blond man working in the field?"

Darwin looked up from his paper. "Who?"

"I think she means Blue Fox," Emaline offered, then stopped short, realizing she should probably have kept her mouth shut.

"Him?" Darwin said. "He's another one of the summer workers from the Meskwaki Settlement. He's been working here since shortly before we came."

Aunt Jo's mouth dropped open. "He is Meskwaki? With yellow hair?"

"Hmm," replied Darwin. "Half French, I believe. Why? He's a good, strong worker. We are lucky to have him."

Aunt Jo turned to Emaline. "I saw you out there talking to him today. I don't want you having anything to do with him. Do you understand?"

Emaline stiffened at her aunt's demand and shot a look at her father.

"Why, Jo?" asked Darwin. "As I understand things, the Meskwaki and the local settlers have a solid working relationship. Everyone gets along just fine. Personally, I find them to be amicable people."

Josephine shrugged and made another face. "They may be good workers and I knew my husband liked working with them, but now he is gone—"

"They are good workers, Jo."

"Well, it's fine. They work during the summers as they always have. Only—I detest them and I want it clear there will be no association between them and this family beyond work. I find them uncivilized."

Emaline could not believe what she was hearing and wanted to say something back to her aunt, but decided it was best not to put more fuel on the fire. When she glanced at her father, he had dropped his newspaper.

"Really now, Jo, don't you think you're being harsh? At least treat them with some civility?"

"I mean the girls. They shouldn't get too, you know, uh, friendly."

"Whatever you say. I don't want to get in the middle of it." Finished with the conversation, Darwin resumed reading his paper.

Aunt Jo shot a harsh look at the two girls. "You understand, don't you?"

"I understand, Aunt Jo," said Emaline. Lucy nodded in agreement, and the girls rose from their chairs.

"Goodnight Papa," they said in unison.

"Sweet dreams," said Papa.

Aunt Jo said nothing more and returned to her needlework.

Lucy and Emaline retired upstairs to the bedroom they shared. It was the nicest room they had ever had. Lucy sat on the pale blue coverlet of her single bed.

Emaline shut the door and went to sit at the dressing table and began undoing her hair. "You certainly were quiet. Can you believe Aunt Jo?"

"What could I say? It was all about you. I wondered what Aunt Jo was watching this afternoon while she sat on the porch in her rocker. Tell me all about him."

"There's nothing to tell, really," Emaline said, not sure how much to divulge, even to her own sister.

"I think not. I've seen him before out there working. He is good looking with his shiny blond hair. I can hardly believe he is an Indian."

Her hair hanging down to her waist, Emaline brushed in long strokes. "Well . . . he was very polite and interested in my drawing. It wasn't the first time I had seen him, either. Before we arrived and were camped on this side of the river, I saw him."

"What? No! Aren't you a secretive thing?"

"He was across the stream and not a word passed between us. But I had strange visions like daydreams, only I didn't make them. They came to me, suddenly."

"Visions? How odd. What were they?" Lucy about fell off the bed, straining to hear Emaline's voice. It was so low.

"Of another time and place, long ago. I don't know, but somehow, they made me feel connected to the young man. Does it make any sense at all?" She stopped brushing and started braiding two plaits.

"No sense to me, but I'm fascinated. It sounds magical and romantic." Her eyes fluttered dreamily. "Like the stories from one of those magazines."

"Perhaps, but nothing will come of it now, what with Aunt Jo spying on me and Papa giving her every right to tell me what I can or can't do. It's infuriating." Her eyes flashed with anger.

"I heard her tell Papa she was going into town tomorrow with the housekeeper to get supplies. Maybe you can go talk to Blue.

Gosh, I love the name."

"We'll see. I don't want to get into any trouble. We haven't been here very long. Blue invited me to his village, suggesting I might do some sketching of his people."

"He did? That sounds like a perfect excuse to talk to him, or plan to go there. Where is the village?"

"Not sure, somewhere near one of the smaller rivers. Walking distance, I'm sure."

Lucy yawned and stretched her arms out wide. "I, for one, am very sleepy." She rose and switched places with Emaline, who had finished braiding her hair and was changing into a long flannel nightdress.

"Thanks, Lucy." She pulled down the bedding on her single bed.

"For what?"

"For being on my side and not berating me like Aunt Jo."

"Of course, we're sisters and bosom friends, too. Who else do we have to be on each other's side?"

"I'm lucky to have you, Lucy. Good night." Emaline rolled over, though sleep was far off from her mind, as it filled with thoughts of Blue.

~ ~ ~

At the end of the day, the Meskwaki field workers left together to make the walk to their village. Blue was thinking of his conversation with Emaline when Keme joined him at his side and slapped him on the back.

"You were deep in conversation with Master Smythe's daughter. What is her name? Ama? You acted familiar with each other. How is it possible?"

"Her name is Emaline. On the journey from the south, I was

fishing at a stream and she was on the other side. We only acknowledged each other, but did not speak."

"Ah, a coincidence both of you end up here?"

"Maybe." Blue divulged the story of the Gypsy he met, expecting Keme would not believe in such things and laugh at him.

"I have never heard of Gypsies. She could see your future? I would be wary of such a person and anything she told you."

"Mother said the same thing."

"You think Emaline is the woman the Gypsy said you would meet?"

"Maybe." Blue tried to read Keme's face.

"If you believe the Gypsy." He chuckled lightly, then turned serious. "I was told the owner who died, the widow woman's late husband, was easy to work for. He accepted the Meskwaki. But the wife is different. I get negative feelings from her. The looks she sends us. I would stay out of her way. You do not want to jeopardize this job, do you?"

"Emaline seems friendly," Blue countered.

"I'm new here, too, and think it best we keep our distance."

Blue thought on his brother's warning, but he could not stop thinking of Emaline. The Gypsy's warning that the happiness would come at great risk crossed his mind. It was unclear to him what risk there could be, not believing someone so beautiful and talented as Emaline would cause him any unhappiness, so he pushed the warning out of his thoughts.

CHAPTER FORTY

Special Plans

The next day, while working in the fields along the road toward town, Blue noticed the surrey with the housekeeper and the old lady with the pinched face passing by. He looked toward the big house, straining to see if Emaline was visible, but he was too far away to tell. The foreman hollered at him to get back to work.

Not long afterward, he heard women's voices. He raised up from his work to discover the cook, Emaline, and her sister had brought food and beverages out to the farm hands. Usually, it was only the cook and another servant, so it was a pleasant surprise to see the two daughters. It was a much-needed break in the warm sun, and the foreman called the men aside to partake.

Emaline approached Blue holding a glass of water and some biscuits in a cloth napkin. "For you," she said. "I wanted to see you today and ask when I can visit your village . . . to draw, I mean." She smiled at him with such innocence and trust, he thought his heart might burst.

"Thank you for this." He took the glass, drinking it down in almost one gulp, then took a bite of a biscuit. "Tastes good. Yes, I want to take you to my village. We have Sunday off. That would be the only time."

"When everyone goes to church, I will beg off with a headache or something."

"You must lie?" Blue gave her a worried look.

"I will explain when I see you on Sunday, day after tomorrow. I must go now." She turned and rejoined Lucy and the cook to go back to the big house.

Blue stood scratching his head, curious about what was going on with her. He did not want her to get into trouble if she had to lie in order to go to the village. But he could not wait for Sunday.

CHAPTER FORTY-ONE

Secret Outing

Emaline thought Sunday would never arrive and, as planned, she feigned a headache.

"I want to go with you," said Lucy, her lower lip stuck out in a pout.

"Not this time. I'm not sure this will even work out. I told Blue I would meet him at the stream beyond our fields, where there are plenty of trees."

"Are you nervous?"

"Yes, can't you see I'm shaking?"

Emaline watched out the window as her father, aunt, and Lucy piled into the covered surrey. She worried the cook was not going, but sighed with relief when the woman wobbled her way out to join them. Papa had said Emaline was old enough to be left alone for a few hours, and she filled with guilt for lying, yet her eagerness to meet Blue won.

She got dressed in her everyday attire, no petticoat, and a straw hat to shield her face from the sun. Her bag of drawing supplies over her shoulder, she crept out through the back of the house. The foreman and the male servant were still around, though she didn't see them.

Emaline lifted her skirts and ran as fast as she could toward the tree-lined stream. Her heart was beating wildly. She had done nothing like it before in her life. Lying to her family, stealing out to go meet someone she had been told to avoid. She found it thrilling.

Blue was waiting, crouched down at the edge of the stream. It was the same as when she saw him the day on the trail.

"Blue," she shouted.

The sight of him with his bright blue eyes, so vivid, she could see them from so far away. They made her heart melt.

"You are here," he said as he rose to his full height.

"You sound surprised." She breathed heavily from running.

"I wasn't sure if you could get away. It bothers me you felt you must lie to visit the village. Were you told not to?"

"Well," she hesitated, not wanting to scare him away if he knew how Aunt Jo felt about him and his people. "My Aunt Jo isn't as open as my sister and my father." She was afraid to share more. When she looked at Blue, he nodded.

"It does not surprise me. I heard about her from my friends. She does not like us much, though she allows us to work on the farm. We don't want to cause trouble or you to get into any trouble, either."

"How sweet of you, Blue. I'm eighteen and old enough to make up my mind. She isn't my mother and I take offense at her trying to control me." Shocked at the words of contempt spewing from her mouth, Emaline hung her head. "I'm sorry. I should not say those things about my aunt."

"I understand. Let us walk now."

For a while, they strolled along the river toward his village, a couple of miles away. Emaline felt awkward. They remained silent until the village came into view.

"My goodness," said Emaline. "It is larger than I imagined. How many people live here?"

"About eighty, but there are others coming and we are growing already, many children." A small boy ran up and wrapped his arms around Blue's legs.

"Blue, come, play with me," said the boy.

"Not now, Ahanu. I brought a friend today."

The boy raised his eyes to Emaline's. "You look like Blue," he said.

Emaline laughed, "In a way, I suppose I do. I am going to draw." She opened her bag and took out the writing board and paper and pencils.

The boy's eyes grew large. "Draw?"

"Why don't you go by the tree and wait for us, Ahanu," Blue said. The boy smiled and ran to the trees, plopping himself on the ground with his hands in his lap, waiting patiently.

"What a charming boy," Emaline said.

"He is my brother's son. Come, they want to meet you."

She followed him through the village where many people were out busy working on various tasks. There was a very large planting area off to the side of the houses. She had never seen such structures before, constructed of long poles and a type of covering on the outside. Blue stopped in front of one house.

"This is where my mother, my brother and his wife, their two children, and I live, along with other families." He went first and Emaline followed.

"It looks so much larger inside than on the outside. How is it possible?"

Blue shrugged and crossed the room to where an older woman sat on a rug on the dirt floor. "This is Emaline," he said to the woman.

The woman stood and extended her hand. "How do you do."

Emaline took the woman's hand and gave it a shake.

"This is my mother, Leoti," said Blue.

"I'm very pleased to meet you," said Emaline, trying hard to hide her surprise.

"You look surprised we know White man's ways of greeting. Remember, my father was White," Blue said.

"Of course, my apologies," Emaline said, embarrassed.

"You will draw pictures of our village?" Leoti asked.

"I will try," Emaline said. "This is my first time visiting an Indian village. It will be challenging to draw. What are you are making?" She pointed at the object Leoti was holding in her hand.

"This is a necklace made with bear claw and otter teeth. You like? I will make you one."

"How nice of you."

Blue showed Emaline out of the wikieup. "What do you want to draw?"

"Oh . . . everything," she exclaimed. "It is all so fascinating. Take me to where your nephew is waiting. I will begin with him and go from there."

Once settled on the ground next to Ahanu, Emaline sketched him, later sketching others while they worked, with a wikieup in the background. She was so engrossed in her drawing, she completely lost track of time. When the shadows changed she realized it had grown later than she planned.

"Blue!" she called out, looking around for him. She was sitting alone. The boy had left much earlier. People turned to look. One woman pointed behind her and Emaline saw him in the distance, helping some men build a new wikieup.

She stood, brushing her dark skirt with her hands, covered with dust. Frowning, she worried how she would explain her dirty clothes.

Blue came toward her. "Are you ready to go now?"

"I didn't realize how much time had passed. I must hurry home. I'm worried everyone is there already and wondering where I am."

"Come, we will ride." Blue ran over to the corralled horses and jumped onto his pinto pony, guiding it over to Emaline. He leaned over, reaching out to her.

"What? I can't get on the horse that way. There is no saddle or stirrups."

"Take my hand, Emaline," Blue encouraged. "I will pull you up behind me."

With disbelief, she grabbed hold of his arm and jumped as he pulled her up and she grabbed onto him, pulling her leg over the horse, her skirts pulled tight, but she eventually loosened them enough to get comfortable.

"You did well!" Blue exclaimed and rode off.

Emaline's hat fell back with the ties tight around her throat. She reached back and pulled the hat onto her head. The bouncing of the horse was so jarring at first, until she found the rhythm, eventually enjoying the ride. Her arms tightened around Blue's waist and she realized she had never been so close to a man other than her father. Her nose twitched from the unfamiliar scent of him, a mixture of dust, smoke, and fish, and she wasn't sure if she liked it.

He rode right past the point where they had met earlier that morning, and the farmhouse loomed ahead.

"Stop!" she cried. "I don't want them to see me on your horse, or you."

Blue pulled the reins on his pony and stopped. "Are you sure? You will be even later if you walk from here."

"I'll be fine. If I think of an explanation or tell the truth. They will want to see my drawings and then they will know the truth."

He dismounted first, and Emaline slid down into his arms. She looked up at him, no longer nervous. He gazed down at her for a moment before he let her go.

"Thank you for a lovely day, Blue."

"I am happy you enjoyed it. You better hurry. I hope they do not punish you too harshly."

Emaline smiled at him, then turned and ran down the road toward the farm.

CHAPTER FORTY-TWO

Lies

The carriage was there, and the horses were already in the barn. Emaline feared everyone would be angry at her, or worried. All the way back, she worked out a story to tell. When she reached the steps to the veranda, she stopped, calmed herself and was taking the first stair when the front door flew open and Lucy came running down.

"They are upset you weren't here when we arrived home." She leaned in to Emaline's ear. "What are you going to tell them?"

Emaline gave a nervous smile. "The truth, pretty much. It will be fine." She put her arm around Lucy, and they went into the house.

"Here she is," announced Lucy.

Emaline put her bag down in the entryway and brushed off a little more of the dust.

"Where on earth have you been, young lady?" sputtered Aunt Jo stomping out of the parlor. "Why your clothes are filthy! What have you been doing, rolling around in the dirt? Let's get you out of those nasty things and get them washed."

She ushered Emaline up the stairs and into her bedroom. Lucy picked up her sister's bag and trailed behind.

"We were worried sick." Aunt Jo said, sounding genuinely worried.

"I'm sorry. I felt better and thought I would go sketching."

"You should have left a note if you thought you wouldn't return before we got home. Shame on you."

"I lost track of time and had gone so far. I was unsure how to make it back."

"You took an enormous risk. It's dangerous. Please don't do it again." She held Emaline's dress out away from her as if it stunk. "I'll take this down to be washed. In the meantime, you clean up before putting on a fresh dress for supper."

"Yes, Aunt Jo. Again, I'm so sorry for upsetting everyone." Feeling very much relieved her aunt hadn't asked to see the drawings—and believed her story, which mostly was the truth—she dropped on the bed.

"Lucky you," Lucy said, holding up the bag.

"Thank you. As soon as Aunt Jo pushed me up the stairs, I realized I left it." She took it and pulled out the drawings. "Take a look."

Lucy looked carefully at each one. "My, my, how fascinating. Were they friendly with you?"

"Of course, I was with Blue, you know. He introduced me to his mother, Leoti. She was very polite and shook my hand, too." She pointed to one of the first drawings. "This is Blue's nephew, Keme's son."

"He looks like Keme. I've wondered about him, you know, Keme looks Meskwaki, but Blue doesn't. Why?"

"I don't know. Blue says it happens sometimes with mixed children, taking more traits of one parent over the other."

"He could pass for White. Why doesn't he?" Lucy queried.

"Why would he? He is happy with his family. It is obvious he loves his mother very much."

"What happened to his father?"

"Rabies, a few years ago, very sad."

"You better clean up. Dinner is soon."

Emaline jumped up and went over to the washstand and poured water from the blue floral ceramic pitcher into the matching bowl. "I'm famished, too! I ate some dried meat Leoti gave me. That was hours ago." She washed her face, arms and chest and looked at the brown water in the bowl. "Dear me, I had no idea how much dust I had accumulated."

They both laughed. Lucy helped Emaline dress, and they skipped down the hall, like when they were little. They had a secret, the two of them, and it lifted their spirits.

At the dining table, Darwin gave Emaline a dour look. "I'm glad to see you are alive and well. Please do not run off again without leaving a note. We were all anxious thinking you were captured, or eaten by a wild animal."

"Papa, I'm sorry. I expected to return in an hour. I promise to leave a note if I am ever alone again and all of you are away. Which I doubt will happen very often."

"True. All the same." Her father turned his attention to his dinner and the rest of the meal was eaten in silence.

CHAPTER FORTY-THREE
Love Possessed

Over the course of the next several days, Emaline grew more and more antsy, wanting to be with Blue. Whenever she would leave the house hoping to find him out in the fields or elsewhere, Aunt Jo would go outside and sit in her rocking chair to watch her. If she got out of sight, Aunt Jo shouted out to her to be sure she could see her. It was infuriating to Emaline to be watched like some kind of criminal. Though her aunt had a reason for her concern, or perhaps she suspected Emaline had lied. In either case, life was becoming more rigid with rules and distrust. Emaline thought she might speak to Papa about it, but he had withdrawn again into the farm business, barely paying any attention to either of the girls.

~ ~ ~

The harvest nearly completed, Blue and his brethren had left the daily farming to prepare for the winter hunting trip. He and Emaline had stolen brief periods of time to be together when Aunt Jo was not watching as closely.

At breakfast, Emaline nervously glanced around the table, everyone eating quietly as usual. Lucy shot her a knowing smile.

"I'm done and going for some fresh air," she announced.

"Of course, my dear. Don't go too far and get lost," said her father.

"I think I know the area pretty well now." Emaline tossed

flippantly, leaving her aunt with her mouth full of food and not able to make an appropriate reply.

Nearly running, she headed toward the wooded area behind the house. Blue was waiting, and she fell into his arms.

"Emma." Blue laughed. "Did you have to run so hard?"

"I couldn't stand another minute in that stuffy house, with people who do not talk to each other, especially when I knew you were waiting." She wanted so much to tell him her feelings for him, but was afraid.

"We should move away from here if you don't want to be seen." Arm in arm, they strolled along the bank of the wide stream that sent trickling sounds across the air.

Birds sang in the trees and Emaline thought it could not be any more romantic. "Blue, there is something I must say to you before we part this last time."

"You sound serious. I hope it is not bad news." He stopped, turning to look into her eyes. "I see sadness and also something else . . ."

"It is love, my dearest Blue." She held her breath, waiting for his reply.

"Could it be? I have longed to hear those words and have wanted to say them to you first, but was afraid."

"Then say them."

"I love you, my beautiful Emaline." He kissed her lightly on her lips.

Emaline swooned from the overwhelming emotions. "Blue, I don't want you to leave. Is there some way you can stay?"

When they neared a darkened place thick with shrubbery and soft green grasses, Blue took her hand and they sat on the grass.

"We won't go for some time yet. Do not fear. But when the time comes, it is expected of all of us. I am Meskwaki."

"I know, but you don't look it, and I admit, I sometimes forget. Please forgive me for even asking. The thought of us being apart for any length of time is more than I can bear."

He touched her face again, and they kissed, long and passionately, their hands moving over each other. The heat of desire rose in Emaline, bursting forth so strongly she could not control it. Passion flooded her body. Blue raised her skirts and Emaline allowed him to enter her, their bodies moving in new and yet familiar patterns.

Visions passed before Emaline's eyes while in the throes of their motions. Images of another couple making love in a darkened cave somewhere in the past, her past? Was it his too? She wondered.

Time sped by. With reluctance, she forced herself to stop. "My love, how will I get through each day without being with you? Especially now we have shared all of this?" She choked on the words, tears filling her eyes.

"Do not fear. We will find time to be together before we go on the hunt. You will live, because you know in your heart we will be together again. You are now my wife, and in my heart, there will be no other."

Emaline's face lit up. "Your wife? Then you are my husband in my heart, as well."

In a fierce embrace, the two entwined once more before they knew they must part. With a tearful goodbye, Emaline insisted she go by herself the rest of the way and left him standing alone, knowing his heart was heavy with the same sadness.

CHAPTER FORTY-FOUR

Consequences

Time dragged along. It became more and more difficult for Emaline and Blue to be together until he left for the hunt. When he left, Emaline fell into a depression. The cold weather came, and it only fed her sadness, despite the vibrancy of the red and gold leaves she so loved. One day, Emaline realized something frightful. Her monthly bleeding had stopped, and she had not noticed. She asked Lucy, but her sister was younger and had even less knowledge. Deciding to keep it to herself, Emaline hoped the monthly would eventually return.

By Thanksgiving, and then the Christmas holidays and all the church events and charity work, Emaline noticed dramatic changes in her body. Her breasts had grown larger and her tummy bulged. She realized it was the same as all the times her mother had been pregnant. The sudden awareness brought her both fear and joy. Fearful others would find her with child, and joy she was carrying Blue's baby. It wasn't long before she pulled herself out of the depression. If she continued growing larger, how would she keep her pregnancy a secret? And Blue was not due back until the end of winter. By then, she feared Papa and Aunt Jo would know of her condition and feared what they would do to her, let alone to Blue.

All her worries came to fruition in January. Her dresses were so tight, even when she cinched in her corset to hide her belly, as much as she could bear, to no avail. She relied on shawls and coats until it was no longer possible. Even her face has grown puffy with the added weight.

"Emaline, you have grown fatter. How is this possible?" asked Aunt Jo one morning at breakfast.

Darwin looked up from his newspaper, and for the first time in months, peered at his daughter closely. "Emaline, there is something familiar about your condition."

"Condition!" exclaimed Aunt Jo, "That's it." She turned to her niece, whose face was red with shame.

Emaline didn't know what to say. Lucy could not hide her knowing look, either.

"Emaline, answer me!" demanded Aunt Jo. "Are you pregnant from that boy, the Meskwaki?"

"What?!" Darwin turned to his daughter. "I am assuming your look of guilt has confirmed Jo's accusation. How far along are you?"

Emaline could not look at her father's face, his look of disappointment and disgust, the same as on Aunt Jo's.

"I'm sorry." Was all she could muster. Hot tears of shame trickled down her cheeks.

"Is that all you can say for yourself? We told you to stay away from him," said Aunt Jo.

"If they weren't all gone on their hunting journey, I would ride over to his village now and beat him to a pulp," Darwin shouted.

Though Emaline knew he would do no such thing, she had never seen her father do anything so aggressive. But she was glad Blue was gone, for she did not know what would have happened to him if he had been there. She was afraid for him when he would return.

Aunt Jo turned to Lucy. "You must have known, Lucy. Why have you not said anything?"

"I would never call out my sister. It was her story to tell." Lucy's eyes flashed.

"Now, now, Jo, Lucy's not to blame. She was being a trustworthy sister. This all falls on Emaline and that dastardly Blue. And here I was defending him and his kind." Darwin slumped in his chair. "Obviously, he will no longer be working on this farm and neither will his brother."

"Oh, Papa, it is not Keme's fault."

"You, Emaline, have no say in this matter, in fact, and I'm sure your aunt will agree with me on this, you are to stay in this house, except for necessary trips to the outhouse, for the rest of your, uh, condition." Darwin's voice was unusually stern and his expression gave Emaline cause for concern. She had never brought on his wrath before.

"Yes, father," said Emaline, her head hung low and hands in her lap, holding onto her baby, afraid for its future. "What will become of me and my baby?" she said, fearing the answer.

"We will need to consider everything. For now, just do as you're told, nothing else.

"I agree with you Darwin, I'm glad you are seeing things clearly." Aunt Jo's smug expression told Emaline everything she needed to know.

Later, in their bedroom, Lucy was extra quiet.

"Lucy, thank you for your support, though I really don't want you punished over my secrets."

"I'm not worried for me, I'm afraid for you and the baby. I'm sorry you'll be confined to this house. It will be months before the baby comes. As much as I understand your feelings for Blue, I must admit, I didn't really see a future with him. It never occurred to me you would become intimate. But I have given little thought to those kinds of things, anyway."

"I appreciate your truthfulness. As I told you before, it was all so sudden, like my body was no longer my own and it belonged to his. It's difficult to explain."

"What will you do when Blue returns? Do you think he'll find out about the baby? It won't be born until May?"

"I don't know. Papa and Aunt Jo will keep it a secret as long as possible. I want to be with him, but I will be a prisoner here. Aunt Jo has control of everything, especially now." She burst into uncontrollable sobbing, consumed by the fear of the unknown.

"My dearest sister," Lucy cradled her, "I wish I could help you."

They sat for a long time until Emaline stopped crying.

CHAPTER FORTY-FIVE

Her Worst Fears

Spring blossomed, and the trees regained their greenness, yet Emaline was oblivious to their beauty. She moped about the parlor wearing one of her mother's old dresses from her pregnancies. Inhaling the scent of the roses on the table next to the bay window, she sighed with sadness, for they did not lift her spirits. Wrapping her hands around her growing belly, she gazed longingly out the window with thoughts of Blue. What must he think of her? He and his brother banned from the farm and she trapped inside the house with Aunt Jo as her jailer. There was no way to contact him.

"Would you like to play some cards?" asked Lucy, coming from the dining room with a plate of cookies. "Here, have one." She held the plate under Emaline's nose. "At least they let you eat whatever you want."

Emaline took a cookie.

"Come on, one hand."

"Oh, alright." Emaline waddled over to the card table and plopped into the armchair. "I feel like an ancient cow."

Lucy laughed, "An ancient one? That's funny. Has your humor finally returned?" Lucy shuffled the deck and dealt out seven cards each.

"Maybe. What's the point? The baby is coming soon, but neither Aunt Jo nor Papa have said barely a word to me the past several weeks as I've grown larger."

"What do you want to happen, Emaline?" Lucy tilted her head.

"I want to keep this baby, and be with Blue."

"I see." Lucy stopped and eyed her sister. "Do you actually think either of those things might happen?"

"No. But I am also afraid of losing it like Mama did. Do you think it could happen to me?"

"Gosh, Emaline, I hope not. Great Aunt Ethel had ten children and only four survived. It is the curse of being a woman, I suppose."

Emaline shuddered, remembering all the women in their family who had lost babies and children by various means. She grew sadder thinking of their poor mama, who had died giving birth the year before. The fear was real.

They had played a few hands of cards when Aunt Jo and their father entered the parlor looking somber.

"Emaline, we need to speak to you. Lucy, would you leave us?" Darwin said.

"No, I want Lucy here. Whatever you have to say affects all of us." Emaline swallowed hard, afraid of what was coming. She reached out and grabbed hold of Lucy's hand. Lucy smiled at her.

"Fine," Darwin said, and sat on the settee.

Emaline could see he was trying to show compassion, but she'd felt his anger about the pregnancy over the past several months. He could not hide it from her. Aunt Jo sat across from him on the matching settee. She was stiff as a board and her pinched face as sour as ever. Emaline braced herself.

Darwin cleared his throat, avoiding eye contact with Emaline. "We've been writing to agencies and churches around the state and other territories."

"Agencies?" asked Emaline. "What kind of agencies?"

Aunt Jo jumped in. "The kind that takes in unwanted children for adoption."

"Unwanted? This baby is not unwanted, at least by me."

"Be sensible. You are unmarried, and we refuse to have the child here under this roof," Aunt Jo said.

"Now, Jo," said Darwin, "you don't need to be harsh. This is a sensitive situation, and I know Emma is hurting." He turned to his daughter. "You understand this is the best option. Don't you? I mean, what if . . . uh, what if . . ."

"It might be dark," Aunt Jo spat.

"Dark?" asked Emaline. She glanced at Lucy, whose face went pale.

Darwin cringed at his sister's words and gave Emaline a sympathetic glance. "Even though Blue is blond and blue-eyed, his mother is full-blooded Meskwaki. The child could look like her, like Keme does." He paused and took a deep breath. "Because of the possibility, it had been difficult finding a family to adopt. But we found a church in Illinois that would handle the situation."

"Illinois?" Emaline could not believe her ears. Were they insane? "You can't mean it. I would never see my baby again?"

"Exactly, Emaline. You must give it up . . . forever. That's all there is to it," said Aunt Jo.

"I won't do it. You can't make me," Emaline cried.

"Calm down, Emma," Darwin said. "It won't happen right away. You'll have a little time with the child before someone arrives to pick it up."

Emaline gripped her belly with both hands as her heart broke into a million pieces. "Please, what if the baby looks like me? Then could we keep it and say it came from a relative or something?"

Darwin gave a beseeching glance at his sister. "I had considered the possibility. Yet, to be completely honest . . . after we discussed it, we don't think it's a good idea."

"What if Blue's tribe takes in the baby? His mother might care for him? She married a White man and her people accepted him and their marriage."

"This isn't the same thing, Emaline," said her father. "I'm sorry. I wish it could be different."

"It *can* be different, Papa. You can make it so. I don't understand why you let Aunt Jo make all the decisions about our family."

Darwin looked as guilty as Aunt Jo was smug.

"Well, Darwin, tell her. She might as well know the truth, and maybe then she'll understand she brought all this on herself."

"What is she talking about, Papa?" Emaline was feeling queasy, like something was cutting through her, but she ignored it. She wanted to understand what Aunt Jo meant.

"Papa, I want to know too." Lucy said.

Darwin didn't look at his daughters. "I made a deal with your aunt, so she would help me out of a difficult situation."

"Difficult? I'd say so," Aunt Jo said.

"Do you mind, Jo? I'm trying to tell them." He rolled his eyes. "Things were bad at the store. There were debts, lots of them. I couldn't pay them."

"Papa, we knew the business was struggling. Why didn't you tell us? What kind of deal did you make with Aunt Jo?"

"I was the one who asked Jo for help, not the other way around. She paid off all my debts so they wouldn't come after me if I agreed to help run the farm. And . . ."

Emaline didn't like how he paused. What more could there be?

"I agreed, along with your mother, Jo would continue to run her house as she saw fit, and . . . I promised you girls wouldn't cause any trouble."

"Huh, no trouble," Aunt Jo sputtered. "This mess you've created for this family, and my reputation, is more than trouble. It's a complete disaster. And you have the nerve to ask for anything."

The girls stared at each other in shock, but Emaline heard some truth in Aunt Jo's words. "I suppose I owe you an apology, Aunt Jo," she said, raising her eyes to her aunt's. "You have done a lot for our family. You are right. I've caused a lot of trouble for you." She didn't know what more to say. She felt bad for her father, for his lack of a backbone, and not being honest with his daughters, and for bringing them to live with this horrible creature, their aunt.

"Darwin, I don't think there is any point in discussing this further. We've decided and the church will send someone when we notify them the baby is born." Aunt Jo stood up as if to signal it was all settled.

"Papa, I understand now, but I don't understand why you won't let Blue's family take the baby."

"Emaline," Aunt Jo interjected, "because then everyone would know what you did and I will not have it!" Her face puffed out and turned red with anger.

Emaline went to stand, but a searing pain shot through her belly. She nearly collapsed on the floor, but her father caught her in time.

"Emaline!" cried Lucy, reaching for her.

"Is the baby coming?" asked Darwin.

"Doubtful," said Aunt Jo. "Probably this heated discussion. She's upset. Take her to her room and I'll send some cold water up."

Memories of the same scene with their mother a year earlier brought fear to the girls, and they yelped in anguish.

Darwin lifted his daughter in his arms and carried her up the stairs to the girl's room where he laid her on the bed. "How do you feel?" he asked.

"Better. Maybe Aunt Jo is right. I was very upset, but I'm a little calmer now."

The maid came in with a bowl of ice water and a cloth.

"I'll take it," said Lucy, as she placed the bowl on the nightstand. She dipped the cloth into the water and rung it out. "Here, this will make you feel better," she said to Emaline and put the cool cloth on her sister's brow.

"Thank you, Lucy. Feels nice," said Emaline.

"Well," said Darwin, "get some rest. Let us know if you don't feel like coming down to dinner. We'll send up a plate." He paused. "I know I don't have the right to ask you this, and maybe I shouldn't, but please, forgive me for not telling you everything about our arrangement with Jo. Regardless of how I feel, I think in time, you will agree this is the best solution."

Emaline said nothing as her father left the room.

Lucy helped her sister loosen her corset, then dropped to her own bed. "I'm so glad you are all right, but I am still in shock finding out about Papa. How could Mama agree to the arrangement when we moved here?"

"It's difficult to understand, though I suppose they didn't have any other options. But what they want to do with my baby is wrong."

"I agree, Emaline, I am so sorry."

"I need to think about this. I had hoped they wouldn't find a place to take my baby," she lamented, letting her head sink deep into the pillow. "Leave me alone, would you?"

"Of course." Lucy got up and rummaged through a drawer, retrieving a small brass bell. "Ring this if you need anything, anything at all." She put it on the nightstand, kissed her sister's forehead, and left the room.

CHAPTER FORTY-SIX

The Secret

It was May, nine months from the day Emaline and Blue had committed their love to each other, and the child was born. Aunt Jo refused to call for the doctor, determined to keep the whole situation a secret. Fortunately, the birthing was normal and easy.

"A girl!" exclaimed Lucy. "Let me clean her up first."

"You did just fine, Emaline," said Aunt Jo, as she busied with cleaning up the bedsheets and getting Emaline washed and changed into another dressing gown.

What a rare compliment coming from her, and Emaline managed a smile.

A knock on the door and Darwin's voice called out. "Did it all go well?" he asked through the door.

"Yes, yes, Darwin, give us some time to clean everything up and we'll let you in. Please be patient." Aunt Jo rolled her eyes.

"Mama's births did not all go well, as you recall with the last one," said Lucy, her voice terse.

"I remember. Didn't know about all the others." Aunt Jo shoved the dirty sheets into a pillowcase and called to the maid waiting in the hall with Darwin. The woman crept in quietly, not to disturb anyone. She had dealt with Aunt Jo's wrath on more than one occasion and she always tread carefully. "Here, take these down straightaway to soak. And tell Darwin, he can enter, now."

Lucy had cleaned up the baby, wrapped her in a soft blanket and carefully placed her in Emaline's arms.

"Hello, little one. She is so tiny and red and look at this tuft of yellow hair." Emaline beamed, for not only did the little girl have blond hair, she was not dark. She was still holding onto the fantasy of keeping the baby.

"Hmph," Aunt Jo grunted. "Now don't go getting attached. The child is not yours. Do you understand?"

"Jo, please," said Darwin as he inched his way into the room and over to Emaline's bed. "What a relief you are well, Emma. You had me worried."

"Papa. I am well." She smiled up at her father. "Isn't she beautiful?" She opened the blanket so he could see the tuft of yellow hair.

He blinked with awareness, then his eyes grew dark. "Emma, it doesn't matter that she has blond hair. Do you understand? We already made the arrangements. My hope for you was for an easy birth, and you would recover. And God answered my prayer. Nothing has changed. I'm sorry."

Her father's lined and tired face tugged at Emaline's heart. He was doing what he thought was the right thing, never mind how much he hurt her. Without a word, she focused on the child in her arms and tried to forget her father and aunt were in the room. Withdrawing was the only thing she could control.

"Well," Aunt Jo gave a huff, "I'll write the letter to the church right away." She turned and strode out of the room as if she had claimed a victory.

Emaline winced at the words, and her smile vanished as she held her baby close to her. Darwin patted her hand, kissed her forehead, and left the room, barely acknowledging Lucy's presence.

Lucy stood at the foot of the bed watching Emaline and the baby. "Now that the baby is here, how you will manage it? My heart is breaking for you and the little girl." She moved to Emaline's bedside and leaned over, and in a hushed voice asked, "What can I do to help? Do you want me to get a message to Blue? I'm sure he's been worried ever since they returned from their hunting season, wondering why he and Keme were not allowed to work here. I could try." Her eyes glistened with unshed tears.

Emaline raised her brows. "Lucy, would you really help? I've been thinking for months, trying to figure a way out of this situation. But I wasn't sure whether to involve you. I don't want you to get into trouble."

"I don't care. What they are doing is wrong and you have my support. I will do whatever possible." Lucy put her head on Emaline's shoulder, gazing down at the little girl in her sister's arms.

~ ~ ~

Blue and Keme had not found other work and went to the Redfield farm early in the morning to beg for their jobs. The foreman shook his head with regret. "I'm sorry, Blue, Keme, but I should have been honest with you the last time you came. You can't be here on this property at all. They have banned you from working here."

Keme and Blue turned to each other, confused. "Is there not enough work here for all of us?"

The foreman made a nervous twitch.

Blue knew that twitch and wondered why he was nervous. "What is wrong? Have we done something?" Blue immediately wondered if they had discovered his relationship with Emaline.

They were standing outside of the barn with the farmhouse within his vision and earshot. The sound of the baby crying wafted down the hill to where the men were standing. The foreman shot a worried glance up at the big house.

"It sounds like a baby crying." Blue said, as he moved toward the sound.

Keme put his hand on Blue's arm to stop him, and shook his head.

The foreman said nothing and shrugged his shoulders.

The crying continued. "It is a baby. Whose is it?" Blue already knew, and he knew the foreman would not tell him anything. Breaking away from Keme's hold, Blue ran toward the big house. When he reached the picket fencing around the small garden area in front of the house steps, he called out, "Emaline! Emaline!"

Keme ran up to Blue and tried to pull him away from the house. "Come brother, you will find trouble here."

Blue pulled out of Keme's grasp. "Do not stop me Keme, you know I must."

Emaline opened the front door, but did not step outside. "Blue, you must leave. My father and Aunt Jo will not allow you here."

"No! I will not leave. Is it our child, I hear?" Blue's eyes flashed a mixture of hurt and anger.

"Please," she said as softly as she could, in hopes he could hear her. "I will send you a message." Then louder, "Please go, now." She closed the door, peeking out the curtained window in the door. He was still standing there. Keme pulled Blue away, and finally they trudged down the hill and off the farm property.

Aunt Jo came up behind Emaline. "You did the right thing, my girl. It is unfortunate he knows about the child, but it won't change anything. If he's smart, he will not spread the news to others."

Emaline could not bear to listen to her aunt's hateful words and ran up the stairs. She went straight to the crib to hold her nameless daughter in her arms. In that moment, she had decided to name the child herself. She would let no one else have her or to name her. She would have Lucy get a note to Blue and they would elope with their child as soon as possible.

CHAPTER FORTY-SEVEN

The Escape

Under Josephine's ever watchful eye, Lucy feared discovery, yet volunteered to go to the fields with the cook taking food and beverages. She slipped a note to one of the Meskwaki field workers to give to Blue. All it said was: "Tonight, as the moon falls on the south side where labor begins."

Emaline prayed Blue would figure out the code, meaning the south side of the barn at midnight. She feared the note might land in the wrong hands.

As soon as everyone was asleep, Emaline and Lucy crept downstairs and to the office at the back of the house to search for cash.

"I think I found it," whispered Emaline, as she pulled out a small lockbox from a cabinet behind the desk.

Lucy smiled broadly, for in her hands were the keys from the center desk drawer. Not very secure, Emaline thought, but she was grateful. She tried several keys until the right one opened the box. There were a lot of bills and coin. She took as much as she dared, for any amount missing would create havoc. She needed enough to sustain the three of them until Blue could find work and support them. They returned the keys and lockbox to their places and went back to the bedroom to get the baby. Emaline had named her Lottie, after their mother, Charlotte.

The sisters went through the kitchen to the back door of the house. Lucy stopped at the door, and Emaline turned around.

"I don't want to say goodbye. It sounds so permanent. I can't bear the thought I might never see you again. I can't write, for fear they will find you out. We need to avoid any suspicion of your involvement." Emaline fought back tears.

"I love you, dearest sister. I will pray for all of you to be safe. Don't tell me where you plan to go, so I won't have to lie. Just know I will be here for you."

Her arms full with the baby and a bag of nappies and clothes, she moved as quietly as possible away from the big house and down the hill to the south side of the barn. As she got closer, her arms aching from her heavy load, she saw a shadow and caught her breath, stopping to wait and be sure it was Blue.

He came around the corner, and she heaved a sigh of relief. It was Blue, her love. He helped with her bag and kissed her on the cheek. Without words, they moved quickly away from the farm toward the tree-lined stream where he had two horses waiting.

They rode due east to the Mississippi River to board a steamboat going south to St. Louis, where they rented a tiny flat. Blue found work right away at a manufacturing plant. Emaline found small sewing jobs using her perfect stitchery, and cared for their little girl who, as she grew older, looked more and more like Emaline and Blue. They appeared as a normal family and were happy.

It was on one of those hot and humid days the following summer, Lottie was running around, laughing and giggling, while Emaline was busy embroidering a collar from one of her customers, when Blue came home from his job.

"Dada," Lottie exclaimed, clamoring at his leg, wanting to be picked up.

Gone were the buckskins. Blue wore work clothes, like all the other laborers at the plant, brown pants, beige collared shirt, and a cap. He had cut his long blond braids before they left Tama County. Setting his lunch pail on the small table, he swooped down and scooped up Lottie in his arms, swinging her around in circles, making her giggle with glee.

"How's my girl today?" Blue kissed her pink chubby cheeks and gave Emaline a loving look. "And how's my other girl today?"

"Happy." Emaline put her work aside and embrace her two loves.

~ ~ ~

Xenia stopped scrying the crystal and cried. "We did it! They are together with a child and very happy." She threw her arms around Yonan and they rocked with joy.

"Finally," Yonan said. "We should celebrate tonight."

"I know exactly how." She snuggled into his neck.

"And you can tell me everything you saw."

"Of course, my love."

CHAPTER FORTY-EIGHT
The Struggle

It was Lottie's second birthday and Emaline added the finishing touches on the birthday cake. Blue would be home soon, and she could hardly wait. They had been deliriously happy and she couldn't imagine a more perfect day, except maybe if Lucy was there. But she didn't want to think about anything negative.

When there was a knock on the door, Emaline gave a start. "Could that be Papa? Maybe he has a special surprise for you."

Lottie giggled, "Papa!"

Emaline opened to door ready to throw her arms around her husband, but what she found were her father and Aunt Jo standing in the hallway. She tried to shut the door, but Aunt Jo pushed right past Darwin and into the apartment.

"Well, it figures you are living in a dump," she said, her nose in the air as if something smelled bad.

"How did you find me?" Emaline asked.

Darwin stepped into the room with a look of embarrassment. "Hello, Emma," Darwin said, opening his arms to embrace her, but Emaline drew back in horror.

"You have no right being here. I'm nearly twenty now and we are married," Emaline said.

Aunt Jo went over to little Lottie, who was sitting on the floor playing with some toys. "Ah," she said, leaning over to pick her up.

Emaline dashed to stop her and picked up her daughter. "Do

not touch my child." She held Lottie tightly in her arms, her eyes flaring. "What are you doing here? You know I won't go back to Iowa." Lottie cried from all the shouting. "Please, let's not shout, it's upsetting Lottie."

"You named her Lottie?" Darwin said. "After your mother?"

"Yes, I know Mama, at least, would not sit in judgment of me. She loved everyone equally."

"We will never really know, will we?" Aunt Jo said.

Darwin sat down on a chair by the table. "We want you to come home. Please?"

"This is my home now," Emaline said.

"You can't continue to live like this," he said.

"We are happy being together. We have a life here, with our child. You won't let us at Aunt Jo's house."

"Sadly, it's true. You can't bring the child or Blue. You must come alone."

"What, and leave my husband and child?"

Aunt Jo gave a look at Darwin. "This is your plan, Darwin. You know I really don't care whether Emaline comes back." She moved out of their way and went to look out the window, peering at the view of the street below, and shuddered with disgust.

"Emma, dear, can't you come back with me? Lucy and I really miss you. You will never have a decent life living like this. Please?"

The door to the apartment opened and Blue entered. "What is this?"

"Blue, I didn't know they were coming. They just showed up." Emaline quick-stepped to the door.

"Why are you here?" Blue asked.

Darwin stood and stared Blue in the eye. "We've come to take my daughter home."

"Your daughter is now my wife, and we are a family. She won't leave us," Blue said.

Emaline huddled close to Blue, while Lottie fussed in her arms. "He's right."

"I don't think you understand. We aren't leaving without her. She can't stay married to you," Darwin said.

"She's a grown woman and has made her choice," Blue said. "Please accept it and we can all move on. All I want is Emma's and Lottie's happiness. You can't give her that."

Darwin frowned, taking a step forward, when Lottie cried again.

"Buhdee cake?" She squirmed in Emaline's arms, wanting to be let down.

"It's Lottie's birthday today. You don't remember?" said Emaline.

"Birthday?" Darwin's brows shot up. "That's right, of course. We came for your birthday," he lied.

"Uh-uh," she cried, and ran from them into the curtained sleeping area.

Emaline went after Lottie behind the curtain and tried to calm her down. Moments later, she heard some scuffling.

"I tell you to leave now!" Blue shouted.

Emaline opened the curtain as Blue was pushing Darwin toward the door.

"Not without Emma." Darwin pushed back, and the two fell to the floor. Darwin punched Blue, and Blue swung back.

"Stop it, both of you. This won't solve anything," Aunt Jo shouted.

"Blue, stop!" Emaline went over to the two men and tried to pull her father off Blue when the glint of metal made her jerk back. Blue had a knife and was trying to stab her father. "No, Blue, don't!"

She stepped back, while the men ignored her, continuing to struggle. Then they stopped. Neither man moved at first.

"Blue?"

"Darwin?" Aunt Jo said.

Darwin rolled onto his back and pulled himself up. Blue was face down and motionless.

Emaline ran to Blue and turned him over. "Blue . . . Oh no!" He pulled the knife from his abdomen and blood gushed down his side. "Ema—line," Blue's voice was ragged.

She turned to her father. "What have you done?"

"I didn't mean to hurt him. He had the knife," Darwin said, panting.

"I told you this was a bad idea, Darwin, but you never listen to me," Aunt Jo said in her condescending tone. "Now look what's happened."

"Please, someone help him." Emaline held Blue, caressing his face, but he had stopped moving. "Wake up, Blue. Wake up, please," she cried.

"Mama, Papa?" Lottie called from the bed.

"Don't let her come out here!" Emaline cried.

Reluctantly, Aunt Jo went to the bed to quiet Lottie, drawing the curtain behind her.

"Papa? Why won't he wake up?"

Darwin checked Blue's pulse. After a few moments, he hung his head. Blue's eyes were still open so Darwin gently closed them with his hand. "I'm so sorry, Emaline. This is not what I wanted."

"It can't be. Please God, no!" Emaline shrieked.

There were knocks on the door and voices in the hall asking if they needed help.

Emaline rocked and rocked with Blue in her lap, mumbling words into his ear—her heart broken into a million pieces. Her mind drifted back into an old familiar place, eons ago, when she lost another great love. Or was it the same one?

CHAPTER FORTY-NINE

New Hope

Xenia and Yonan were celebrating with the other couples, bragging how they had finally succeeded in helping their future selves get together, married and in-love, living with their first child.

"How wonderful, Xenia," said one of the other women. "Does this mean you will be joining us on the first ship? I noticed your names weren't on the manifest. It leaves the day after tomorrow."

Xenia stopped short and turned to Yonan, who had heard the woman's question, too.

"We will probably wait for the next ship," Yonan said.

"Well, I wish you both well and hope to see you on higher ground." She bid them farewell and left with her husband.

Xenia pulled Yonan aside. "Are we going on the next ship?"

"Depends on you. Are you ready?"

"I'm still curious about Blue and Emaline."

"I don't understand the need to check up on them. Let it be, Xenia," said Yonan. "We succeeded. I'm happy, aren't you?"

"I can't help it. It feels like something went wrong again. I need to know for sure."

Yonan finally agreed. The scrying room was empty, and she went straight to the crystal and into her routine to connect. Her hands moved over the surface. "I'm there . . . just want to see one little . . . No! Not again!"

"What is it? What will happen?" asked Yonan.

Xenia ran from the room. She went to the Temple, finding it full of people meditating. Gayeena was leading the session. Xenia took a seat in the pew up front, but she could not calm down, and burst into tears. When a few people looked over at her, she ran outside to the garden. She sat at the Koi Pond for a few minutes and wiped away her tears.

"My dear, Xenia, whatever is the trouble?" Gayeena's soothing voice washed over Xenia.

"It isn't working. I give up. I don't want to try it anymore."

Gayeena sat on the bench next to Xenia. "Now, tell me what happened."

"We thought we had finally succeeded, we celebrated and told other couples. Our future selves were together, married, with their first child, for two years."

"What good news," Gayeena said, squeezing Xenia's hand in comfort.

"It was not to last, like the last lifetime. Only this time it was Yonan's self, killed in a fight. I am afraid we will never be together for a long, happy life in the future," Xenia lamented.

"So, you intervened in two lifetimes where the death time did not change. I suggest you concentrate on the good you have done, not what you think are failures."

Xenia hiccupped and gave Gayeena a strange look. "What do you mean?"

"The two of you successfully brought your future selves together. They never would have met if you had not been there. They found love and happiness, even for a short time. Is that not a reason to celebrate?"

"I suppose."

"You bought joy to yourselves in a future lifetime. Why not try one more time. Go to the twenty-first century, to what is called Los Angeles. I have a good feeling about things."

"H-how do you know this? I thought you could not see my future, only your own."

The high priestess smiled. "While scrying my future recently, I met your future self. Though you didn't know who I was, but I recognized you."

"Recognized me, but how? Didn't I look different?"

"Remember, I have a higher vibration than you, and I can see things you cannot."

"That is right," Xenia conceded. She thought for a moment. "If you insist, then we could continue. Did you see Yonan's future self, too?"

"I did not, but I felt his presence in the area when I recognized you. Now, dry your tears, and give it one last go, yes?"

"Thank you, High Priestess." Xenia returned to the scrying room to see if Yonan was waiting for her. She had a renewed sense of the future. It might still turn out.

Yonan had his head in his hands when she entered, and when he looked up his face flooded with relief. "My heart. I hoped you would come back here once you had some time alone. Will you tell me what is going on?"

She filled him in on what happened with Emaline and Blue, and the talk with Gayeena.

"I understand, and I'm fine with giving it another go."

"Gayeena has scheduled us to use the device tomorrow. But before we travel again, I should go down to the beach once more to check on the status of new ships. Do you want to join me?"

"You go ahead. I should visit the silk farms. They suggested we put our process into a manual to include with the scrolls and your art in the tubes."

"Excellent idea. I'll see you at home later." She kissed Yonan and headed to the ships.

~ ~ ~

When Xenia reached the beach, everyone had stopped working to stare across the ocean toward the distant island. Billowing dark clouds spewed from the top of the volcano. The earth rumbled and waves grew higher than they had ever been, nearing the unfinished ships.

Suddenly, the volcano erupted, shooting red rocket-like bursts, and molten lava spilled over the sides. The sky turned dark as the smoke and ash blew toward Zorathia. In terror, those on the beach ran in all directions, screaming in fear of a premature end. Elder Ziros tried to calm them, but they could not hear him over the frightened voices of his people.

<My people,> Gayeena said. They stopped to listen. <Do not be afraid. The eruption of this volcano is not the end coming sooner. It is part of the planet preparing for the Great Shift. The air will change. Wear cloth masks to filter the smoke. There may be quakes. Be at peace.>

The people quieted and went to their homes, and so did Xenia.

As soon as she entered their home, Xenia found Yonan and ran into his arms.

"Dear, dear, Xenia. I heard the message from Gayeena and we can see the volcano from the veranda. Do not fear."

"I cannot help but wonder if we should change our plans, give up on our future selves, and do the End-of-Life Ceremony. Have you thought about it, too?"

"Fleetingly, maybe once. If it is what you want. We have choices, though they all have the same end."

They stepped out onto the veranda and gazed with sadness at the red lights coming from the distant volcano. The sun had set, and the sky had a spooky grayness as the moon peeked through.

"The view of the volcano forces me to face the reality of our situation. Despite all we know, I have been in denial," he said.

Xenia leaned her head on his shoulder. "How much time remains? Weeks?"

"Just a few."

Xenia put a finger to her lips, thinking. "Gayeena suggested we go to the twenty-first century. Shall we try one last time? If we accomplish nothing substantial, we will give up and come back to face our fate." Her eyes glistened as she spoke.

"I agree. We will go tomorrow as planned. One last time."

PART SIX: LOS ANGELES, CALIFORNIA

21ST CENTURY

CHAPTER FIFTY
Divination

Xenia and Yonan hovered in the apartment of Jessica Le Fleur, Xenia's future self.

<Yonan, you should go to where I found Greg your future self, and I will stay here and help along Jessica.>

<That worked well before,> he said.

<Good luck to you.> She watched him float off through the ceiling.

Xenia heard Jessica's voice coming from another room, so she moved around the living room, looking at all the paintings on the walls. My goodness, she thought to herself. She gazed around at exact duplicates of her own paintings of Zorathia. *How is this possible? Is Jessica dreaming of Zorathia?* If she could have cried in her astral body, she would have spilled an ocean of tears. Overjoyed her art would somehow survive, and seeing it all on Jessica's walls, gave her renewed hope that this was the lifetime that would "click."

Jessica entered the living room holding something to her ear. Xenia noticed Jessica's appearance was very much like herself as a Zorathian, tall with long, straight, black hair and gray eyes. She didn't know it could happen. How surprising.

~ ~ ~

"I'll talk to you tomorrow . . . yes, I have the address." Jessica said, "I don't know how you talk me into these things, an Astrologer? But, thanks for the birthday gift, Judy. It is a generous gift. What? . . . Okay, okay, I promise to keep an open mind. You know something. I'm thirty years old and still haven't found my so called 'true love,' which, by the way, does not exist, at least for me . . . okay, gotta run, or I'll be late."

Jessica put the object into her pocket, grabbed her shoulder bag and left.

Xenia followed as Jessica got into a strange vehicle and drove through the busy city streets while Xenia hovered above.

"Is this the right place?" Jessica said out loud. She parked on the street and went up to the entrance of a quaint little house that was converted into a business in an older residential area of Los Angeles. There was a sign on the door listing the astrologer, along with a physical therapist and an esthetician. A reception desk was in what would have been the living room.

"May I help you?" said a perky, young girl, as she removed one ear bud.

"I have an appointment with Carol," Jessica said.

"She's about done with a client. Please have a seat."

Brochures for the three businesses fanned out on the small glass-topped coffee table. Jessica sat on the rattan loveseat and picked up the one for Carol. A woman came through the waiting area and left out the front door. A few moments later, a tall, thin woman, fifty-ish, stood at the hallway entrance.

"Jessica? I'm Carol, come this way."

They went down the narrow hall and to the back room.

"This is very nice," Jessica said. The room gave her a comfy feeling and smelled of lavender and vanilla.

"Thank you." Carol looked over Jessica's shoulder. "I see you brought one of your spirit guides?"

"Huh? I didn't bring anything with me." Jessica turned around. In the corner of her eye she saw a flash of golden light but it disappeared.

"I guess you don't know you have one. I can see them with some people. Yours is a golden light being. I haven't seen one like that in a while." Carol sat down in a recliner and motioned for Jessica to sit on the other upholstered chair. She picked up her tablet and flipped through it until she stopped, finding what she needed.

Jessica shrugged her shoulders, not having a clue what Carol was talking about. "This is the first time I've ever been to an astrologer, uh, or any type of, I don't know what, New Age kind of thing. My friend Judy referred me to you. This was her idea."

"Oh yes, don't you love those kinds of ideas?" The astrologer flashed a radiant smile. "I received your birth information and have prepared your astrological chart along with some other information. You know I am also an intuitive reader?"

"A what? I don't know what you mean?" Confused, Jessica became irritated at Judy.

"It just means I sometimes get additional information from what I find in your natal chart through my personal guides."

"My natal chart?"

"Your birth chart."

"Uh, right? Judy told me about it. She was pleased with the one you did for her. Who are your personal guides? Do they work in another office?"

"No, they are spiritual guides who speak to me. You know, from the 'other side,' like how I can see your guide next to you, I can hear mine."

"Judy tried explaining to me. It's hard for me to comprehend things I don't see."

"I understand, and you aren't alone. So, let me ask you a few confirmation questions. You are thirty and single?"

"Painfully so."

"How do you mean?"

"I've tried for years to find the perfect man, and all I found is, there isn't one, for me at least. I've pretty much given up on men. That's when Judy suggested you, in hopes you will change my mind." She laughed.

"Exactly what I see in your chart, many short-term relationships having gone nowhere."

"Yeah, figures." She laughed again.

"Only up to this year, though."

"Really? This year. What a coincidence, because I'm here or what?" Leaning in, suddenly very interested in what Carol had to say.

Pretending she didn't notice the doubt, Carol continued, "Someone from your deep and distant past will appear soon, and he most likely is your soul mate."

"There is no such thing as soul mates. I read an article about it in Cosmo. Besides, there isn't anyone from my past I would ever want to see again."

"Not someone from this life, someone from a past lifetime."

"I'm confused. A past life?" Jessica barely held in another laugh. "I'm sorry, I really don't believe in all of that hocus pocus stuff."

Carol kept a straight face. "I understand. Many people don't, but you don't need to believe in it for it to be true."

Jessica couldn't laugh at that and grew quiet.

"Now, according to the aspects right now, you will travel soon to where you will meet this man."

"I don't have any trips planned. Or the time to travel. So, how? But, just for the sake of knowing, if I end up traveling somewhere,

where would it be?"

Carol closed her eyes briefly. "I'm getting it will be east of here."

"Ha, seems pretty vague, since we are on the West Coast. East of here covers a lot of territory."

"I'm sorry. I can't be more specific. I did your full chart and prepared a report." Carol went through Jessica's chart explaining things from her past which had already happened.

"Wow, Carol, this is very interesting and so true, especially what you mentioned about my relationship with my mother. How am I going to remember all of this? I should have been taking notes."

"I've printed it out for you." Carol handed her a bound report along with a color version of the chart. "Also, the fee Judy paid covers up to three questions you may have after this session. Do you have questions now?"

"I have a ton of questions, like, what does he look like? How will I know I've met him? What if I don't travel now, like you said? Does this mean I will never meet him?"

"All excellent questions. The only one I can answer today would be, what does he look like . . ." She closed her eyes again for a few moments. "He has a most unusual color of blue eyes and he will look familiar to you, though you have not met in this lifetime."

"Okay, well, it's something, I guess. More than I had waiting for Mr. Right." She chuckled. "Sorry, I keep laughing, but I'm not sure about all of this. I do hope you are right, though."

Carol handed Jessica the report and bid her good luck.

Her mind full of doubt and curiosity, Jessica headed back to her apartment, where she worked from home. She threw her purse on the counter and went straight to the home office set up in the extra bedroom. Shelves of drawing materials lined one wall, and a drafting table sat at the window. As a freelance illustrator, she mainly did book covers for romance novels. Some were historical, but all had either a couple on the cover or a manly, handsome man. People had asked her why all the men on her book covers looked so much alike. It was true. They might have different color hair, or skin, or eyes, but they looked like the same man. She didn't know why, but with every cover she created, she fantasized about the man in the illustration and being in a loving relationship. Even when she used a male model, it still happened. But the publishers and authors loved her work, so it didn't really matter. Judy told her it must be her "dream man" and Jessica replied, "He doesn't exist."

She looked at the book cover she was working on and thought, *if this is my dream man, there is no chance a real human man would ever look like this.*

~ ~ ~

Intent on her illustration, she nearly jumped out of her skin when the phone rang. She saw it was her mother, so put it on speaker.

"Hi Mom, what's up? I'm kinda busy right now on a cover."

"Sorry, dear," her mother sniffed, "but I have bad news."

"You sound upset. What's happened?"

"Your grandmother. She had a stroke and died this morning."

"Oh, no! How awful. Are you flying out there right away?"

"Yes, there isn't any family left to take care of things. Just the housekeeper and the farm employees. How will I manage everything and the funeral arrangements, too?"

"You want me to go with you, don't you?"

"Would you? You never really got much of a chance to get to know your grandma, except for the brief summer trips we took when you were little, before the divorce."

Jessica cringed. The divorce was a touchy subject, though she was completely supportive of her mother's decision to leave her father. She was only ten when they stayed with her grandmother for a few weeks.

"Let me make a call to my client to see if I can get a delay in the deadline, okay? And I'll call you back. When did you want to leave?"

"Tomorrow."

"Tomorrow! Geez, the tickets will cost a fortune."

"Don't you worry about the tickets. I'll pay for them. Having you with me would be payment enough."

"Thanks Mom, get the tickets. What airport will we be flying into?

"The Toledo Municipal Airport in Iowa is the closest one."

"You can count on me, Mom. My client will just have to understand."

"Okay, I'll let you know the time and I'll pick you up," her mother said, and disconnected.

When Jessica dialed her client and explained the situation, they understood, and she went to pack. It was June, so the weather would be warm and humid. She hated packing for winter travel. Suddenly, she stopped packing and thought about what the astrologer told her—that she would travel *east* soon! Was this a coincidence, or would the rest of the prediction come true too?

~ ~ ~

Oh dear, Xenia thought, *she is traveling somewhere else?* She would need to wait for Yonan to return to Jessica's apartment before she could follow. *Where is this place in Iowa? Is it in the same place where the other lifetime was? Is there a connection?* She hadn't looked into Jessica's future, only where she was at the time Yonan's future self was located.

She waited until the next morning when Jessica left. Yonan appeared and sensed Xenia's distress.

<Is something wrong? I have very interesting news about Greg.>

<Jessica left to fly to Iowa today. Her grandmother died.>

<What a coincidence. Greg is flying to Iowa. Something about his family too, though it made little sense to me. Iowa, same place as where the other lifetime was. What is the connection?>

<I don't know, but we need to find Jessica there.>

CHAPTER FIFTY-ONE
Iowa—Again

Jessica's mother, Sarah, insisted on renting the car and doing the driving, especially since she knew exactly where they were going. It was a long drive and Sarah filled her daughter in on what they needed to do when they arrived.

"I'd forgotten how beautiful it is here." Jessica gazed out the window as they passed rolling green hills and fields with the occasional farmhouse. They crossed covered bridges over streams and rivers until their family farm loomed in the distance.

"There it is," said Sarah, "a little run down, isn't it? Mom refused to spend any money to fix it up. She insisted there wasn't anyone to take it over anyway, so she didn't want to spend my inheritance on the house."

"Are you going to sell the farm?"

"Of course. I have no intention of moving back here. I left all this before you were born, remember? I never really missed it. I was a city girl in the country. L.A. is still my place of choice."

Jessica smiled at her mom, so young-looking and energetic. She kept in shape at the gym and jogging. She was the epitome of the California girl, plus thirty years.

They pulled up alongside the large rambling farmhouse, which sat on a hill overlooking the fields of corn and wheat. Several field hands milled about the barn, as if they knew something was brewing. A woman opened the screen door at the back of the house and waddled down the steps, her arms held out for Sarah.

"Sarah! Look at you!" She hugged Sarah in a tight embrace.

"Aunt Jen," Sarah said. Though Jen wasn't an aunt, she had known the woman since she was a little girl, a housekeeper and part-time nanny. "You haven't changed a bit since my last trip."

"It's been a few years. Your mother never stopped complaining about how she never got to see you and . . . looky here," she turned to Jessica. "Jessie, how grown up you look, it's been what fifteen years since you were here. Shame on you," she chuckled, but there were tears in her eyes.

"More like twenty years, Aunt Jen, I'm sorry so much time has passed. I feel so guilty. Grandma is gone and I didn't see her for so many years. But, then, she never came out to Los Angeles to see us, either."

"Well, it's all water under the bridge now."

"Guess so." Jessica had always wondered why her grandma had never visited them in California.

"Well, let's get our things into the house," said Sarah, looking peeved by the references to her mother's complaints.

The house smelled musty, like old houses do, with all the antiques and old stuff everywhere. It looked like nothing new had been purchased since World War II. Just like it looked when Jessica was last there. She dragged her suitcase up the stairs and stood at the landing, looking around and wondering which bedroom was available.

"Now," said Aunt Jen, "I prepared the two extra rooms for you. I'm still cleaning the master bedroom, after, well, you know—after."

"She died in her bed here?" said Sarah, shocked. "Not at the hospital?"

"She never made it to the hospital. She refused to go, said it was her time, and she laid there for two days waiting to die."

"Oh my God. That must have been terrible for you, Aunt Jen."

"I'm fine dear. You go along now."

Sarah nodded and took the room across the hall from her mother's room, pointing Jessica to the other.

It was still as Jessica remembered, and her favorite room, everything in pink and dark raspberry—the four-poster bed with its covered canopy in pink with matching bedspread with ruffles all around, a skirted dressing table, and a matching upholstered stool. She plopped down on the bed, exhausted from the travel. An early morning flight, all the hustle and bustle of the LAX airport, and the stress of flying coach. The time difference made it late in the day and she was hungry.

After unpacking and freshening up, she checked her mom's room. It was empty, so she went downstairs to the kitchen. The aroma of roast chicken made her stomach grumble.

"Hmm, smells divine Aunt Jen. Where's Mom?"

"She's in the office looking through stuff. I took care of what I could, ya know, getting your grandma picked up by the mortuary. Your mom said she wanted to have a memorial. Your grandma wanted cremation. That's being done." She turned to the antique stove and stirred the gravy.

"Thanks." Jessica went into the office and found her mom with her head in her hands, slumped over the desk piled high with papers in complete disarray. "Mom, are you okay?"

Sarah raised her head and there were tear stains on her cheeks, smearing her blush, and her mascara had run. "Guess I should have worn waterproof mascara," she laughed, holding a black-stained tissue.

"Oh, Mom." Jessica hugged her and pulled up a chair. "What are you doing? Man, what a messy desk. Did you do this?"

"Not me. This is my mother's fancy work. No wonder she was having problems. Why she wouldn't hire a manager is beyond me. She insisted she could do it."

There was a tap at the door. "Sorry to interrupt," said Aunt Jen. "She was losing her memory toward the end. I didn't have the power to do anything about it."

"Why didn't you call me?" asked Sarah.

"She wouldn't let me. I know I should have ignored her, but you know how she was. Dinner's ready."

"Mom, let's get some food in us. You can look at all of this tomorrow. Okay?" Jessica stroked her mother's bleach-blond hair, pulled her gently up, and they went into the kitchen.

"In the dining room, if you please," said Jen, her hands full with the platter of sliced chicken.

The dining table was set with the best table linen and silverware. "Why all the fuss, Aunt Jen?" asked Jessica. "It's just us."

"Aleen would have wanted it this way, that's why. And it's special having both of you here, despite the reason."

She had set three places, since Jen was like family. They enjoyed the meal and the company, and all three worked together cleaning up the dishes and the kitchen. "You've earned a rest, Aunt Jen."

"What do you mean, am I fired already?"

Sarah looked guilty. "No, at least not right now. I need you through this tough time. You realize the farm will have to be sold."

Aunt Jen's face fell. "Yeah, I figured, and I know my time to retire has come, now Aleen's gone. It's hard to imagine a life anywhere but here. This is where I've lived nearly all my life, too."

CHAPTER FIFTY-TWO

A Discovery

The next morning after breakfast, Sarah said she would be in the office and suggested Jessica go up into the attic to look for some photos for the memorial. She thought her mother had moved all the albums up there since there wasn't anyone around to look at them.

Jessica grabbed a flashlight in case the lighting wasn't good. She couldn't remember ever going into the attic. The last flight of stairs in the three-story house—the third story and the attic were added around 1890—was narrow, with a short set of steps. The door squeaked when she pushed it open and turned on the flashlight. A long string hanging in the center of the room connected to overhead lighting. When she pulled it, the room flooded with light, which was a good thing since the tiny windows allowed very little in.

The room was much more orderly than the office. There were boxes piled high with neat handwriting on the sides, listing the contents and dates, and shelves filled with unused items, probably as old as the house itself. Jessica scanned the boxes for albums or photos and found one dated 1990-2015, Albums. She pulled it off the stack, and it was so heavy, she placed it on the floor and dragged it in front of an old sofa by one of the tiny windows. She pulled off the sheet protecting the sofa, causing a flurry of dust that made her cough. It revealed a lovely burgundy colored brocade settee she guessed was from around the 1840s or 1850s, looking very Victorian, and she positioned herself on its edge to open the box.

Jessica pulled out several albums and, leaning up on the inside of the box, she found a journal. It looked way more interesting to her than the albums, so she opened it first, wondering which of her ancestors it had belonged to. In the upper right corner of the first page, was the name Emaline Smythe. Jessica recalled her great-great-great aunt was Emaline and read through the journal dated from 1857 to 1858. Emaline recorded their arrival in Tama County after moving from Ohio to live with her Aunt Jo, her father's sister. Page after page of entries of her mother's death, how horrible it was living with Aunt Jo, and how her father had changed. Then the tone of the entries lightened. She had met a young man who worked on the farm, and visited his village to draw pictures of his tribe.

What? Tribe? Entranced, she read further. There was mention of some drawings and a portfolio which had been hidden. Jessica checked the box again. No portfolio. She looked at all the other boxes. She checked all the shelves and then she found it, a dusty brown leather-covered portfolio tied together with faded brown ribbon. Inside were sheets of paper with pencil drawings of a Native American village. In the lower right-hand corner of the drawings, in Emaline's hand: 1857, Meskwaki Village. Several drawings were of individuals, including one of a boy labeled "Keme Lascaux's son," and then the last few were of one man. The name on these drawings was Blue Lascaux, and Jessica's mouth dropped open. She couldn't believe her eyes, for the face she was looking at was the face of the man she had been illustrating on the covers of all those romance novels. What did this mean? Her mind was spinning. She grabbed the diary and the portfolio and ran down the stairs to find her mother.

"Mom! Mom!" she hollered as she sprinted to the office.

"What the hell is the matter with you? I told you I'd be in here."

Sarah gave Jessica a frustrated look. "I'm trying to make sense of all of this."

"I was so excited to show you this." Thrusting the journal and portfolio to her mother, "Have you ever seen these before?"

Sarah put her pen down and took the two items. She opened the journal and looked at the drawings. "Emaline." She tapped her finger on her temple. "I seem to recall that was my great-great-great aunt, maybe? These drawings look a little familiar, but you know how not artistic I am, and I probably didn't find it very interesting when I was a child. But, this journal. I would have remembered, and I've never seen it before."

"Well," said Jessica, "it only covers about a year from the time Emaline, her sister, our great-great-great-whatever grandmother Lucy, and their parents came here from Ohio. I read the whole thing. She fell in love with one of the farm hands, who happened to be a Meskwaki tribesman and she got pregnant! Imagine that. I don't recall hearing any stories about her. Did you?"

"Actually, I remember my grandmother telling us about some family scandal way back. Someone had an illegitimate child, but to find out it was Emaline is a surprise to me. You know how family tales get morphed over the years. But, this journal, where did you find it?"

"It was in the same box as the photo albums from 1990 to 2015. Odd it was in there, isn't it? Almost as if I was supposed to find it." She gave a nervous laugh. She had never had those kinds of thoughts before she met the astrologer.

"Yeah, weird. Aunt Jen said my mom was having memory problems. Anyway, let's go back and see if we can find anything about what happened to the child."

The two returned to the attic and for hours searched through boxes and shelves but found no other references to Emaline, Blue, or the child.

"It's a dead end. I guess we'll never know," Sarah said with resignation.

"Bummer," said Jessica. "Anyway, we've got the memorial to plan, and at least now we have all these photos of Grandma and Grandpa, and when you were little. I think these will do nicely." Jessica spread out the photos they had selected on a small table.

"Sounds good. Tomorrow, you can go into town to buy some presentation boards and stuff. You know all about those." She winked, and the corners of her eyes crinkled. Jessica wondered when she last had a Botox treatment and chuckled to herself.

CHAPTER FIFTY-THREE

A Strange Meeting

In her grandmother's SUV, Jessica drove into town to pick up the materials she needed for the memorial display and to find some real coffee. Aunt Jen's bitter brew was undrinkable. After a quick stop at Michael's Crafts, she hopped in the car and a flash of golden light appeared in the corner of her eye. She turned to see what it was, but it was gone. Instead, she noticed a coffee place nearby. The sign boasted fresh roasted coffee, and she pulled in.

While mulling over the quite extensive coffee menu, she overheard someone say the name Lascaux. Her ears perked up and looked around to see who had said it. There weren't very many people in the shop at that hour, but it was a man's voice and there were two sitting by the window. One man wore jeans and a leather vest, his long graying hair tied back in a single braid. The other man was dressed a bit more formally in black slacks and a collared shirt. She noticed a briefcase on the floor next to his chair.

She placed her order and walked over to the men's table. "Excuse me," she said. "I didn't mean to eavesdrop, but did one of you say the name Lascaux?"

The younger of the two men looked up at her. "I did."

Jessica took in a sharp breath, for his eyes were the most unusual blue color she had ever seen. "It wouldn't happen to be a relation to a Blue Lascaux?"

"How did you know?" he said as he did a double-take at her.

"Have a seat." He pulled the empty chair out for her.

"Thanks," Jessica said, taking the seat and draping her shoulder bag over the back of the chair. "I'm Jessica," she said, sticking out her hand. She couldn't take her eyes off him, the thick dark brown hair trimmed close, clean-shaven, not the bearded look that was in fashion, and a brilliant smile. She liked it.

"I'm Greg." He shook her hand and turned to the other man. "This is my new friend, Dan."

Dan gave her a nod. "Well, Greg, I think you have all I can tell you." He got up to leave.

"Wait, not just yet. Stick around. I'm curious what Jessica knows about the Lascauxs and you would be, too, right?"

Dan sat back down and waited quietly, observing Greg and Jessica.

"So, Jessica, how do you know about Blue Lascaux?" asked Greg.

Her coffee had arrived. "Thanks," she said to the girl and turned back to Greg. "This is such a coincidence, because I just learned about the name last night while going through my late grandmother's things. She passed a couple days ago." A lump formed in her throat. Everything had happened so quickly she suddenly realized she hadn't cried since learning of her grandmother's death. She swallowed. "The name was mentioned in a very old journal or diary from the 19th century."

"My condolences on your loss. Personally, I don't believe in coincidences, but I'm here in Tama because of information I found in a diary. I'm doing some genealogy work on my family."

"Really. A diary? All I know is Blue Lascaux was half French and half Meskwaki and apparently had some kind of romance with my great aunt, several times over, from way back in 1857."

"You got all that information from an entry in a diary?" Greg eyed her curiously.

"There were a lot of entries about him and the Meskwaki Village." She took a sip of her coffee and swooned. It was better than she expected. "The coffee is wonderful here," she said. Glancing at Dan, she noticed he was wearing an unusual necklace. "Is that a bear claw on your necklace?"

"It is. An ancient one handed down through my people. I am Meskwaki."

"Dan was telling me of some old stories from his family about a French fur trader who married one of their people and they had two sons. Dan is a descendant of one of those sons. What was his name?" he asked Dan.

"Keme Lascaux," Dan said.

"Keme?" Jessica exclaimed. "Now this is getting way too weird. I saw the name written on a portrait drawing of him, drawn by my aunt."

"No kidding," said Greg.

Dan smiled. "Interesting. I agree. There are no coincidences."

Greg reached into his briefcase and retrieved a cloth-covered object. "This is the diary of my great-great-great grandmother. What she wrote in here prompted me to have one of those DNA tests done from a genealogy website. I'm part Meskwaki, it seems."

Jessica's eyes grew large. "I see. May I ask what you found in the diary?"

"Sure." He opened it to a page he had flagged with a post-it. "Says here, she and her husband adopted an orphaned girl through the help of a church in Illinois. Her name was Lottie Lascaux. Later," he turned to another page, "she wrote when they discovered the girl's father was half Indian, they almost changed their minds about adopting her. But because she looked white and so beautiful, they agreed to take her. The rest of the diary is written with love for the little girl."

"Did she mention the name of the mother?" Jessica asked.

"Oh, yes," he turned the page, "uh, it was Emma Lascaux."

"Emma? My aunt's name was Emaline. Oh my God."

"Oh my God, is right!" said Greg.

Dan looked pleased. "It appears we are all related. I'll let you two continue. I need to get going. Greg, you have my number. When you are ready, you come visit the rest of the family. And you too, Jessica."

Dan stood to take Greg's hand. "I look forward to it. This had all been overwhelming. Thank you for your time." Greg sat back down shaking his head as though he could not believe his luck.

"Greg, you really must come to the farm and meet my mother. We are in the middle of planning a memorial for my grandmother and you should be invited, because oh, wow, we're cousins! How bizarre is this?" She shook her head, overwhelmed by it all.

"This is unbelievable. First, I find out my family tree isn't what I thought it was, and now I have two new families to get to know. I'm so glad I made this trip." Greg leaned back in his chair and ran his hand through his hair.

"I'm visiting too, from L.A. Where did you come in from?"

"L.A? I live in L.A. Unreal."

"Yeah, unreal," Jessica said, staring into his eyes. "Aside from us actually being related, distantly, so, I feel like we've met before."

"L.A. is a big place. But anything is possible. I kinda feel the same way, too."

"Let me give you directions on getting to the farm, and my cell. It's the Collins Farm, has been for generations. Oh, and my last name is Le Fleur, Jessica Le Fleur."

"Greg Benton," he said, and they shook hands again—only this time they lingered a moment longer than necessary—before they exchanged cell numbers and Jessica texted him the address and directions to the farm.

"Bring the diary and we can compare the two stories, okay?"

They finish their coffees and Jessica practically flew back to the farmhouse, and not by speeding. It was because of Greg. She remembered the astrologer saying she would know him because he was familiar and had the most unusual eyes. Who would have guessed the man would be a relation?

"Wait until Mom hears this." And she hit the gas down the rural road toward the farm.

~ ~ ~

Xenia and Yonan floated above the table in the coffee shop. <I did not see all this in my scrying,> she said to Yonan, in disbelief. <I hadn't gone far enough forward in time. This is amazing. They are connecting all on their own without our help at all.>

<This must be the lifetime we have been searching for.> Yonan's astral body was glowing more brightly with emotion.

<Yes, I agree. We can return to our time now and check on them from there. They have already connected, and I could see a spark between them.>

<Yes, my heart, let us return. The time is growing short for Zorathia.>

CHAPTER FIFTY-FOUR

Connections and Family Secrets

They held the memorial for Aleen at the farmhouse instead of the church. They would bury her in the family cemetery, a short distance from the big house. Neither Sarah nor Jessica had siblings, but there were a few cousins who lived in nearby townships who came. Aleen was active in the church, sang in the choir, and served on several committees over the years. She was well known and loved by many, which surprised Sarah considering all her differences with her mother.

When Greg arrived, Jessica stuck close to him, introducing him to her mother and other family, helping him to feel welcome and at home. The service was mostly a few words said by the pastor, a few friends, and family, and then they all filed out to make their way up the short hill behind the farmhouse to the cemetery.

After they placed Aleen's urn in the small crypt, Jessica, her mother, and Greg remained in the graveyard to look around at other ancestors buried there.

"Here's your three times great-grandmother, Lucy," said Sarah, pointing to a low headstone that read Lucille (Lucy) Smythe Collins, 1841-1915. "Greg, this was Emaline's younger sister. I think Emaline's grave is out here somewhere, but I forget where. I never cared much for this cemetery. Aunt Jen might be able to find it."

"I didn't know Aunt Emaline was buried here," said Jessica.

"There's nothing in the diary I have either, about what happened to them and why Lottie was an orphan," said Greg.

"Hmm, I recall some stories told about them by my grandmother, but I paid little attention when I was young. I should have shown more interest." Sarah sighed.

"I can tell you some of it," said Aunt Jen.

"Aunt Jen, I didn't see you come back up. Everything okay at the house?" asked Sarah.

"The last of the guests left, and I saw you all still up here. About Emaline, Aleen would share family stories with me." She stopped and wiped her face with a handkerchief. "I seem to recall there was a scandal surrounding Emaline. She got pregnant and ran off with the father, a half Meskwaki. He died, and they put the child up for adoption."

"Yeah, we have some information about it. But how did the father die?" asked Greg.

"Don't recall. Emaline was brought back here. Shortly afterward she killed herself, very young. Very sad. They tried to keep it all hush-hush, but you know how hard it is to keep something like that a secret."

Jessica shot Greg a glance, and he looked disheartened. "How awful," she said to him. "I'm sorry. I had no idea Aunt Emaline committed suicide."

"She was your relation, too. The entire story is terrible. I guess it was the times," Greg said.

"Why don't I remember the story?" asked Sarah. "I should have remembered. Aunt Jen, do you know where her headstone is? We didn't see it."

"It's up here somewhere, probably in the back row. She was one of the first ones to be buried in this cemetery, alongside her mother, and next to Josephine's husband. Forget his name. Last name was Redfield. He's the one who started this farm."

Heading over to the back row, the others followed, looking for headstones. "Okay, here's Charlotte's. She was Lucy and Emmaline's mother. Yeah, she died in 1857. That's when they came here, Josephine's brother's family," Aunt Jen said.

"Yes, in Emaline's diary," Jessica said.

"You found it? I haven't seen it in years. Never read but a page or two, felt kinda strange to me, peeking into someone's private thoughts. I seem to recall a photo of the sisters in one of the albums." Aunt Jen kept looking.

"Really?" Jessica said. "We'll have to look through those. Wouldn't that be great, Greg?"

"Uh, yeah . . . Wait, what's this?" Greg said getting down on his knees and starting to pull grass. "I think I found it."

There, in the back row in the corner, a small headstone was partly overgrown.

"Emaline's?" asked Jessica. They all crowded around.

Emaline Smythe b. 1839 - d. 1859,
Beloved daughter, sister, mother.

"Why is it smaller than the rest of the stones?" asked Sarah.

"I was thinking the same thing, and her married name wasn't included, though it says mother. Which is interesting," said Jessica.

"I don't know, don't recall anything said about that," said Aunt Jen. "Well, I best be gettin' back to the kitchen to finish cleaning things up. I'll see you all later for dinner. Greg, you staying?"

He shrugged.

"Of course, he is," said Sarah to Jen, turning to Greg with a questioning gaze.

"Yes, please stay," said Jessica, smiling.

"Very kind of you," said Greg. "This has been an enlightening day of discoveries."

"Well, it isn't over yet, because I want to show you Emaline's diary and the drawings. There are some old photos of them, too," said Jessica.

"Okay, I'd love to see those, and let me get the other diary from the car."

They returned to the house, and Jessica guided Greg up to the attic. They mulled over the two diaries, and Greg found the drawings of great importance.

"It's frustrating," said Jessica, "to not have the missing pieces about Blue and Emaline and why their child was an orphan. And, if writing diaries was common back then and Emaline had one, where's Lucy's?"

"Let's keeping searching. Has to be here, right?" Greg said. "Have you looked at the furniture in the back?"

Jessica looked at where he was pointing. Behind some stacks of boxes and a tall bookcase, there were some pieces of old furniture. "No. I couldn't get to them."

"Let me move this, okay?" While moving the tall bookcase with a drawer and two doors on the lower half, the drawer fell out and broke. "Well shit! I'm sorry." Both of them bent down to pick up the drawer pieces. "Wait, this is odd. It looks like a false back." Greg jiggled the drawer, and the back slid off. "Another journal," he said, and pulled a book out of the compartment.

"It says diary on the front."

Greg put it in her hands.

"I'm almost too excited to open it." She caressed the leather binding. "Excellent condition, too."

"Well, open it," he chuckled. "I can't wait either."

Jessica opened the cover and there was writing on the first page.

"It's Lucy's!"

"Let me get Emaline's diary. I want to check those dates again." Greg hurried to the small table where the photos and drawings were scattered and picked up the diary. When he handed it over to Jessica, he fumbled and it fell to the floor. "Geez, I'm such a klutz."

"It's okay." Jessica picked it up by the back cover, and she noticed some pages in the back with writing. "There is an entry on the very last page. I thought the rest of the diary was blank." She read it.

"Read it out loud, Jessie," said Greg.

At first his familiarity with using a nickname startled Jessica, but when she glanced at him, she suddenly felt relaxed and comforted by it.

"Sorry, is it okay if I call you Jessie? It feels more natural to me?"

"Sure," she said, "I like it." She smiled.

"Are you going to read the entry?"

"Okay. Here's what Emaline wrote."

August 1860

It's been two months and my heart bleeds a little each day till I have nothing left at the end of it. I have nightmares of you, my only love, dying in my arms. I know you were trying to protect us from my father, but I see the flash of metal, your knife in the air, and then it was gone, you wrestling with father and he stands up and you on the floor, blood spilling from your body. I cannot bear to be without you and Lottie. She is gone, too. They gave her away. Aunt Jo's doing, and father did nothing to stop it. What a weak man. I hate him and her and everyone else in the world. There was a terrible confrontation when your family learned about your death. I thought they would kill father. Somehow your family heard the truth in the story. They were upset your body was buried so far away and Lottie was with strangers. None of your people work here at the farm anymore. It's just as well. But I will see you soon, my love, soon.

Tears trickled down Jessica's cheeks as she held in a sob, her hand holding her stomach. "Oh, how gut-wrenching."

"Suicide, like your Aunt Jen said, and Blue died in a fight with Emaline's father. Wow! Rough times." Greg leaned back on his heels. "I guess that pretty much fills in the blanks, huh?"

"I suppose."

"Jessica!" Sarah scurried up the stairs to the attic doorway. "Guess what I found?" she said, holding up some papers.

"We found something, too."

"Me first, okay?" Sarah overcome with excitement, plopped on the burgundy settee. "While clearing out the cupboards in the office, I found a lockbox with old wills and testaments. This one is Aunt Josephine's. It states, because of Emaline's suicide in 1860, none of her offspring, in perpetuity, could make a claim to her inheritance. She made it clear, if Lottie, or any of her children, ever showed up wanting money, the will prevents it. What a horrid, hateful woman!"

"I was thinking how much Josephine must have hated poor Emaline, and it might explain the extra small headstone for her." Jessica said.

"Guess so. Well, I had to share this right away," Sarah said.

"I hope you don't think I'm here to collect anything from this estate," Greg said, looking concerned.

"Oh God, no!" Sarah said. "From the looks of the accounts, there isn't much left of this 'estate' anyway. What did you find?" she asked Jessica.

"Two things, actually," Jessica held up the two diaries. "Lucy's diary, and on the last page of Emaline's, a sort of suicide note."

"Amazing." Sarah took Emaline's diary from Jessica's hands to read the page herself. "Wow, how heartbreaking."

"We were getting ready to read some entries in Lucy's diary when we found the note by Emaline. What was the date again? I want to look for it in Lucy's diary."

"August, 4, 1860. God, she was only twenty-one years old." Sarah lamented.

"Here's an entry on that day," Greg announced.

August 4, 1860

My hand is shaking. I can barely write these words. Emaline, oh my dearest sister, why oh why did you do it? And why was I the one who found you—hanging from the beam in the barn? How will I ever forget the way you looked? You left me alone now, with them. Could you not have talked to me and let me help you somehow? How will I bear it without you? I know you were in pain. Please forgive me for not having the right words to help you. I will miss you so terribly, terribly much.

"Then a couple of days later, she wrote."

August 6, 1860

How wicked she is. I can barely call her aunt, but I must. Father is beside himself over Emaline and he told me about the child. We were alone. He needed to talk. Aunt Jo was in town at the lawyer's office. Who knows what for. Emaline barely in the ground and no funeral. Unconscionable! The pastor and the few of us. So afraid of how it would look. Who would care at this point? Most people knew about the elopement for the last two years and then dragging her back here alone. Now this.

Anyway, father told me Aunt Jo forced him to take the child, Lottie, to Illinois for the adoption. I wish I could have seen the little version of Emaline at two years. Father said she looked just like her mama.

"Aunt Jo was really something, huh." Jessica said.

"I recall some not so nice things said about her when I was a child. I wondered if any of it was really true. I guess they weren't exaggerating." Sarah said.

"Oh, here's one about the headstone, though, years later." Greg continued to read from the diary.

May 1875

Only two days until the wedding. I was thinking I would never marry, but God loves me, after all. When I take Stephen's name, I'm going to change the name of the farm to his—Collins Farm. I want so to wipe out all the terrible memories of Aunt Jo and Father, now they are gone, too.

The headstone came today. I had it modified for my dear sister by adding the memorial, which should have been included years ago. I am at peace now and can live my own life with my new husband.

"I guess that covers it," said Greg, as he closed the diary and handed it to Jessica.

"Thanks for reading those entries. I'd like to read more of it later, but I've got to get back to the books. I'll catch you a little later, Greg?"

"Sure," he said.

Sarah smiled at Greg and gave her daughter a wink, then left the attic.

CHAPTER FIFTY-FIVE

Falling in Love

Greg and Jessica spent as much time together as possible until she needed to return to L.A. On the last night, they strolled down to the river near the farm and walked along the riverbank.

"Will you be going home soon?" Jessica asked, taking in the late afternoon breeze.

"Eventually. You know I work remotely, so I could stick around here if I wanted to. Do you really have to leave?"

"There is a project I need to complete and only so much of it can be done here."

"Too bad. I was hoping to spend more time with you." He stopped and turned, taking her hand, looking deep into her eyes.

Jessica thought she would melt right there and then. Those eyes of his held her spellbound. Until then, they hadn't even kissed. She was thinking he was only interested in her as family—then he drew her into his arms and kissed her.

It was the most magical kiss she had ever experienced. The world around them fell away. The wind picked up and it felt like they were floating in space. She saw flashes of Greg in different time periods, Egypt, a cave, next to a beautiful waterfall that looked like the painting she had done. Though his face would change, she knew it was him. She wrapped her arms around his neck and allowed herself to be caught up in the passion.

When he pulled away for a moment, he took a breath. "Wow,"

he said. "That was some kiss."

"It was, and I don't want it to stop." She pulled him closer.

"Are you sure you can't work something out with your client?"

"I'll call her tomorrow," Jessica giggled, and they kissed again.

Jessica gazed at Greg and thought about the astrologer. "I've been wanting to tell you something," she said hesitantly.

"Oh? About what?"

"Well, you might think I'm nuts, but before I came here for my grandmother's funeral, I visited an astrologer about my love life, or I should say, lack of one." She chuckled.

"No kidding. And what did the astrologer tell you?"

"She first confirmed what I already had experienced: dead-end relationships to the point I had given up. I thought finding an honest and committed man was not in my future. But she told me I would travel to the east very soon, and I would find my soul mate."

"Really? When did you see her?"

"The night before I flew here. Wild, huh?"

"Wild. I guess not crazy at all. Because it happened."

"Do you believe in soul mates?"

"I never did before I met you. Because you are my soul mate."

"I think so, too."

"I love you, Jessica. I can't believe this is happening so fast, but it's true." He took her face in his hands and kissed her nose, then her forehead, each cheek and then her lips, in a long, soft, loving way.

"I love you too, Greg. I never thought I would find this kind of feeling."

"What kind of feeling?"

"A sense of wholeness. I've always been so independent, though I wanted love. Guess I thought it meant giving up who I am. I don't feel that with you."

"And you shouldn't. My love accepts you for who you are and how I feel when I'm with you. Which is amazing. I think I feel the wholeness you mentioned."

Their arms entwined, they continued to stroll along the bank, gazing up at the moon as it rose from the horizon.

~ ~ ~

By the time Sarah had the financial situation straightened out and the farmland sold to a large co-op, Jessica and Greg were engaged and returned home to plan the wedding. Sarah turned the farmhouse property over to a realtor so she could return to L.A. to help with the wedding and go back to her job.

After they were married, Greg gave up his apartment and moved into Jessica's.

"You know, Greg, this apartment isn't big enough for the two of us and our work at home jobs."

"I was thinking about it, but homes are so expensive here."

She pulled him down onto the sofa with her. "I know. However, the farmhouse is still for sale."

"Uh-huh? What are you getting at?"

"I'm suggesting we move to Iowa. The farmhouse is in the family trust. The land sale covered all the back debts, and there is plenty in the trust to pay for improvements. It's big enough for two home offices and a nursery." She stopped and gave him a sidelong glance to see his reaction.

"Nursery? Is that another hint?"

"No, I'm not pregnant . . . yet! Just thinking ahead, ya know." She punched him lovingly. "And we can both do our jobs at home there, right? Why here in noisy, dirty, and crowded L.A. when we were so happy on the farm?"

"I miss it and getting to know my Meskwaki family. I think it's a possibility."

She wrapped her body around his and snuggled close. "Really? You would do it?"

"I would," he said, and kissed her passionately.

"I'll call Mom tomorrow and tell her."

CHAPTER FIFTY-SIX
Closure

"Come on, go with me," Xenia implored.

"I am convinced Jessica and Greg's relationship will last, but we can scry the crystal one last time. Then we must go straight to the Temple for the final congregation with those who are still here."

"Agreed," Xenia said.

Going up the crowded mountain path, they bid farewells, knowing their deaths would happen any day.

Instead of entering the Temple, they went around the building to the scrying room. It was empty. Xenia took her place with her hands over the crystal for the last time. With her eyes closed, she centered her mind, then peered into the future. "I found them. They are back in that place, Los Angeles, together, planning a wedding!" Xenia could barely contain herself. "I'm going to speed forward several years . . . They are still together, though it looks like they are living at the farmhouse in Iowa, not in Los Angeles, and they are much older, with children."

"How wonderful," Yonan said, as he clasped his hands together excitedly, "go further."

She sped through time further. "I see them very old, still living at the farmhouse, but with grandchildren and great-grandchildren all surrounding them, and they look happy."

Xenia stopped and embraced Yonan. "We did it, finally!"

"I knew we would," Yonan said, laughing, "though I had no idea it would take so long. It was quite an adventure, though, wasn't it?"

"It was. Despite my resistance in the beginning and getting so discouraged. You maintained your optimistic attitude we would succeed, and we did. You know what?"

"What, my heart?"

"You are pretty smart for such an old, old man." She laughed.

Yonan looked thoughtfully. "I have thought about all the lives we visited and all the work we did to get our future selves together, only to have them not be together, or die."

Xenia relaxed on the sofa and poured two cups of fresh juice. "Yes, I thought about it too, and then this last one with Jessica and Greg. All we did was nudge them into the right place at the right time. Then, it all fell into place."

"Well, there was the time I guided Lascaux to return to Leoti, or Blue would not have been born and Greg and Jessica would not have connected later." Yonan settled back into the cushions next to his love and took a sip of papaya juice.

"But the reason Lascaux left Leoti was because she saw our astral bodies and was so afraid she told Lascaux. That never would have happened if we had not been there. So, what you did was to correct the error we made by forgetting to hide ourselves."

"Do you now agree going to the future made a difference for the better, or changed things for the worse?"

"Not sure." She pondered. "Gayeena said we did a good thing by bringing love into our future lives by intervening. Bessie would not have had a fortunate marriage, even though it was cut short. The same with Emaline."

"It is one way to look at it for sure."

"And . . . if we had not intervened to get Blue and Emaline together, regardless of the outcome, Greg would not have been born and Jessica would not have met him."

"All in all, it was a success."

"Whether it was for a brief period or for a long time, helping them find each other is what was important. I see that now," Xenia said thoughtfully.

"What I learned was thinking living a long and happy human life in the future wasn't easy to accomplish."

"The journey was a learning process for me, too." Xenia said. "I wasn't sure going in, but I believed in you and what you wanted. I got caught up in the emotion and thinking we failed. There was no failure. We helped our future selves experience the same deep and abiding love we have now."

"Our love will continue through all those lives. That is something to celebrate. Our souls may live forever, but knowing our love is eternal is the best discovery." He snuggled up to Xenia.

"Isn't it wonderful?"

~ ~ ~

In the great hall, Gayeena stood at the altar, waving her arms and chanting the mantra while the congregation held their last session. She shared the devastating news that all communication with the ships had ended, confirming through her crystals that they did not make it to higher ground. Prayers were said for the perished and for themselves.

Gayeena bid farewell to all and especially to those who time traveled, ending with her favorites, Xenia and Yonan.

"We will see you in the future, High Priestess," Xenia said.

"Yes, we will, won't we," she said.

Xenia and Yonan returned to their home to celebrate their success in securing a happy union of their future souls. They danced to their favorite music, drank their favorite wine, and made love for hours and hours. When the continent of Zorathia rocked and shook, a massive earthquake split open the lands.

"See you soon, my love," Yonan whispered in Xenia's ear.

"Yes, my love, soon."

And a great tidal wave consumed them.

EPILOGUE

For months, Jessica and Greg had been making improvements to the old farmhouse. The painters had arrived that morning and were already working on the exterior. The kitchen contractor had finished installing the new cabinets and counter tops when the doorbell rang.

Jessica dropped what she was doing to answer the door. "Greg! It's the delivery truck. They're here!" She ran out the front door and down the steps, jumping with glee, directing the driver and his assistant while they removed the twelve large and narrow wooden crates. "Careful, those are very valuable," she said.

One by one, they carried the large flat packages into the living room. She signed on the unit and the men went on their way. "I'm excited they've arrived. Help me, please?"

Greg and Jessica opened the crates and slid out the bubble-wrapped art work. Carefully, they unwrapped each one, and Jessica instructed Greg where to place them. They leaned the paintings against the furniture and spaces along the walls. When she was hammering a hanging nail into the wall, the television in the living room beeped that there would be a special report at the end of the news program. Oblivious to the announcement, she continued to hang the painting until something in the voice on the TV claimed her attention.

This Special Report will reveal details of an underwater archaeological expedition in the Indian Ocean, which has uncovered a submerged landmass where there appear to be remnants of an ancient city. In a cavern beneath the city, the team has found dozens of strange metal containers. Preliminary testing on the metal reveals it is an unknown substance. Among other things, the tubes have been found to contain hundreds of scrolls written in an unknown text.

Curious, Jessica stopped to watch the program.

Among the most startling of the other contents are twelve paintings on silk fabric of scenes, presumably of the continent as it looked before being submerged under the ocean. Some scientists theorize there was a cataclysmic shift of the earth on its axis which caused the continent to sink. This theory has been suggested for decades, but with no verifiable confirmation.

The discovery is said to be the most significant in the twenty-first century, since it provides evidence of an advanced civilization dating back possibly millions of years. The exact carbon dating is yet to reveal the time frame. But some ancient aliens theorists are already considering this to be proof of a pre-historic alien colony on Earth.

Images of the scrolls and containers appeared in a montage across the screen, ending with the twelve paintings.

Jessica gasped, her eyes riveted to the television—then she looked at her paintings around the room.

"Jessica!" Greg cried. "Those paintings look exactly like the ones you painted. How is this possible?"

Jessica thought of all the men she had painted for those book covers and how they looked like Blue Fox from the nineteenth century—and now her paintings looked like those from ancient times. She recalled the visions she had seen when she first kissed Greg, and that the astrologer said Greg would be from a past life. An understanding look slowly spread across her face.

AUTHOR BIO

An award-winning author, P. L. Jonas, has a creative spirit with a passion for literature, art, and music. She began writing fiction after a long career in marketing and technical writing and editing. A native Arizonan, she has traveled all over the U.S. and ten other countries. Drawing on her personal experience, a fascination with history, and a love of research, she weaves intricate stories of romance, fantasy, and suspense. In 2021, she received First Place in the Chanticleer International Book Awards, Goethe category, for late historical fiction. When not writing, she is reading or painting while her beloved cat looks on.